THE PENNY WARS

Also by Elliott Baker / A FINE MADNESS

Elliott Baker

THE PENNY WARS

G. P. Putnam's Sons   New York

THE PENNY WARS

Part One

I

IT was in Tuesday's paper.

> *June 22, 1939*
>
> *To the Editor.*
> *Dear Sir:*
>   *It is exactly one year since Joe Louis successfully defended his heavyweight championship against Max Schmeling. Since then the myth has grown that Louis was fighting for democracy and Schmeling in behalf of Nazism.*
>   *Isn't it about time everyone realized that these two palookas were only fighting for money?*
>
>   *Sincerely yours,*
>   *Tyler A. Bishop*

They'd left out the last sentence, the most important sentence, the dirty. . . .

"Three cents for the paper," croaked old Mrs. Mintz.

He put the pennies on the candy store counter and went outside. The hot sun fuzzed the type, and he had to keep blinking to clear the words as he read them again.

The missing sentence hurt, a hole that couldn't be filled in. He was already composing a protest. "I'd rather have been ignored than censored. Are you so afraid of truth?" But on the third reading, it didn't seem so bad. His point was still obvious to anybody with half a brain. And ending with the question was kind of effective. He knew the letter by heart, and it still hit hard. Imagine the impact on someone reading it for the first time!

He looked around, wondering if any of the people on the street had noticed it yet. The old woman waddling around the corner, Fedorchak lettering today's bargains on plate glass and spelling rhubarb without an *h,* the Negro hunchback who was the lookout for Blacky Roche lounging on the crate in front of the barbershop. None of them would even know that newspapers *had* an editorial page.

A number eleven streetcar came down Granite Street, and he made the usual bet with himself that it wouldn't stop at the corner. He lost. The doors flapped open, the step dropped down, and a priest got off, all pale and shriveled from never getting any.

Other faces stared at him through the streetcar windows like they'd never seen a left arm in a sling before. Some of them were bound to read the letter today, never suspecting they'd gawked at the writer of it. Not that he could blame them. It didn't sound like something by a sixteen-year-old with a busted wrist. Especially "myth" and "behalf." He could have found a way to use "idiosyncrasy" or "concomitant." But that would just have been showing off.

The streetcar whined away, its cable pole swinging behind like a broken tail, and the intersection hadn't even twitched. Tyler stared at the paltry cluster of shops. The movies would put Pat O'Brien and Henry Armetta and J. Edward Bromberg in them and toss in a good crisis, and the street would come alive, everybody pulling together because way down deep they were all good and decent. But this bunch, with their signs bidding for immortality, Fedorchak and Pitkin, the druggist, and Ryan, who owned the saloon, and Dalesandro, the barber, and Yunkes in his little delicatessen. If the German panzer units were thundering down Granite Street right now, would they all fight shoulder to shoulder behind a barricade of orange crates and beer kegs and pickle barrels? Or were they all as lousy as his father said?

He was reading his letter to the editor again when Howie

Clevenger turned the corner on his bike, the meat deliveries piled in the basket.

"How's the wrist-ola, Ty?"

Tyler just shrugged.

"Don't it itch?"

"Like a bitch," he said for the millionth time, and when Howie got close enough, he held out the newspaper and pointed where to read without comment.

"Terrif!" said Howie, just skimming it.

"The crapheads left out the last sentence."

"Hold this, will ya?"

Howie leaned the bike toward him, then took the paper in both hands and read the letter again.

"So what'd they leave out?"

"The struggle going on in the world today is not a sporting event but a conflict of ideologies."

"Oh," said Howie.

"The bastards," said Tyler. "It makes no goddam sense the way they have it."

"Aw, take it easy, Ty!"

"Easy! Did you hear Gabriel Heatter last night?" Howie shook his head. "Well, you should have."

"He gives me a pain in the ass."

"At least he knows the score," said Tyler. "We just happen to be going through one of the most crucial periods in the whole history of civilization, that's all. And when someone censors a letter to make sure it won't start people thinking, what do you say? You tell me to take it easy."

"So don't take it easy."

"You're as bad as everyone else around here," said Tyler. "Even at my house, what's important? Danzig? Hell, no. Just whether my father's going to get on that stupid *Amateur Hour*."

"Is he?" asked Howie, anxious to change the subject.

"Jesus!"

"No kidding. Can he really sing?"

"He sounds okay in the bathroom," said Tyler.

"Hey! That's a good idea. We got the Street Singer, why not

the Bathroom Singer?" Howie cupped his hands over his mouth and started croaking:

> *"Martaaaaaaa,*
> *Rambling rose of the toilet."*

The Negro hunchback raised his head and gave them a dirty look, and Fedorchak came out of his store to see what was going on.

"It ain't funny," said Tyler.

"Aw, come on," whined Howie. "What d'ya want, anyway?"

"I just want to get laid and save the world," said Tyler. "In that order."

But Howie, looking past him, just let out a low whistle. Tyler turned around. Two girls he'd never seen before were coming toward them. Both carried tennis rackets and wore shorts, the tall one's orange, the stocky one's white.

"And a lookie, lookie, lookie," chanted Howie.

"I get the one with the biggest boobs," muttered Tyler.

The girls neared them, pretending they weren't there.

"Well, what d'ya know?" said Howie, but they didn't break step.

"It's pretty hot for tennis," said Tyler.

"Sure," said Howie. "How about a soda?"

But the girls strode right by, noses in the air.

"Or a sundae," Howie called after them. "My favorite is *cherry*."

"Hell with them," grunted Tyler, but Howie wasn't through. "Maybe it's gold-plated," he said loudly.

"Some technique," said Tyler.

"I'm doin' okay."

"Not for me, you ain't."

"I'm working on somethin' for you."

"Yeah."

"Just gimme time." Howie gave him back the newspaper and got on his bike. "You don't want some Dracula."

"In my present state," began Tyler, but Howie was pushing off.

"See ya."

"See ya."

Tyler watched him ride away. You don't compete with a best friend. But being strictly objective, he was better-looking than Howie. Howie's porcupine hair had never been trained, and his head was too big for the rest of him, and his eyes were close-set, and he still had pimples. Not that Tyler thought of himself as handsome, not exactly. But he'd had several compliments on his thick, wavy hair, and he was only a half inch away from six feet, and though he was underweight, he was rangy more than skinny. Sometimes, in the mirror, he'd practice getting the same mixture of confidence and skepticism on his face that Clark Gable had, and it looked identical to him. But Howie still got the girls. The dirty wisecracks hadn't paid off just now, but there'd been other times when they had, when the girls pretended to be shocked or insulted while Tyler tried to cover his own embarrassment with serious talk. But it was Howie they'd always be interested in, not him. And Howie had made it lots of times while he was still looking for his first.

Of course, they had different standards in girls. That was the answer. The ones Howie scored with, the gigglers, the shriekers, making noises instead of words, fluttering their eyes and scuffing their saddle shoes—Tyler couldn't make small talk small enough for them. But there were other girls in this world, too, girls who would be intrigued by what he had to say and who wouldn't even breathe in Howie's direction, girls like Rowena.

Did Rowena read the editorial page? He took the long way around the block on his way home in order to pass her house, hoping she'd be on the porch. The letter in the newspaper would be a perfect way to start a conversation. But the green and white striped awning hung over empty chairs. Was she behind the lace curtains, stretched out on the couch in only halter and pants? Or maybe taking a bath? He tried thinking himself invisible, but it didn't work in broad daylight.

Then he saw the folded newspaper lying against the screen
door. The Keyhoes had theirs delivered. Tyler stopped and
bent over to tear a weed from the edge of the lawn. No one was
watching. All he had to do was pop up the front steps and
dog-ear the editorial page of the paper. But an anonymous
phone call, handkerchief over the mouthpiece, would also do
it. "Miss Rowena Keyhoe? This is a friend. Read page twenty-
two today." And click!

Mrs. Swerdlov made a poor substitute for Rowena. But the key
in the milk box meant no one was upstairs, and the only sound
in the house was the slurping of the washing machine in the
cellar. Tyler went down and found Mrs. Swerdlov feeding
sheets through the wringer, always a fascinating sight, always
the prospect that part of her pumped-up bosom would get
caught between the hard rubber rollers and the explosion
would be heard around the world.

"I happened to notice this in the paper," he said casually.

"What, what?"

He repeated it, louder than the machine this time.

"My hands are wet. Hold it so I can read."

He held the paper up, and she leaned forward to peer at
the print, coming close enough to the wringer to make
him wince. No skimmer, Mrs. Swerdlov. She sucked in every
word.

"That rotten Schmeling," she said. "The nigger shoulda
killed him."

"Negro," corrected Tyler, but she was still reading. He
timed her getting to the end before speaking again.

"You don't mind my showing this to you."

"Why?" She looked worried. "I should?"

"I mean, your being of German origin."

"What's with you? All of a sudden you don't know I'm a
Jew?"

"Your religion is Jewish," explained Tyler. "But your
nationality is German, just as Mr. Swerdlov is Russian."

"Listen," she said, "a Schmeling I ain't. Besides, what about my cousin, Dr. Axelrod, over there I ain't heard a word from for two years, if he's still alive."

She lifted a fat, puckered arm to blot her eyes. Just like Pavlov said. With mice a bell. With Mrs. Swerdlov mention of her dentist-cousin in Düsseldorf.

"Anyway," said Tyler, "they left out the last sentence."

Upstairs he wandered the rooms aimlessly, tried reading some more of *Stover at Yale* but couldn't concentrate, tried soap and water on the blackening cast on his wrist but only made it dirtier, took a chair to his bedroom closet to stand on and grope toward the back of the shelf, behind the folded frayed curtains and worn-out mackinaw and other remnants saved without purpose, under the hatbox and the imitation leather suitcase, stretching and balancing until his fingertips gripped *Naked Beauties of the World.*

It fell open to the right pages by itself. Force of habit. There she was, at least the top half of her, Miss Solomon Islands herself, still smiling unashamedly at the camera with only her wrists, throat, and earlobes covered; but the goddam South Pacific sun had bleached out the details. What he'd first thought were nipples were only vowels showing through from the back of the page. Not so with the Arunta woman. With her every pore was visible. Fine, if she wasn't about sixteen months pregnant. He read the caption again:

The Arunta women of southeastern Australia do not know the cause of birth.

So what? Neither do some of the people in the Granite Street section of a certain city in upstate New York. A Mrs. Horowitz for example, bulging with her seventh. And what was America discussing while Europe smoldered? Last night it was the Horowitzes.

"I don't know what they live on *now*," said his mother.

"They live on relief," said his father.

"He must be getting money from some place," she said.

"He's always going into the barbershop. And he doesn't get *that* many haircuts." She lobbed the hint over her sons' heads. As if he and Ross didn't know what went on in Blacky Roche's back room.

"He could pick horses that win," said Tyler.

"Shut up," snapped his father.

"Seven children," sighed his mother. "And the oldest is only twelve. You'd think they were Catholics."

"Maybe they're Aruntas," mumbled Tyler.

"What?" His mother with her sharp sense of hearing.

"Never mind."

"Your mother asked you what you said."

"I said, 'Maybe they're Aruntas.' "

That look they'd been exchanging all his life, that "what have we released on the world?" look.

"Then why didn't you say so?" said his father.

"What song you gonna sing in the audition, Dad?"

"Just shut up. Will you just shut up?"

Three bucks he'd spent on the crummy book. Months of nickel saving, then dogging the mailman until the parcel arrived from Chicago, not to mention sneaking it into the bathroom where he could examine it in peace and the hiding of it afterward. And for what? Argentina—woman peeking over fan; Brazil—woman peeking through fan; Ceylon—woman in native costume; Denmark—ditto; England—Queen Victoria; France—finale of the Folies Bergère photographed from five miles away. He'd pawed the pages frantically for the "never before views" promised in the ad. Then, nearing the end, cheated, disgusted, turning pages by rote, he passed the buxom, braided farm girl of Rumania and came to the letter *S*. On the left the woman of the Solomon Islands, washed out. And—facing page—the southeast Australia Arunta mother, complete with leprosy, beriberi, and at least three more little Aruntas yammering to get out.

That was all. Tibet to Zanzibar were buttoned up to their chins. And he still had the problem of how to get rid of the book. If he didn't, it was bound to be discovered eventually, and there'd be accusations. "Sex maniac! I'll bet it was you peeking in Eunice Swerdlov's window." How could anybody be that hard up?

One possibility kept occurring to him. He could plant the book in Ross' dresser. Let the stupe get out of that one. But Ross never had three dollars. And even if he did, no one would ever believe he'd spent it on a book. Tyler put *Naked Beauties of the World* back in its hiding place and went into the parlor. Sprawled on the lumpy davenport, he stared at the chandelier, at the framed pictures of cows grazing in front of a farmhouse, at the dust hanging in the ray of light slanting across the room from the porch window.

Rowena. What was she doing this very second? Did she have a book hidden in her closet, too, something she'd sent away for? And did she take it down and sneak looks at a photograph of a naked cannibal with tattooed testicles? No, not Rowena. He closed his eyes to see her better. Then he managed to think himself invisible.

He had a potion. Never mind from where. And it was different from the one in the movie. The smoking one that Claude Rains drank made him invisible permanently. But Tyler's invisibility only lasted an hour or two. All he had to do was drink something ordinary to set off the potion after it was in his bloodstream. Nothing too ordinary, though, or it could happen when he didn't want it to.

How about a chocolate malted? *Come on, get to Rowena.* But he had to work out the logic first. He'd take the potion, then go into Pitkin's Drugstore and order a malted, waiting until the store was empty of customers and the druggist's back turned before sipping the drink. *Whfft!* Immediate invisibility. But how about his clothes? Even the idiots in this neighborhood might notice clothes floating through the street. He backtracked. It would take ten seconds for the chocolate malted to be effective, long enough to get into the phone booth at the back of the store. And once invisible, he'd strip off his clothes and hide them in a secret compartment at the top of the booth. What secret compartment? *Nuts! Get to Rowena.*

The sidewalk would be hot on his bare soles as he walked to her house, her front vestibule when he reached it cooling to his skin. He'd ring the bell and press himself into the corner so she wouldn't accidentally touch him as she came out. He couldn't help imagining her face if she did. But she wouldn't. She'd just stare puzzledly at the empty vestibule, then push the door wider to look out—wide enough for him to duck inside. Now what? He couldn't sit on a chair or sofa in the parlor because she'd see the indentation. No, he'd just stand drinking in her beauty. And what would Rowena do? Scratch her head, paint her fingernails. *Jesus. Will you stop drawing it out?*

Okay, she'd turn on the bath water, then go to her bedroom, pull down the shade, and start undressing. Off would come her blouse, off would come her skirt, and in walked his moronic kid brother all sweated up and puffing like an advanced asthmatic.

"That scummy Seymour called me Crisco again. I'm gonna paste him one."

Tyler kept his eyes closed tight, struggling to stay in Rowena's bedroom, resisting speeding up the picture.

"Whose newspaper?"

Tyler jumped up and snatched it out of Ross' hand. He wasn't chancing any stupid comments from him about the letter. He flopped back on the davenport and pretended to read.

"You weren't using it 'til I wanted it."

Tyler ignored him. Not that he was talking to him more than necessary anyways, not since the dope had dropped the pole when they were putting up the awning and his wrist had cracked from the blow. If it weren't for Ross, he'd be spending the summer playing ball and maybe with a part-time job like the one Howie had, instead of writing letters to editors that got mutilated.

He was still buried in the newspaper when his mother staggered in with the groceries.

"Sixteen blocks," she said, "to save eighty-five cents."

"Coolie wages," muttered Tyler, taking the bag from her and carrying it into the kitchen.

"But it paid for these." She pulled two song sheets out, "The Boulevard of Broken Dreams" and "I'll Never Smile Again."

"Dad can't read music."

"He doesn't have to. He knows the melodies. But if he holds the sheet music, it will look more professional."

"It's supposed to be an amateur hour," said Tyler, folding the newspaper so that his letter was up and putting it on the table facing her.

"Tell him you think he should hold the sheet music," she said, unpinning her hat.

"All I know," said Tyler, "is what I read in the paper."

She didn't pick up the hint and instead started taking off her gloves with little tugs at the fingertips. The end of June, and she still wore hat and gloves, and would all summer no matter how hot it got.

"You buy any doughnuts?" Ross started taking the groceries out of the bag and putting them on the table. A box of cream of wheat came down right on the letter. Tyler pushed it away.

"Look," he finally said.

His mother leaned worriedly to see what he was pointing out, probably expecting an obituary.

"It's yours," she shrieked. "When did you write them a letter?"

"Where?" Ross crammed in, trying to peer over her shoulder as she sat down, but Tyler pushed him away.

"Let Mom read it first."

As she started to, her eyes kept darting up toward him as if trying to link him with the words on the page. He watched her closely for a reaction, and as if aware of this, her narrow face became impassive, and she lowered it closer to the paper, leaving him looking at the top of her head. Gray hair was mixing with the brown, all pulled tightly back and into a bun. But the little wisps of hair at the front and sides had a copper tinge, sustaining her boast of having been a natural redhead in her younger days. This was important to her, this and the fact that her weight hadn't varied more than three pounds since she was eighteen (pregnant eras excepted)—both meaningless morsels of pride delivered repetitiously the same as his father always telling about seeing McKinley shot.

"Very good," she said, about halfway through the letter. Then, at the end, she said it again. "Very good." But with less conviction, and when she looked up at him, her mouth was sucked in, disapproval forming a line at each end like parentheses.

"What's the matter?"

"Nothing," she said.

"You don't think it sounds priggish." It was a word he'd learned from *Stover at Yale*.

"No. But I wish you'd shown it to me before you sent it."

"Why?" He could feel his own mouth tightening.

"Not that it isn't very good."

"But?"

"But the way it's worded, some people might get an anticolored implication."

"Anticolored?" He looked to the ceiling for support.

"It's really very good," she said quickly.

"It's not my fault if they left out the most important sentence."

His father didn't make it any better. He wouldn't even read it when he got home, not until he washed up. So it was left on the kitchen table. When he came back in, buttoning the clean shirt he'd put on, he kept moving around the table, throwing sidelong looks toward the newspaper, almost snorting at it through his small, flat nose. Then, when he finally sat down and picked it up, he just stared at it through glazed eyes. He'd been staring at everything like that since the postcard came from Major Bowes about the audition.

Tyler waited for his comment, knowing it would be something fatuous. But his father just coughed about ten times.

"Isn't it a good letter?" prodded his mother.

His father gave another cough, then turned to Tyler.

"Would you call Joe Louis a palooka to his face?" he asked, even more fatuous than Tyler had expected.

"That's supposed to be an adult reasoning with a child," he said to the calendar hanging over the sink.

"I warned you," his father slammed a fist on the table. "Stop making remarks at me when I'm sitting here."

"Frank." His mother could get all kinds of inflections into names. This time it was soothing.

"That's his way of getting at me. The kid's a goddam sniper."

"There'll be no swearing at the table," she said, putting the plates around as if dealing cards. "Besides, they left out the most important sentence."

His father coughed again. "I think I'm coming down with a cold," he said huskily. "I feel all congested."

He tapped his chest, trying to produce a congested sound. "See how hoarse I'm getting."

"You'll have to sing through a megaphone," said Ross and got a look that would have killed anything human.

"Summer colds don't last," said his mother. But she wasn't taking any chances. She took the pint of whiskey from the top shelf of the cupboard and measured a quarter inch of it into the water glass.

Tyler watched his father swig it down, wondering if they'd get the New Year's Eve routine. Yes, here it came—the squeezed eyes and vibrating head, the *aaahh,* the hiccup, the hand massaging the collarbone. Then the snorting and mumbling, the "Where am I?" and "Who are you?" and "I kin lick any man in the house."

It was an act Tyler had seen a hundred times before. But now suddenly there was anxiety in it, a desperation to please, as if their acceptance of this performance would excuse him from doing something more. A few seconds of it would have been bad enough, but he went on reeling around the kitchen, stumbling into icebox and door, rumpling his thinning hair so it stood up in a peak in front.

"Frank!" This time a gentle warning.

But he kept it up, posing like John L. Sullivan and swaying in big circles as if his shoes were nailed to the floor.

"Around, around she goes," chanted Ross, trying to sound like Major Bowes. "And where she stops, nobody knows."

That got a yawn from Tyler and a grim smile from his father and a rewarding laugh from his mother. Then she made the mistake of bringing out the song sheets.

II

IN 1939 they'd been living upstairs from the Swerdlovs for eleven years. And though there were fragments of things before—lemon sherbet when he had his tonsils out, thick headlines about Lindbergh, some kid with eczema who got him in a headlock in the middle of the toy section of Mathiesson's Department Store—though there were dozens of fragments like these, full memory for Tyler began in 1928 with his first visit to the flat below.

That night the Swerdlov parlor had been another country, a room as rich and perfumed and heavy and ugly as the woman presiding over it; boxes made of bone, purple lamp bases strangely illuminated from inside, six bronze animal-cracker lions on a candlestick holding fat white sticks of tallow in their upraised mouths, a hundred strands of clicking colored beads dangling in the archway to the dining room, cushions—countless cushions of velvet and silk which made sitting up straight impossible—and most of all the eagle ready to swoop from the top of the piano, already singling him out.

On that first visit Mrs. Swerdlov had been a tireless hostess, tottering across the Oriental rug on surprisingly small feet at two-minute intervals to proffer candy to him or black syrupy coffee to his parents, and on one trip, noticing his glance, lifting him in her flabby arms and carrying him to the eagle, coaxing and coaxing until he touched the glass button eye. And, interspersed, was the apology for Mr. Swerdlov not being home because he was working late in his fur shop downtown.

Then they circled the piano and she slid open its secret panels and threaded a roll of punched paper inside. More magic

21

as the keys jumped without being touched and music started
coming out, impossible until he saw her feet moving.

> *"Let the great big world keep turning.*
> *Never mind if I've got you."*

The three grown-ups sang away, but all his attention was
glued to Mrs. Swerdlov as she gripped the piano bench for leverage and furiously pedaled away, gulping in big globs of air
and calling encouragement between lines, her voice the loud-
est and even lower than his father's.

> *"For I only know,"*

"Ev-ry-body!"

> *"That I love you so,"*

"Sing, Tyler, sing!"

> *"And that no one else will do."*

And afterward, puffing for breath.
"Such a voice, Mr. Bishop. You should do something with it."
"He's going to," said his mother.
That was the first Tyler knew of their trump card, the voice
that would someday get them onto Easy Street. But at the time
he'd just whined for a turn at the pedals. They'd let him, and
since his feet didn't reach, he had to stand and push one pedal
at a time, making short, jangling bursts of music until Eunice
Swerdlov stuck her face through the clicking colored beads and
asked if they could please make less noise since she was trying
to study for her finals.
Eunice had been in her third year at State Teachers College
then, an angular sour girl with a receding chin and strong
glasses, refusing to come in and be introduced, stamping
back to her room and slamming the door. Now Eunice was
thirty-one, disadvantages still intact, her mother's prophecy
that night in little danger.

"My good-natured daughter. Such a personality, we'll never have to pay for a wedding."

There'd been many other nights around the player piano during these eleven years, always without Mr. Swerdlov being home and often against Eunice's protests. And every time Mrs. Swerdlov would compliment his father's singing and his father would beam smugly and his mother would promise that someday something would be done with that fine tenor voice. How fine Tyler wasn't sure. He didn't think his father was as good as Allan Jones or Richard Crooks. But he sure sounded better than the contestants on *Major Bowes'*.

They were tough on the contestants. They rarely had a good word for the tap dancers and impersonators that Major Bowes introduced, not to mention the birdcallers and one-man bands. But it was the singers they were hardest on, the men singers that is, especially the tenors warbling "Mother Macree" and "Danny Boy" and "Did Your Mother Come from Ireland"? As soon as one of them finished, his father would *lah-lah-lah* the last couple of lines of the song they'd just heard, always sounding better than the contestant. And his mother would say, "You should go on that program," and his father would answer, "They never come here."

He had said it again that night, not two minutes before the announcer recited the list of cities where the *Amateur Hour* would be holding auditions, and there they were right between Toledo and Pittsburgh.

"Box Six Thirteen, Grand Central Station, New York." His mother kept repeating the address the announcer had given, hopping around the room until she found a pencil and wrote it down. Meanwhile, his father had sunk down in his chair as if he'd been sledgehammered.

"Carrie, I'm forty-three." He pulled at one sideburn as if the grayness there was Exhibit A. "They want young people."

"That plumber who won last week was in his fifties." Tyler tossed it in for the sake of accuracy.

"You shut up," barked his father.

"He sang 'Polly Yachi,'" added Ross.

"And you, too!"

But it was only a token resistance. The whole Wehrmacht couldn't have stopped his mother from writing to Box 613, and a week later the postcard arrived. It was still propped on the pantry shelf, telling his father to report for an audition to Studio D of the radio station downtown. He was to be there at one o'clock Saturday.

In comparison with what was going on in Europe the audition was about as important as a flea's family tree. But as Saturday got closer, Tyler felt a vague curiosity about it, not so much the audition itself but about how his father would worm out of it. The Camille coughing act before dinner obviously wasn't going to work. Acute laryngitis might, but he'd bet his mother would summon Dr. Lessing to authenticate it. In his father's position he'd gargle with something to make his throat red—Mercurochrome maybe.

The question of the lyrics had occurred to Tyler. His father never knew more than three consecutive words of any song, and he couldn't go down to the audition and just go *lah-lah-lah-de-do*. Several times Tyler almost pointed this out. But he'd vowed not to show any interest in the audition. And it wasn't until his mother brought home the song sheets that he realized she was way ahead of him. She stood now, waving a song sheet in each hand like she was sending semaphore. And the look on his father's face showed that she'd just closed his last escape hatch. He'd probably been planning to get up Saturday morning and claim he couldn't go audition because he didn't know any lyrics. You'd think after almost eighteen years he'd know her better.

"Woolworth's has a new woman at the piano," she said. "She's got this trembling voice that's always a little bit flat."

Tyler watched his father. What once had probably been an easygoing manner had matured into pure weakness. But the chin was trying to make one last thrust of defiance.

"After dinner," she said, "you can sing them both for us, and we'll choose which one we like best."

"The hell I will."

"You've got to get used to singing in front of people."

"They ain't people," said his father, pointing toward him and Ross.

"But if you can't sing in front of your own family, how are you going to face a whole audience of strangers?"

She waited for a logical answer, but he just concentrated on buttering a piece of bread. "Frank?" She almost sobbed it.

"I'm not going Saturday."

"You've got to. You said you would."

"I never said."

"You're on their list for the audition. You've got to go."

"I don't have to do anything."

"Famous last words," muttered Tyler.

"You keep out of this," yelled his father.

"Would it be too much to ask to have our supper before it gets cold?" asked Tyler.

That led to a temporary cease-fire. Nothing was said while his mother put the creamed tuna on the table, and they dug in. She just toyed with hers, reloading her battery of arguments, waiting until they were almost through before starting again.

"The winners go into those traveling road shows," she said. "They pay them up to a hundred dollars a week. Imagine having that much money coming in. Just a few months would pay for Tyler going to college."

"Look," said his father, "if I thought making a fool of myself would give him an education—"

Oh, no. They weren't going to use him. And he said so.

"You aren't martyring yourself for me. Sing or don't sing. But if you do, it isn't for my benefit."

"No?" asked his father. "Who else?"

"It'll be because you don't want to be a clerk in a trucking company all your life."

"Why, you little punk!" His father started to get up until she put a hand on his arm.

"We're all talking at cross-purposes," she said.

"The only reason I even considered it," grumbled his father, "was to get them out of this lousy neighborhood."

"I'll get myself out," said Tyler.

"I don't know what everyone's raving about," she said.

"We're raving about this goddam neighborhood," yelled his father.

"There's nothing wrong with this neighborhood." She went to the pantry for the salt and pepper shakers.

"Not much," said his father. "All the scum right off the boat makes a beeline here. I'm surprised these kids can even speak English."

"It hasn't hurt the boys to grow up here. This is a melting pot."

"Yeah, yeah," scoffed his father.

"People of all kinds living side by side," she said. "That's what a melting pot is." Tyler wished she'd drop it already, but she didn't, going on about how it was good for Ross and him to grow up in a melting pot, and even if they could afford to move out of the melting pot, she didn't have any regrets about living in a melting pot. But she said melting pot once too often, and his father got the last word.

"If this is a melting pot, then America's cooking shit!"

Well, not quite the last word. He'd never said *that* word to her before, and he wasn't inaugurating it while they were eating creamed tuna fish. Tyler watched the blood drain from her face as if a plug had been pulled out of her big toe. Then her wrists went limp, and the salt and pepper shakers hit the floor. But no one moved to pick them up. She's going to faint, thought Tyler. He tensed, ready to spring from his chair and catch her. But she just turned and walked with a brink of suicide stiffness into the parlor.

"Now you've done it," said Tyler.

"Shut up! Shut up! Shut up!" Some vocabulary.

His father drummed his fingers on the porcelain tabletop and stared down at the spilled salt and pepper. Then he turned on Ross.

"Well, sweep it up before it's ground into the linoleum."

"I'm still eating," moaned Ross.

the song for the audition. Ross voted for "The Boulevard of Broken Dreams" and his mother for "I'll Never Smile Again."

"Well?" His father turned to Tyler.

"You want my honest opinion?"

"Come on. Vote." He stood flushed with victory. He knew he'd sounded good.

"For the first time in my life," said Tyler, "I agree with Ross."

"Two votes for 'The Boulevard of Broken Dreams,' " chirped Ross.

" 'I'll Never Smile Again' is prettier," insisted his mother.

Then there was a knock on the back door. Ross went to answer it and came back with Mrs. Swerdlov.

"I liked the one with the broken dreams," she said. "So did Eunice."

But before they went to bed, his father had been talked into singing "I'll Never Smile Again."

III

THEY put on their suits Saturday morning just in case he changed his mind and let them come along. She kept looking over at the clock while they ate breakfast. And when it said eleven, she let out a "Frannnnnnk?" like a mating call. His answer was a dull moan, promising enough to make her reheat the coffee and wait another five minutes before marching back to the bedroom. Tyler could hear them mumbling there, then a few loud words.

"You've got to."

"Let me alone."

She came back to the kitchen with a face of chalk, and Tyler felt that if her lips could be pried open, he'd learn some new words, but beauts.

"He claims he's sick," she finally said.

"Holy mackerel!" piped Ross, quick on the uptake. "How about the audition?"

"Tyler," she said. "Go see if you can talk sense to him."

It had a football coach's ring to it, and he found himself at the bedroom door without planning what to say. His father was balled up in the sheet and blanket, his face burrowed in the pillow and facing the wall.

"What's the matter, Dad?"

"I'm sick."

"Maybe if you took some Bisodol."

"I've been telling you for days, I'm sick. I got this pain in my chest."

"It's just nerves."

"Go 'way."

"Mom's all upset. This means a lot to her."

"Go 'way!"

Tyler stood there trying to think of something else to say. The wallpaper just above his father's head had a faint brown patch spreading. He studied the pattern, alternating red roses with some kind of drum major or grenadier. The paperhanger hadn't even come close at matching seams, splitting the drum major right up the crotch on one and giving him a rose for a left leg.

"You sounded terrific the other night," Tyler said.

He waited until it was obvious he'd get no answer, then went back to the kitchen and shrugged a sign of failure. This set his mother in motion as if he'd passed her a baton. She ran out toward the bedroom, unleashing her first words like a battle cry.

"Get out of there and get dressed."

"Carrie!"

"You heard me!" Her voice was rasping and shrill, meaner than Tyler had ever heard it. "I'm not letting you throw this chance away, too."

"I'm sick, Carrie."

"Sick!" The one, scoffing word wiped away any doubt.

"My chest—"

"There's nothing wrong with your chest. Get up!"

"I'm sick."

"You're not sick. You're yellow! You're butter! You're jelly! Big shot! Tell me all the things we were going to do. Like going to California. Like having your own business. Tell me all the things you were going to give me."

"I'm not faking, Carrie. This pain—"

"I don't care about your pain. Do you hear? I don't care how much it hurts. You're going down there and sing."

"I can't."

"Get up! Right now! Get up!"

Silence then. Nothing moving, no creak of bed or floorboard. Tyler realized he was holding his breath and let it out, then heard Ross do the same. He felt that he shouldn't just sit there, that he should either find a solution or absent himself from the problem. But he stayed in his chair, wetting a finger to magnetize crumbs from the table. Then he heard it, the sickening, clicking sound of bone on bone, the sound of playground or alley while the onlookers yelled. But now it was coming from his parents' bedroom, drawing him down the hall toward it.

She was kneeling on the bed, leaning over him, her small fist bunched and pounding, driven by the "Get up!" she hissed between blows. And his father just lay there, a helpless hand raised to protect the back of his head. Then she saw Tyler, and her fist remained high. She stared at him, puffing hate and exertion, her face flushed, her hair a wild spray. It was an animal pose, distracted by a camera or crushed twig, and he was sure he'd get her venom next. But still the animal, she turned and looked down at the carcass beneath her. And the whimper muffled in the pillow, the beaten puppy's cry, unclenched her fist.

Tyler stood rooted as she brushed past him and stalked righteously toward the parlor. The straightness of her back, the way she regroomed her hair with one toss of her head, as contrasted with the huddled form on the bed, almost made him follow her, to console her for what she'd been forced to do. For the worst of it was it hadn't worked.

He went back to the kitchen and sat down. He could feel Ross watching him, waiting for a sign. Just taking off his suit coat would be enough. And Ross would change his clothes and trot off to the playground, leaving him with a father hiding in bed and a mother staring blankly out the front window. But that wasn't what really bothered him. There'd been plenty of times when he couldn't see how his parents would ever be able to make up. What was different now was his own sense of disappointment. He was no longer detached about the audition. He wanted his father to go, and he wanted him to win. He sat hoping that any moment he would come into the kitchen, dressed and shaved, and say he was going through with it. But the clock was heading toward noon. And the postcard was propped near it, taunting him.

*Please report to Studio D Station WBEZ, 1140 Huston Street
at 1 P.M., Saturday July 1 to be auditioned for THE MAJOR
BOWES AMATEUR HOUR. (Bring this card with you.)*

And next to it lay the song sheets. He went and picked them
up, the postcard, too—passports to the future while time, un-
stoppable time rendered them useless.

"What we gonna do?" whispered Ross.

Tyler turned to him, intending to convey his own heavy
sense of resignation and defeat. But instead he found himself
trying to see his brother through new eyes. To a stranger the
face might not look so dumb and round. To some people he
might be just a plump little fourteen-year-old boy with big
blue eyes and freckles like thumbtacks. After all, Mrs. Swerdlov
often patted that bristly red hair.

"Come on," he said.

"Where?" Ross didn't budge.

"With me."

He thought he should tell his mother they were going out,
then decided that thundering down the backstairs would let
her know.

"Come on, will ya?"

He shoved Ross ahead of him. And it wasn't until they
were on the streetcar that he brought out the song sheets.

"Learn these words." He handed Ross "I'll Never Smile
Again."

"What for?"

"Two bits says you can't learn them by heart by the time we
get downtown."

"What we goin' downtown for?" Ross edged away from him
suspiciously.

"You want to bet or not?" challenged Tyler, shoving the
song sheet under Ross' nose until he looked at it.

"I hate that one."

"That's right. You like 'The Boulevard of Broken Dreams.' "
Tyler gave it to him. "Same bet."

"Two bits," said Ross, his face determined.

Tyler turned to look out the open window. The shiny straw seat was hot, and he felt the seat of his pants sticking to it; but he tried not to fidget, afraid to break Ross' limited power of concentration. The sights passed were as familiar as their house: the auto supply stores, the printing factory, Karl and Kurt's Brau Strubel where Bund meetings were held, the huge Churchill Tabernacle, the stadium with the first trickle of men going through the turnstiles for today's doubleheader with the Red Wings, then the beginning of the downtown area, the cheap nightclubs you had to show a driving license to get into, Danceland which hadn't changed the displayed pictures of its hostesses since the Charleston, the movie houses—the Granada, the Mutual, the Princess—the smaller shops merging into the department stores, all as he had seen them a million times before, but this time they seemed closer together, the ride shorter. It didn't seem possible for even a normal brain, let alone Ross', to memorize a whole song in such a short time. When they got off at Huston Street, Tyler led him into a doorway and tested him.

> *"I walk along the street of sorrow,*
> *The Boulevard of Broken Dreams.*
> *Where Gigolo and Gigolet. . . ."*

"Not gig," said Tyler. "Jig."
"It's spelled with a *g*," whined Ross.
"Will you stop arguing?"
A tapping on glass interrupted them. The doorway belonged to a small lingerie store, and the owner was peering out at them between the brassieres and girdles, waving them to move along. So Ross rasped the rest of the lyrics on the way down Huston Street, talking more than singing them and getting about every other line right. Then, as they neared the red brick building of Station WBEZ he suddenly stopped and demanded his two bits.
"You got half of it wrong," said Tyler.

"Then give me thirteen cents." Instead, Tyler gave him the postcard. "What's this for?"

"Now listen," said Tyler. "Concentrate hard. You're Frank Bishop."

"Huh?" Boy, the doctor must have used forceps when he delivered him.

"For the next couple hours you're Frank Bishop. You're taking Dad's place in the audition."

"Me?" Almost a scream.

"You."

"But I can't sing."

"Sure you can. You've got a swell voice."

"But it's changing," croaked Ross.

"That's what makes it unusual."

"I'm goin' home."

Tyler hung onto his arm for half a block before managing to drag him to a stop.

"Will you smarten up?" he said. "You heard what went on this morning. They could get divorced because of this. But if you win, they'll be so glad they'll make up."

"Why me?" whined Ross. "What about you?"

"I'm not the type they want. You are."

"What type?"

"Look"—Tyler started steering him back toward the radio station—"this could be a big break for you."

"What type?" repeated Ross.

"You know. You're kinda . . . cute."

Ross stopped dead and socked him, but Tyler caught it on the shoulder of his good arm.

"I mean," he added quickly, "some people would think so. They're always after your type for the movies."

"Who wants to be in the movies?"

"Everybody does."

"I don't."

"Not much you don't."

"Speak for yourself."

"Well, I'll tell you one thing," said Tyler. "You won't get discovered staying home or in the playground. You've got to be *seen*. Remember how Lana Turner was discovered at a soda fountain?"

"Okay," said Ross. "Let's go to Rexall's and get a soda."

"You kill me."

He'd hoped to keep up the banter long enough to get Ross inside the building. But Ross stopped dead again in front of the entrance, staring at the revolving doors as if they were the gates of Sing Sing.

"If you get to Hollywood, you might meet Deanna Durbin."

"She's older than me."

Ross stood with his feet apart and firmly planted, ready to parry whatever he said next. Flattery had failed; reason would never dent that thick skull. What was left?

"Tell you what," said Tyler, desperately. "You do it and I'll treat you to lunch and a movie."

"I choose the movie?"

"You choose it."

Ross thought about it. "Naw," he finally said. "It ain't worth it."

"What *is* worth it to you?" persisted Tyler.

"Nothing."

"You do this," said Tyler, "and I'll see to it that nobody ever calls you Crisco again."

That made Ross blink, but he still held back.

"How you gonna do that?"

"Never mind. I'll do it."

"You gimme your word?"

"So help me," said Tyler.

But he had to raise his right hand and swear to it before Ross believed him. Then they went in.

No problem in finding Studio D. All they had to do was follow the commotion. He kept a firm grip on Ross' arm all the way down the corridor just in case he tried to bolt again.

The scene inside the studio was just as he'd expected, all noise and confusion, like in the musicals when Frank McHugh tried to get the chorus girls lined up to be looked over while George E. Stone played the piano and it seemed as if they'd never notice Ruby Keeler. Well, not *exactly* like that. But something like it. And the little man in shirt sleeves at the piano, the one being called Bert, looked a *little* like George E. Stone.

The one in charge, the tall, thin pansy with mottled skin whose name was Lester, had about a hundred people pressing around him, all yammering and waving their postcards. There was one enormous colored woman, dressed for a wedding, who stayed clear of the mob, but whose voice boomed out over all the others. She sat in the back row of folding chairs, spreading over two of them and fussing with the little girls she'd done up, pulling at their skirts and the yellow bows in their wiry hair and calling out every half minute, "Da tree pickaninnies —hyah we ah!"

But it was the musicians who caused the biggest mess, clogging the aisles with bass fiddles and drums and a xylophone. And there was one guy who'd set up a table with about thirty glasses, each with an exact amount of water so it would sound a certain note when tapped. He kept going off to fill a pitcher from the water cooler in the hall, and every time he came back, he claimed somebody had been drinking from the glasses he'd already filled. And Lester would yell, "Stop drinking his water!" before turning to the next complaint or question.

The only one who seemed calm was the woman named Tucker. She circulated in the crowd with a clipboard, collecting the postcards and writing down names and looking all cool and fresh in her navy blue dress. When she got to them, Tyler had to admit she looked better at a distance, but she still wasn't bad.

"And who have we here?"

Tyler had to jab Ross in the ribs before the jerk woke up and handed her the postcard.

"Frank Bishop," she said with a reassuring smile and wrote it down. Then she turned to Tyler inquiringly.

"I'm with him," he said.

"His manager?"

He caught the twinkle and wanted to say something clever, that he was a concert pianist or a juggler, then hold up his broken wrist.

"His brother," was all he said.

"Well, good luck," she cooed to Ross. "And don't—" But before she could tell him what not to do, Lester shrieked her name. One of the contestants had taken off his coat and was only wearing a leopard skin with flags and arrow-punctured hearts and names tattooed on his arms and a hula dancer on his chest.

"But this is radio," said Lester. "People can't *hear* muscles." He said it pleadingly, afraid to antagonize the man. Then Tucker went to his rescue.

"What did she mean?" asked Ross. "Don't what?"

"She was gonna say, 'Don't be nervous,'" said Tyler. He led Ross away to an empty section of seats far from the three pickaninnies and their hog-calling mother and told him to study the lyrics some more.

"I got a better idea," said Ross. "She didn't know I'm supposed to sing. So why don't I recite instead?"

"Recite what?"

"I know all the words to 'Gunga Din.'" Ross leaned closer and started rattling them off.

> *"You can talk of gin and beer*
> *When you're quartered safe out here*
> *And go to penny fights at—"*

"You'd better sing," said Tyler, and Ross sulked a little before turning to the song sheet again.

Meanwhile, Tucker had convinced the muscleman to put his coat back on and follow her out, leaving Lester to flap his arms helplessly and say to Bert, the pianist, that this was worse than Minneapolis. It was about the tenth time he'd said it.

"I wonder what happened in Minneapolis," said Ross.

"Learn the words," barked Tyler.

It was after one o'clock, but no attempt had been made to start the auditioning. Then the burly man with the cigar and John L. Lewis eyebrows came in, and as soon as he saw him, Lester started screeching for quiet. The burly man was called Mr. W. In fact, he was called it at the end of every sentence by Lester and Bert and even Tucker. But Lester did most of the brownnosing. "Yes, sir, Mr. W." "Would you like to sit here, Mr. W.?" "Anything you want, Mr. W.?" It was obvious who was the big shot and who would decide which ones got on the program.

"He don't look like Major Bowes," said Ross.

"Does Bowes begin with a *W?*"

"I thought Major Bowes'd be here."

"You won't see him until the broadcast in New York," explained Tyler. "Mr. W.'s in charge here."

The other contestants had realized this, too, and were finding seats instead of milling around, as if to show how quiet and cooperative they could be.

"Ready when you are, Mr. W.," chirped Lester, and the burly man nodded his double chin over his starched collar and polka-dot bow tie.

"Oh, one other thing," remembered Lester, addressing the whole room. "You singers." Tyler could feel Ross stiffen at the word. "There are some songs we can't clear with ASCAP, so you'd better have an alternative."

"What's ASCAP?" whispered Ross.

"How do I know?"

"What's alternative?"

"You'd better learn the words to 'I'll Never Smile Again.' "

"I don't know all of 'Boulevard of Broken Dreams.' "

"Keep memorizing," said Tyler.

" 'I'll Never Smile Again'?"

"The one you're doing."

He'd tried to sound calm and confident to Ross. But all the time the others were auditioning, he sat worrying about "The Boulevard of Broken Dreams" being cleared with ASCAP.

The first one called was a chubby kid about nine who

thought he could imitate Al Jolson singing "Sonny Boy." As if all it took was getting down on one knee and spreading your arms at the end. The kid's parents were with him and they must have told him to play up to Mr. W., which he did, rolling his eyes at him while sounding as much like Al Jolson as Mrs. Swerdlov did. In fact, less.

When the kid finished, Lester looked at Mr. W., and the burly man just moved his cigar back and forth like a windshield wiper.

"Thank you," called Lester. "We'll let you know."

So this was the turndown, the back and forth motion of the cigar and the "Thank you. We'll let you know." For a while it seemed the only reaction anyone was going to get. Then a man in a plaid shirt, accompanying himself on the guitar, finished "Home on the Range." And this time Mr. W. pointed the ash end of his cigar toward the singer, and Lester said, "If you'll just go over to Miss Tucker," and everybody knew that the man in the plaid shirt had made it.

Between "Sonny Boy" and "Home on the Range" there was a fluttery little woman with a huge straw hat singing "In a Monastery Garden" and the guy with the water glasses playing the "Blue Danube" and a quartet called the Ebenezer Four that harmonized "That Old Gang of Mine" and a skinny giant about seven feet tall with an enormous Adam's apple bobbing up and down as he did barnyard impersonations. Roosters at dawn, pigs oinking, chickens laying eggs. Some talent in this world.

"Frank Bishop," called Tucker, and Tyler was caught by surprise. But Ross wasn't. He just handed Tyler the song sheet, stepped on his foot as he lurched to the aisle, and lumped to the front of the room, where Lester directed him over to Bert at the piano. While they huddled there, conferring, Tyler suddenly hoped "The Boulevard of Broken Dreams" wouldn't be clear with ASCAP so they could forget the whole thing. But Bert started hitting different notes, searching for Ross' key. And the way his forehead creased, it was obvious that Bert didn't often get a singer with a changing voice. Then Ross turned around to face the audience and took a deep breath.

"I walk along the street of sorrow."

"Hey!" chirped Bert. "Wait for me."

He trilled an introduction up and down the keyboard and nodded toward Ross as he began playing the melody. But Ross just stared at him. Bert stopped and shook his head wearily.

"You're fighting me, boy," he said. "Here." He kept thumping one chord over and over. "You come in here."

Then he trilled the introduction again and nodded the cue, and, wonder of wonders, Ross started at the right time.

"I walk along the street of sorrow,
The Boulevard of—"

The voice which sounded something like Andy Devine's dwindled as Ross became aware that Bert was waving him to stop.

"Wrong key," sighed Bert, partly explaining why it had sounded so awful, and a few people giggled.

"Okay," piped Lester, "let's get off the street already." This got some laughs, and Lester looked over at Mr. W. for approval. But Bert had started playing again.

"I walk along the street of sorrow,
The Boulevard of Broken Dreams."

Ross kept singing, never noticing that the piano had stopped and that Bert was sitting back with his arms folded.

"Look, Ma, no hands." But Ross didn't seem to hear Bert's crack or the laugh it got. He stood stiff as a statue, his eyes transfixed at some point on the ceiling near the back of the room, his face squeezed in concentration as he struggled to remember the words.

"Where Gigolo and Gigolet. . . ."

He mispronounced them again. But Tyler hardly heard. He was staring too, all prayer and will power and body english fastened to the top of Mr. W.'s cigar, urging it to point instead of wave back and forth. But even miracles have limitations. The cigar started waving, furious and final.

"Thank you," said Lester.

"Could share a kiss without regret."

"We'll let you know," called out Lester.

"And forget their broken dreams."

Lester had to pounce over and shake Ross' arm to stop him. "We'll let you know," he repeated.

"I can recite 'Gunga Din,'" said Ross.

"Some other time." Lester almost shoved him toward the aisle.

"And I can imitate Major Bowes."

Then Tyler managed to catch his eye, waving him to come toward the door. As Ross walked up the aisle, there were a few handclaps. The old story. Cheer the guy after he's bleeding.

"That piano player loused me up," grumbled Ross.

"He couldn't play with the Salvation Army," said Tyler, good and loud.

Outside he counted the change in his pocket, just enough for hamburgers and Cokes if they ate fast and got to the movie before the prices changed. Since Ross was choosing which one, they wound up looking at *Dodge City* again instead of *Goodbye, Mr. Chips,* which was supposed to be terrific.

"They're gonna let me know," said Ross, right when Alan Hale was going to get hung. More problems. His mother and father finding out about this would only make things worse.

"We'd better intercept the mail until it comes."

"What comes?" asked Ross, intent on the screen.

Then Ann Sheridan was singing "Marching Through Georgia" flipping her short frilly skirt up over her can and giving all the drunks in the saloon the come-on. Ross wasn't interested in this part.

"The letter," said Tyler. "About whether you made it or not. You don't want Dad to know what you did unless you made it."

"I guess," said Ross, not sounding very convinced.

"So we don't say a word, okay?"

"Okay."

But he was already dead.

IV

MRS. SWERDLOV took over from the beginning, an affinity with death imbedded in her fat. It was she who opened the door when they got home, her thick arms hugging them into an awkward bundle, her bloated face squeezing out sobs and tiny, intermittent squeaks about God sending for their father and how the neighborhood had been scoured for them.

There was a frozen time, raw and white, like a slash before the blood appears, only longer—much longer—while they lingered in the kitchen and Tyler tried to reorient the house gone lopsided. He managed a few questions, stiff and direct, enough to learn that his father had a heart attack, that it was too late when Dr. Lessing got there, that the body was now at the undertaker's. Mrs. Swerdlov kept assuring them it would be delivered back by five o'clock in the cheapest coffin. A vague thought that she could have said "least expensive," but Mrs. Swerdlov was still gasping facts, trying to convey in a hoarse whisper the intensity of their mother's screams. Dr. Lessing had given her something, and she was fast asleep now —in Tyler's bed. The sleeping arrangements seemed to concern Mrs. Swerdlov most. Tyler would have to move in with Ross. After all, they couldn't expect their mother to stay in *that* bedroom now. How about the other rooms? Didn't his father haunt those, too?

Then Ross started to blubber, and Mrs. Swerdlov picked up the sound. It was contagious like seasickness, and Tyler, feeling his face start to melt, walked quickly down the hall to the empty bedroom. Someone had made the bed, Mrs. Swerdlov probably. But it didn't take much imagining to see it as it had

44

been—her balled fist, him cowering—and hear the hollow, clicking sound of the blows.

It wasn't right that this should have been his last view of him. Heavy indignant globs twisted up from Tyler's stomach. Crying would let them out, or he had only to turn away or close his eyes. But he kept them riveted on the bed, reliving the scene, making the pain inside him bulge unbearably until Mrs. Swerdlov enveloped him from behind, soothing him with pieces of words and dragging him back to the kitchen for a glass of tea.

Tea was Mrs. Swerdlov's cure for all troubles, and she kept the kettle boiling for two days. It was the only thing that remained constant. Everything else dwindled, from Sunday afternoon, when the parlor was full and grief was high and all expressions of sympathy sounded original, to Monday morning, when they sat alone. Even his father's face against the white satin of the coffin, that gradually dwindled, too. At first it seemed very much alive, only sleeping, and Tyler watched it carefully. He'd read a story once by Émile Zola about a man who was believed dead but had only suffered a cataleptic fit. He'd regained consciousness after he was buried and had to claw his way out of the coffin and grave. It *could* happen. So he watched his father's eyelids for the faintest flutter and his chest for the slightest rise, several times sure he'd seen one or the other and almost calling out, "He's not dead—look!" But moving closer, holding his breath, there was neither flutter nor rise, and gradually the face began to yellow and shrink.

During the whole time he avoided his mother's eyes, looking at her only when the others came, the men almost always taking her hand between both of theirs, the women leaning over to interlock necks with her and pat her shoulder. They all came, the Lorenzos, the Brennans, the Novaks, the Goldsteins—the roll call of the World War movies. All except the Keyhoes and daughter Rowena. And why? Sometimes the way they swigged down Mrs. Swerdlov's tea he made thirst their motive. Sometimes, as they stood a full ten seconds staring down at the corpse, he decided it was just a gesture of respect that they hoped to have returned someday. But when Mrs. Mintz, who had entered with a long wail, later came back into the parlor from supposedly using their bathroom, he heard her whisper to Mrs. Kuyava, "Such wallpaper in the bedroom." Snoopers, spies, seizing on death to gain admittance and pry in closets. The measure of a man is his wallpaper!

Did his mother know how phony they all were? If so, she didn't show it, enthroned in the easy chair facing the door, tearless and dignified, thanking each and every mourner who came in and never the same way twice. Then they'd come over to him and mumble something about him being the man of the house now. The implication was always that a happy family had been dismembered, a contented home disrupted. This was the great hypocrisy. No, there was an even bigger lie than that. His father hadn't just died. He'd been killed, murdered by skepticism. If they all hadn't thought he'd been faking those chest pains and called a doctor, he might still be alive.

Sneaking glances at his mother, he wondered if she were suffering the same pangs of guilt. She should have a few extra ones to contend with. At least he hadn't hit him. When he first heard his father was dead, crazy questions jumped through his mind. Would the undertaker notice bruises on the back of his head? Would there be an autopsy? Could a boy testify against his mother? He'd kept telling himself that one-hundred-and-twenty-pound women didn't hit that hard. If a guy could die from a few little punches like those, football players would be dropping like flies. But the questions didn't go until he heard Dr. Lessing say that the heart attack had been coming on for a long time, probably months. Still, he wasn't going to forget what had taken place—ever.

At first it was easy to revive the scene and the sick shame that went with it. He'd begin by envisioning himself standing over his father, goading him to get up. He saw himself with a sneer, heard a cocky, challenging edge in his voice. Then he'd see her kneeling over him, slugging him. At first it was unbearable to think about. But by Sunday morning it was losing its vividness, and by late afternoon it was getting dim. Going back to look at the bed where it had happened didn't even crank it up. Something else was needed. And he found it in their top dresser drawer.

He'd sneaked looks at its contents for years, always hoping for something that had been withheld from him: adoption papers, a Luger, an 1820 Indian Head nickel worth a fortune. But the drawer had always yielded the same untraceable lavender smell, the same pocket watch with the big hand broken off at the source, the same marriage license and photographs.

He knew all the photographs, but he now studied them more deliberately. The one of the baseball team always interested him most. His father had identified the men for him—the bald, squat one in the business suit holding the trophy was the owner of the brewery that sponsored the semi-pro team; the lanky one next to him was the pitcher; the giant on the other side was the first baseman who once had been to spring training with the St. Louis Browns. His father stood at the end of the second row, his uniform too big, his cap tilted back. He'd always claimed he'd been the shortstop, the spark plug of the team. But his placement in the group was that of a utility infielder. Still, he looked a lot happier there than in the wedding picture.

She dominated this with her huge bouquet and the train of her wedding dress swirled on the floor. She'd been all ready for the camera shutter, her chin raised, her smile just right. But no one had told his father to relax or that his pants needed a little hoisting to make the creases hang straight. The one thing that had always nagged Tyler, though, was the bodice of her dress. The way she stood at an angle it was obvious that there was nothing filling it out. She'd been as flat-chested then as she was now, and that was the big puzzle about his father. Why would a man marry a flat-chested woman? What would be the point?

Then Tyler noticed something new in the drawer, a ball of tissue paper tucked at the back. He unfolded it slowly, realizing what it was before it was fully uncovered but forcing himself to go on. The thin gold bar was turning black, and the

artificial teeth at each end were worn almost smooth. Tyler
turned the bridge over in his hand. It wasn't repellent any
more. Now it was a hot coal of indignation. He thought of the
countless times his father complained about his bridge being
loose without getting any sympathy from them and how often
his mother told him off for the noise it made when his tongue
flicked it against his upper teeth. The sick, fierce feeling was
back now. He had a bellyful of all the pretending that had been
going on. The next person that started droning soap opera
clichés at him was going to wind up in a state of shock. Tyler
set a grim face in the dresser mirror, a face that had seen everything and wasn't going to put up with any crap. Holding it,
mouth and eyebrows firm, he went back to the parlor, a tough
marshal walking through swinging doors. And there was Howie,
his face as long and sad as all the others.

"Tough, Ty," he said.

"Howie?"

"Yeah?"

"You lined up some tail for me?"

He should have said it loud enough to make everybody in
the room fall off their chairs. But he'd whispered it, and it
was only Howie's eyes that were doing somersaults. Tyler
crooked a finger to make him lean closer.

"Tell me a dirty joke," he said.

"Quit kiddin' around." Howie tried to move away, but
Tyler grabbed his sleeve.

"Tell me a joke." Slightly louder this time.

"I can't." Howie looked at the coffin, then quickly away.
"Not here."

"Okay."

Tyler walked back to the kitchen, and Howie followed him,
fidgeting and jingling the coins in his pocket.

"Make it good and dirty," said Tyler.

"What d'ya wanna hear a dirty joke for?" Howie cringed.

"To get things in proportion. To clear the air."

"A dirty joke clears the air?"

"Will you quit stalling?"

"Look, Ty, I ain't no expert on funerals, but—"

"For chrissake!" exploded Tyler. "I'm not asking you for a million bucks."

Howie kept chewing his upper lip and sneaking looks at him, debating whether to humor him or beat it. Then he leaned closer and lowered his voice like he always did when talking about sex.

"There was this farmer who had hot nuts for this broad, ya know—"

"I know," said Tyler.

"And he kept takin' her out, but he couldn't get up enough nerve to make the first pass."

"The story of my life," said Tyler.

"You sure you want to hear this?"

"Sure, I'm sure."

"Well, this farmer meets this guy who makes Errol Flynn look like a rookie, some travelin' salesman, see, and he asks him for advice on how to begin, ya know. And the traveling salesman tells him it's a cinch. 'Remember,' he says. 'Women want it just as much as we do. All you gotta do is bring up the subject naturally.' "

"This is dirty?" said Tyler.

"This is screwy," said Howie. "Let's go back to the parlor."

"Finish the joke."

"Anyway," said Howie, "the farm kid keeps tryin' to think of a way to bring up the subject naturally. Then he gets this idea, and he takes a horse and paints the whole thing white except for a certain part, which he paints black."

"A mare or a stallion?" asked Tyler.

"A *male* horse, jerk," said Howie.

"Where'd he get it?"

"What's the difference where? From his farm."

"Okay."

"You want to hear this or don'cha?"

"Continue."

"Well, he ties this horse to a fence at the end of a road. And that night he takes the broad out and drives down this road and parks with his headlights on the horse. But she don't say nuthin', and he don't say nuthin', and they just sit there until he drives her home." Howie was warming to the story. "So the next day the farmer takes the same horse, and he paints the whole thing green except for the certain part, which he paints orange. And he takes the broad out again that night, and they park with their headlights on the horse, and she still don't say nuthin', so he drives her home."

"So the next day," prompted Tyler.

"So the next day he takes this poor old horse, and he paints the whole thing red, white, and blue."

"How about the organs?"

"Purple," said Howie. "And quit interruptin'."

"So that night?"

"That night"—Howie chortled—"he drives down the road and parks with his headlights on the horse. And the broad stares at it, and after about ten minutes she says, 'Gee, look at that funny-lookin' horse.' And the farmer says, 'Yeah, let's fuck!' "

Howie didn't see Mrs. Swerdlov come in to refill the teapot just before he delivered the last line. But when Tyler didn't laugh at it, Howie turned to see who he was staring at, and the hinges of his jaw broke. Mrs. Swerdlov just stood there, a puffed-up red-faced statue. But the look she gave Howie practically blew him out the kitchen door and down the stairs.

Still, he came back Monday for the funeral, which was more than the others did.

V

THE rain stopped about nine o'clock. Then a few minutes later, as if he'd been waiting in his truck for it to end, the florist delivered the wreath. There was a card attached, signed by a jumble of names: John Esher, Lily Halliwell, T. T. Margussen, Angie (from the switchboard), and about a dozen more. At the bottom, just in case his father had never mentioned any of them, someone had written, "from all his fellow workers at Wing Trucking." There was a verse, too, and with nothing else to look at, Tyler soon had it memorized.

> *Today the world is a sadder place*
> *Because he's no longer here.*
> *Today the sun shines not as bright*
> *As it did when he was near.*
> *We'll miss his jokes and ready smile,*
> *We'll miss his warmth and love,*
> *For he has taken all these things,*
> *To a better place above.*

He wondered who'd picked out the card. Angie (from the switchboard) probably. He remembered his father once saying that her halitosis came at you right over the phone. He'd never seen her but he imagined her scrawny and bowlegged, thumbing through stacks of greeting cards in a stationery store until she found this especially disgusting one.

Just after ten, Mrs. Swerdlov came in. Then Howie showed up, his hair slicked down for once. And after that, nobody, except Reverend Sickles. Because of the minister's bulging frog eyes, it was hard to tell if he was surprised to see the parlor so empty. But if so, he quickly recovered. He was a spindly man who bubbled at the mouth when he spoke, and his woolly gray hair seemed tinged with mustard. After whispering somber greetings to each of them, the reverend sat down and started studying a worn prayer book he'd brought. You'd think after all the people he'd buried he'd know the dust-to-dust stuff by heart.

Reverend Sickles closed the book as if he'd heard Tyler's thought. Then he padded across the room and sat on the couch next to Ross, who watched him uneasily.

"Ah, I'm afraid I didn't know your father too well," said the minister quietly. "Perhaps you could tell me some things so I can make the service more personal."

Ross nodded and cleared his throat.

"Did he have any special interests?"

"Baseball," said Ross, and Reverend Sickles jumped. No one had told him the kid couldn't whisper.

"Oh, yes." The minister's smile looked a little stiff. "The game of life. Hits, runs, errors."

"He once played for a brewery," said Ross.

"Ah—anything else he was particularly fond of?"

"Singing."

"Music. Good, good," muttered Reverend Sickles, "gone to join the heavenly choir."

"He sang pretty good," said Ross.

"Thank you." The minister seemed glad to stand up. "That will do nicely." But instead of returning to where he'd been sitting, he came over and leaned his face down toward Tyler until their noses were almost touching.

"Are there any other members of the family?" The question was barely audible. "Yet to arrive," was added on the next breath.

"Our only living relative is my grandmother," Tyler whispered back. "My mother's mother. And she's got a kidney condition, so she couldn't make the trip from Baltimore." His voice went husky from trying to keep it *sotto voce,* and he was afraid Reverend Sickles would think it was from emotion, as if he was bemoaning the barrenness of his family. "My father had two brothers," he added offhandedly. "One died in Boston—from eating bad clams. The other was on his way to California. We were going to move out there too after he got settled. That was nineteen thirty-one."

"What happened to him?" Reverend Sickles looked as if he was still thinking about the bad clams.

"His car went over a cliff in Colorado," said Tyler, adding a loose finger snap to his shrug to indicate the flimsiness of life.

Reverend Sickles nodded and fluttered back to his chair before Tyler could pile on any more grisly tales. Just in time, too. Tyler had already made up one about a beautiful young aunt, dead from illegitimate childbirth.

They were supposed to leave for the cemetery at noon. From eleven thirty on, the man driving the hearse kept creeping up the stairs and peeking in as if somebody might have sneaked in when he wasn't looking. And each time he did, as the steps creaked, they all leaned to look, hoping it might be a possible pallbearer. He was a paunchy man, who must have been hired for the job because of his mournful face.

The fourth time he came up he crooked a finger at Reverend Sickles, and the minister went out to the hall to huddle with him. The hearse driver kept wiping his forehead and the inside of the chauffeur's cap with a soiled handkerchief and tried to keep his voice down, but they heard every word.

"I'm supposed to take this one, then have my lunch, then pick up anudder over on Geneva Street."

They couldn't hear Reverend Sickles' reply. He'd mastered the soft word. But whatever he said, the man wasn't reassured.

"What if nobody else shows up?"

Tyler went out to the hall.

"We can manage it," he said. "The three of us and Ross and Howie."

"I'm sure that won't be necessary," said Reverend Sickles, oozing patience.

"I think it will," Tyler persisted.

"I got a hernia," wheezed the hearse driver. "I can't lift anything."

"You go have your lunch," said Reverend Sickles, and the man limped down the stairs to emphasize his alibi.

Tyler looked back at the parlor, at his mother and Mrs. Swerdlov all in black, at Ross and Howie, at the casket, now closed and squatting heavy.

"Maybe the four of us can carry it," he said.

"No," said the reverend. "You and Ross can't be pallbearers for your father."

"Why not?"

"It just isn't allowed. And I can't either."

"No one else is going to come."

"Of course, they will. It's early yet." The minister tried to sound confident but missed by a mile.

At twelve thirty the room felt desperate with anxious glances going from the mantel clock to watches to the casket to each other. Finally, Mrs. Swerdlov spoke.

"My husband said he'd try to close his shop and be back in time." Then a mintue later. "Nobody realizes a furrier is busy in summer. Alterations, repairs. . . . July's a big month."

Again she got no answer. Again the glances went around the room, helpless, resigned. Anyone else would just shut up. But not Mrs. Swerdlov.

"You never know," she sighed. "Even a strong ox like Lou Gehrig, in the prime of life." She focused on Reverend Sickles. "Did you hear on the radio what he's got?"

"Lateral sclerosis," said Ross.

"Tomorrow's the Fourth," said Reverend Sickles to no one in particular. "I don't think gravediggers work on holidays."

Tyler stood up. "I'll be right back," he said. As he went downstairs, he heard Mrs. Swerdlov offering another morsel of comfort.

"Listen, there are worse things. Like my cousin, Dr. Axelrod, in Düsseldorf. You don't think he's better off if he's dead?"

The paunchy man was slouched behind the wheel of his hearse, eating a sandwich (liverwurst) and reading the newspaper it had been wrapped in. Parked behind the hearse was the minister's car, a '34 DeSoto, simonized to a gleam. Across the street the women waited in clusters, two here, three there. He counted nine in all, nine vultures watching him with beady eyes, knowing there weren't enough pallbearers, waiting to see what he'd do.

Tyler walked out to the middle of the street, looking first one way, then the other. At the far end toward Humber Parkway, two kids were grinding around in circles on their box scooters. From a greater distance came the popping of a chain firecracker. Some pyromaniac couldn't wait until tomorrow. Otherwise, there was no sign of life. He started for Granite Street, broke into a trot.

The stores at the intersection seemed deserted, too. But their doors were wide open. Then Fedorchak came out of his, lugging a bushel basket of potatoes, and Tyler ran over to him.

"We need some pallbearers, Mr. Fedorchak."

"Pallbearers?"

The grocer looked around as if trying to remember what shelf they were on

"To carry my father's casket out of the house and at the cemetery."

"They'd have to go to the cemetery?" Fedorchak pushed back his greasy felt hat and scratched the top of his head.

"It will only take a couple of hours," said Tyler.

"Still, you should have six pallbearers. How many you got?"

"Just one," said Tyler, meaning Howie.

"So you need five more." A mathematical genius, Mr. Fedorchak.

"How about you?"

"Me?" He almost laughed. "I've got a store."

"We're good customers of yours."

"You're customers," grudged Fedorchak. "But I can't close up my business for two hours on a Monday."

"Thanks anyway," said Tyler, heaping the words with contempt.

He kept his fingers crossed that there'd be some men in the

saloon this early. But there was only wiry, little Mr. Ryan standing on tiptoes between the bottles behind the bar, tacking a
flag up over the mirror.

"Sorry, kid," he said, not missing a stroke with the ham-
mer. "But I got a beer truck comin' any minute."

"And my father never got drunk in here," added Tyler just
before he went out the door.

But at least they'd tried to sound sorry. Pitkin, the druggist,
didn't even do that. He just sat at one of his two round tables,
scooping the ice cream from the bottom of his soda with a long
spoon.

"No kiddin'," he finally said. "What you gonna do?"

"If I can get three more men," said Tyler.

"Three? That's a lot."

"Any suggestions, Mr. Pitkin?"

He watched the druggist's chinless Andy Gump profile bending over to sip the straw. He watched him thirstily.

"I think you'll have to wait until tomorrow," said Pitkin.
"Then all the men will be home."

"We can't wait," insisted Tyler. "The hearse is here now, and
everything's been arranged. Besides, gravediggers don't work
on the Fourth of July."

"I don't know what else you can do," said Pitkin.

"Would you be a pallbearer if I can get a couple others?"

"Me? I'm from the wrong tribe, kid. Besides"—he waved
a hand toward the back wall lined with jars of chemicals—"I
got prescriptions to fill."

"Yeah," said Tyler. "I can see you're busy."

"Still," Pitkin called after him, "you're a bright boy. You
should be able to think of something."

The number eleven streetcar was coming, carrying possible
pallbearers. Tyler trotted over to the stop, trying to get up
nerve to flag it, then decided to let fate decide. If the streetcar
stopped to let someone off, he would jump up the steps and
appeal to all the men inside. Some were bound to have the
decency to help. His determination wavered as the blank face
of the streetcar bore down on him. He was sure it was slow-

ing, that there was a change in the pitch of its whine. But then
it was swaying by, the yellow and black of its sides blurring together, its windows one long fuzzy pane. And now he was sure
there were plenty of men riding inside who would have been
glad to help. He should have waved it to a stop. He'd had the
solution in his hands and failed. If his father didn't get buried today, the blame was his.

What now? He could wait for the next streetcar and do what
he should have done this time. But they came at twenty to
twenty-five minute intervals, and the man driving the hearse
might not wait that long. He had to produce at least three
able-bodied men right away. How? Pitkin's parting shot ran-
kled. He should be able to think of something. Going house
to house, appealing at every door? There wasn't time for that
either. Running to the cinder lot and asking the biggest guys
in the ball game? No. His father wasn't being carried to his
grave by kids in sweat shirts and sneakers.

And all the time he stood there, rejecting possibilities, he
was looking at the powder blue Cord convertible with the top
left up because of the morning rain. Blacky Roche had parked
it well down the street from the barbershop as he always did,
as if he was fooling anybody.

Tyler shifted his gaze to the barbershop. The hunchback
lookout wasn't there. The lazy spinning red and white pole
beckoned. He marched stiffly across the street and pushed
open the screen door.

Mr. Dalesandro stopped, his razor poised in mid-air, the
thumb and forefinger of his left hand pinching the loose, lath-
ered neck of the man in the chair. Tyler saw that it was the
colored hunchback being shaved. Dalesandro looked surprised. Tyler hadn't been inside his shop for three years, not
since Dalesandro put a Landon poster in his window. He'd
also had a brush cut only a week ago. But Dalesandro didn't
seem to notice. He just gave Tyler a "won't be long" nod and
bent studiously to scrape away another inch of lather.

"I want to see Mr. Roche," blurted Tyler.

The hunchback, popping up, almost got his throat cut.

"Who?" said Dalesandro.

"Mr. Roche."

"Never heard of him," said the hunchback. But he didn't lean back in the barber chair. And Dalesandro couldn't keep from glancing toward the door at the back of the shop.

"Will you give him a message?" asked Tyler.

"We told ya," said Dalesandro. "We gotta no Mr. Roche here."

"Tell him we need five pallbearers for my father," said Tyler.

"If you don't beat it, kid," said the hunchback, "you're gonna need pallbearers for you."

Tyler ignored him. "We need them right away," he said to Dalesandro. "At Ninety-one Woodward Avenue, upstairs. They'll have to go to the cemetery, so tell Mr. Roche to bring his car."

"What's with you?" yelled Dalesandro, waving his arms and pointing to all the corners of the shop. "Where'sa five men? You can't count?" He jabbed a finger toward the hunchback, then at himself. "One an' two. So how you make five? You're crazy! Scram!"

The more excited Dalesandro got, the calmer Tyler felt. He walked to the screen door before delivering the *coup de grâce*.

"Ninety-one Woodward Avenue, upstairs," he repeated. He looked at the clock on the wall and checked it with the Ingersoll on his wrist. "I'll wait five minutes. Then I'm calling the cops, and your back room's getting raided."

"What back room? Hey! Com'ere."

Tyler tried to slam the screen door behind him, but it was cushioned. Dalesandro's yelling had stopped, and he didn't wait to find out why. He wasn't calm now. His heart was thumping in his throat, but he fought against walking away too fast and wouldn't let himself look back until he reached the intersection.

The screen door was pushed open, and there were hazy shapes and colors behind it—Dalesandro's white jacket and a blue suit. Tyler raised his good wrist deliberately and looked at his watch. Then he walked quickly home.

The vultures were still across the street, but the driver wasn't in the hearse. Tyler stopped on the downstairs porch and looked back toward the corner. His watch told him three minutes had elapsed since his ultimatum. Were they calling his bluff? The sound of a motor made him think he'd won. But it was a Railway Express truck, stopping way up the block. He kept staring, his eyes aching for the color blue: the blue convertible, the blue suit. Another minute must have passed by now. He didn't look at his watch to verify it. And what if another elapsed, and five more, and a half hour? Would he use the Swerdlovs' phone to call the police? He'd made the threat without realizing he might have to carry it out. Had he ever intended to? Had Blacky Roche, who was used to sizing up poker faces across a card table, been able to tell from that one look through the screen door that he was dealing with a gutless punk who would never go through with it? And what if he didn't call the cops? Maybe if he steered clear of the intersection for about six months, they'd forget about him. But if the place ever did get raided, even though it had nothing to do with him, they'd think he'd ratted and come looking for him. On the other hand, what if he went in right now and dialed the operator and asked for the police? They probably wouldn't give Blacky Roche more than thirty days, but he could be far away by then. Of course, there might be a syndicate that would track him down, even if he was working at a gas station on some New Mexico highway under an assumed name. Or more likely, Blacky was paying off the cops not to raid his place, in which case the phone call would get nowhere.

It was all knotted in his mind now. Nothing he could do seemed right. The only solution was for the blue convertible to turn the corner with five men inside. If only it would. Please. Please, Blacky. Do something decent for once in your life. As his mind begged, he knew that he'd never carry out the threat, that it had been nothing but a grandstand play, and the men had known it. If he hadn't been so goddam melodramatic, if he'd just gone in and asked Dalesandro and the hunchback to help out of common decency, they might have. And maybe they would have brought along some other men from the back room. That had been the intelligent way to do it, to put himself at their mercy. But not him. No begging for big shot him. Instead, he just screwed everything up. It would serve him right if they found him some night in an alley with his head cleaved open.

There was no point in putting off the inevitable. Tyler went into the vestibule and up the stairs. When he entered the parlor, his mother was crying and Reverend Sickles was bent over her, mumbling about how it didn't reflect on the esteem with which her husband was regarded by the community. Not much. The hearse driver was there, too, fingering his cap and with his face set like all the tears in the world couldn't change the orders he'd received from his boss.

"No one came," whimpered his mother.

Howie walked across to Tyler. "We could manage it, Ty, you and me and Ross and them." But Tyler shook his head. "Why not?"

"Because the stupid church has stupid rules," said Tyler loudly.

This straightened up Reverend Sickles, but he just turned on an understanding face as if you could throw horse turds at it and he'd forgive you.

"The day after tomorrow," he said. "And I'll make arrangements for the pallbearers."

"No one came," repeated his mother. "No one cares about us now. What's going to happen to us, Frank?"

Everyone waited as if they expected an answer to come out of the casket.

"What's going to become of us?" She turned to Tyler this time, her face suddenly haggard and old.

"We're going to struggle," he said, "and suffer, and eventually die—like everybody else." He said it flatly, and it would have been effective if the end of it hadn't been drowned out by the thumping on the stairs. Then they marched in, the five

of them. Tyler knew four of them by sight, Blacky and Dalesandro and the hunchback and Mr. Horowitz who kept his wife
permanently knocked up. The fifth man, the huge barrel-
chested thug with a bent nose, was a stranger. All five stood staring at him, like rival gangsters waiting for him to make his
move.

"Hi, Blacky," said Tyler feebly.

Everybody could act, everybody except Howie. He kept
shaking his head as if seeing triple. But the others didn't bat
an eye.

"You're friends of the deceased?" said Reverend Sickles.

"Yeah," said Blacky Roche, and motioned the others toward
the coffin.

Reverend Sickles followed them. "If I could just have your
names."

"What for?" Blacky eyed him suspiciously.

"For the church records."

"Oh." Blacky mulled this over before adding, "Eugene
Roche."

The others identified themselves. Mr. Dalesandro's name
turned out to be Anthony (what else?), and Mr. Horowitz's
was Leon. The hunchback even included his middle initial.
"George W. Johnson," he said. And the big thug's name was
William Witowski.

"And who is the sixth pallbearer?"

"Howard Clevenger," said Howie, and took his place at the
casket.

They hoisted it easily, five of them carrying the brunt of it
while the hunchback just reached it with his fingertips. An-
gling it around the banister of the stairway wasn't as simple,
and they cut a deep groove in the woodwork.

"Christ," mumbled Witowski, "this son of a bitch weighs a
ton."

Tyler heard it distinctly, but the others pretended not to.
Still acting. Academy Award performances all. His, too. Coming down the front steps, with his mother hanging on his arm,
he knew he wasn't walking naturally. Something halfway be-

tween a coronation and a beheading. The vultures were still watching, waiting for a rush of tears and hysteria. He could feel his mother trembling and thought she was going to oblige them. But she didn't.

It started raining again as they drove to the cemetery. Reverend Sickles shifted gears as if churning butter. His reflexes were slow, too, and several times they nearly ran into the back of the hearse. Tyler kept glancing at the rearview mirror to see if the blue convertible was still behind them. Other vehicles deferred to their small procession. Pedestrians stopped and watched as they went by. One old man took off his hat. Homage to a father—a few stopped cars and a doffed hat.

The rain increased and was really pouring down by the time they got to the cemetery. The pallbearers hunched against it as they pulled the casket out of the hearse, and it was slippery going carrying it toward the tent which had been put up over the open grave. Tyler walked holding his mother's elbow, aware of the picture he made, hair matted, arm in sling, the Confederate soldier with only pride left. Just ahead, Blacky Roche's new suede shoes splashed in the mud.

When they circled the grave with the casket propped above the rectangular hole, he tried to concentrate on what Reverend Sickles was saying, deep sonorous praises to his father—a man not of fame or great accomplishment but something more important, a good husband and father. But he couldn't keep his eyes from traveling to Blacky. The rain had left dark specks on the powder blue suit. Should he offer to pay for the cleaning? He studied Blacky's face, wondering what it would say to that. The cheeks were slightly pocked, and there was a faint scar, like a question mark, on the left side of his neck. The bookie's nickname was unavoidable, dictated by his eyes and wiry hair. The only surprise had been his voice when he gave his name. It should have been gruff, but it was high and squeaky. Blacky arched forward to look down at his shoes, all soaked and caked, and Tyler suddenly felt guilty. He'd had no right to pull this stunt. Blacky could just have had him beaten up. The fact that he didn't showed he was regular. Tyler resolved he'd make it up to him someday, maybe provide him with an alibi.

"Who took his pleasures from the simple things of life, the crack of ball on bat, the sound of spontaneous singing—"

Reverend Sickles stopped as if aware of how boring he sounded and took a long look around the group hemming the grave. In the corner of the tent the two gravediggers leaned on their shovels and smoked. The minister opened the back of his prayer book and looked at the names he'd written there.

"Roche," he said, "Dalesandro, Horowitz, Johnson, Witowski, Clevenger." He intoned each name, and Tyler watched the men as they were called. Each looked up, then down again sadly at the casket.

"It is fitting," said Reverend Sickles, "it is altogether fitting that those who carried Frank Bishop to his final resting place represent different races and creeds of the melting pot. For it was in the melting pot that Frank Bishop chose to live."

When they got back to the cars, his mother insisted on thanking the five men individually. But she shook the hunchback's hand more than the others. She didn't realize that cripples resented getting extra attention. Tyler wondered if he should thank the men, too. They were getting into the convertible so he had to make up his mind fast.

"Mr. Roche."

Blacky, about to get in behind the wheel, stopped and turned to him.

"Thank you very much, Mr. Roche."

Tyler went to him and held out his good hand. Blacky took it, and Tyler braced, ready for a bone-crushing handshake. But Blacky's fingers felt limp, and his voice was again high and thin when he spoke.

"You just pray my place never gets raided, kid."

The best knockout punches are the ones that travel a few inches. And the left fist that Blacky drove into him didn't travel any more. Not outside it didn't. But after hitting his stomach, it kept going, and Tyler was sure he felt the knuckles touch his spine.

The convertible drove away, leaving him bent in half with nothing to lean on. He sucked desperately for an inch of air, but his lungs were sealed, his throat corked. He managed the three steps to the nearest headstone and grabbed it with both hands to prop himself up. *"Max Somebody 1862-1928."* He tried to subtract the dates and figure out Max's age, but the numbers kept dissolving in his brain. The cemetery was darker, almost purple, the people silhouettes. He made out his mother getting into the car, the driver closing the doors of the hearse, the gravediggers already filling in the hole, alternating quick shovelfuls as if it were a race. Then he gagged, dumbly watching the line of spittle descend from him, unable to move his head so that it wouldn't land on Max's pitted marble slab. But some air had squeaked in. Not much. A molecule maybe. Then another.

"Steady, my boy." Reverend Sickles was patting him on the shoulder and cooing into his ear. "No time to get faint. Remember, you're the man of the house now."

VI

DANZIG dominated the rest of July, Danzig and the dentist of Düsseldorf—alliteration.

His mother decided that their period of mourning should last thirty days, *sans* movies, *sans* games for Ross, *sans* radio. So Tyler had to get all the news from the paper, poring over the front page every night, trying to keep track of Ribbentrop's movements, struggling with pronunciations—Teleki, Csáky, Doumenc, Ciano, Voroshilov.

The time dragged. The heat set a new record during July for consecutive days over ninety, and the air hardly moved. Every few days he went up to the branch of the public library to return four books and take out four more, which he read in the orange rocker on the veranda, his feet propped up on the railing, shadowed by the awning but with a clear view of the street below in case she walked by.

She did, three times—slender, graceful, poised. Her route was always the same. She'd stay on the far sidewalk on her way to Granite Street but come back on this side so he was looking right down at the neat parting of her page boy hair. The first time she returned with a pair of shoes she'd had fixed, the next time with a small grease-stained bag from the delicatessen. The third time he went downstairs to be there when she came back.

As she turned the corner, he bent over, retying the rag tails Mr. Swerdlov kept on the wire bordering the small front lawn, and retying them, and retying them. Where was she? Nobody walked that slow. She might have crossed the street to avoid him. He turned to look and almost rammed his head into her hip.

"Hello, Tyler."

"Hello, Rowena."

"I'm very sorry about your father."

"Thank you," with a slight gulp.

Her arms were deeply tanned. Her shins, too. She'd been spending a lot of time at the beach. Thousands of guys had seen her in a bathing suit, everyone but him. He wondered where the tan ended, imagined beyond its borders while staring into her sunglasses. The snub nose supporting these was peeling a little. Otherwise she was perfect. She smiled faintly and started sidling away. If he didn't say something interesting she'd be gone.

"Uh." The sound slowed her. "Uh, do you know how to pronounce C-S-A-K-Y?"

She lifted her sunglasses and repeated his spelling, frowning. "I don't even know what it is."

"It's a name," he said, trying not to sound superior. "He's the Foreign Minister of Hungary."

"C-S-A-K-Y?"

"There's two dots over the *A*," he said.

"An umlaut."

"Is that what it's called?" As if he didn't know. But it made her stop sidling. She even took a half step back toward him, tucking the bag she carried behind her. From the smell, she'd been to the delicatessen again. It was sausage or bologna—the thick pink kind. He looked at the mouth it would soon enter. Had she ever been French-kissed? He appraised the glistening teeth that would chew the bologna and followed the stuff down her esophagus, unrepelled by anything of hers, willing to kiss her appendix—full of stomach poisons and toothbrush bristles.

"You having a nice summer?" she asked, then caught herself. "I'm sorry, I—"

"That's okay," he said. Then, when she still looked apologetic, he held up the cast on his arm. "At least this comes off next week."

"Does it itch?"

"Like a b— b-b-big mosquito bite." Close call. "You having a good summer?"

"Kinda dull," she said with a brave smile. But she didn't ask him to come over to her house to make it less dull. She on her porch, he on his, both bored stiff when all they had to do was get together. But he couldn't invite himself over. And he couldn't ask her upstairs to see his etchings.

"But I'm going to Alexandria tomorrow," she said.

"Egypt?" He felt like he'd been slugged.

"No, funny. Alexandria, Virginia." Well, how was he to know? Anyway, his was a global view of the world. "I'm visiting my cousin for three weeks."

The hemispheres rejoined, he should have been relieved. But instead he thought of some sophomore from the University of Virginia giving her the rush. Who ever heard of their lousy football team?

"Have a real good time," he said.

"I will," she promised, tossing him a half-hearted wave as she turned to walk away, knowing he was watching her, knowing her calves rippled with every step, knowing what he was thinking even though she'd never admit it.

Aside from her, what he missed most during the month were the news commentators, Kaltenborn and Dorothy Thompson and Gabriel Heatter, even if Gabriel Heatter did get pretty mushy and hysterical sometimes. Most of the time he could hear Mrs. Swerdlov's radio through the parlor floor, muffled—but enough to make out *Fred Allen* and *Doctor I.Q.* and *One Man's Family* and *Charlie McCarthy* and the *Kraft Music Hall* with Bing Crosby and Ken Carpenter singing "Hail K.M.H." like a couple of zombies. Mrs. Swerdlov turned the volume way up for the Louis-Galento fight because Ross had been moaning about not being allowed to listen to it. But whenever a news broadcast came on, it would remind her of

Dr. Axelrod, her cousin in Düsseldorf, and she would turn down the radio so she could yell at her husband.

It was right after Hitler had become a new name that Mrs. Swerdlov brought out the box of old photographs and showed them the one of her cousin. She bought a frame for it at Woolworth's, an ornate silver frame with clover-leafed corners which, for display purposes, held a faded picture of Clara Bow pouting over her bare shoulder. Tyler was there when Mrs. Swerdlov crumpled this into her garbage pail and slid her cousin's photograph into the frame. Then it was propped on the mantelpiece, a sepia-toned portrait of a sad young man with a widow's peak, a bushy mustache, and a high celluloid collar.

At that time, dentists ranked first on his shit list, so Tyler took an instant dislike to the face. Looking at it, he imagined it above him, a mirror strapped to the forehead, the sad eyes suddenly gleaming as the drill descended. But later, as the stories emerging from Germany got worse, Tyler felt guilty about this. And whenever he was in Mrs. Swerdlov's parlor, he would stand for long minutes staring at the photograph, consciously secreting sympathy for the man who posed for it, trying to guess what horrors he was enduring that very minute.

The Dentist of Düsseldorf was Mrs. Swerdlov's only living relative, the son of her father's brother. But there was a hitch in the relationship—for the dentist's mother, the woman Mrs. Swerdlov's uncle had married, was not Jewish. As Mrs. Swerdlov put it, her cousin was not a full-blooded one of them. She didn't say it with contempt—a Cherokee chief dismissing a half-breed—but with a choke in her voice as if the poor guy had incurable anemia or something.

This business of Jewish blood was a favorite topic with her. It wasn't enough to brag about Governor Lehman and Albert Einstein and Judge Samuel Rosenman who wrote a lot of Roosevelt's speeches. Mrs. Swerdlov was convinced that anyone she found especially attractive had to be at least partly Jewish. So her list of *Lantsmen,* as she called them, included people like John Barrymore, and Eddie Duchin, and Anthony Eden. Nothing Tyler could say would dislodge any of them. Even when she claimed Shirley Temple.

"Now you've gone too far," he'd said.

"Why? You think Temple is her real name?"

"So what if it isn't?"

"Temple is a Jewish name, that's what."

"How about Temple University?"

"A rabbinical school."

"Aw, come on, Mrs. Swerdlov."

"What? You're so smart. So why did they call her Shirley Temple? Why not Shirley Church? Who goes to Temple—Pope Pius?"

Before the Nazis took over, Mrs. Swerdlov had only mentioned her cousin a few times—when he opened his office, when he got married ("so late," she said; he was forty-four), and when his wife had a baby daughter. News of these things came in letters, in German of course, always arriving in the morning mail so that they'd get the translations at breakfast. Mrs. Swerdlov would clump up the backstairs and into their kitchen, brandishing the thin blue stationery with the slanted writing, always pretending she'd brought up the envelope so Tyler could have the stamps when she knew damn well he never saved stamps.

It was all bragging then, not the letters themselves but her interpolations while reading them. And the way she did it, like pointing out that Dr. Axelrod's office was in the best part of Düsseldorf, always made it sound as if all his accomplishments came from the Jewish half of him. The wife bothered her though. She knew her first name was Inge, but not her maiden name, and though Mrs. Swerdlov claimed she wrote asking point-blank what the woman's religion was, her cousin never told her.

"Not that it matters these days," Mrs. Swerdlov finally said. "Everybody marries everybody." Then she added with a heavy sigh, "As long as she isn't a *Schwartze*."

Tyler felt his face redden but kept his temper down.

"There are three girls in school named Inge," he said. "All black as coal."

Mrs. Swerdlov stared at him over the cup of coffee she was blowing on to cool.

"In Europe," she said, "Tyler is a woman's name." And her face was as straight as he'd kept his.

"I'll bet," he scoffed. But it took him a couple of hours to get over it.

During the summer of 1936 the letters became more frequent, and though the contents didn't seem very different, they had to take Mrs. Swerdlov's word that he was telling her things between the lines.

"Who knows what they're doing to him?" she sobbed. And the newsreels and pictures in the papers backed her up, showing storm troopers beating up Jews in the streets and making them wear a Star of David on their sleeves. Dr. Axelrod's Aryan mother wouldn't count either. The Nazis, like Mrs. Swerdlov, regarded anyone with a drop of Jewish blood as Jewish.

Then, after many months of silence, another letter arrived. Mrs. Swerdlov was crying openly when she came upstairs with it, summarizing it because she couldn't bear to read it aloud. Her cousin had lost everything, his practice, his wife, his child, everything! Tyler had images of leather-booted thugs throwing a dental chair out of a window, slapping the protesting woman out of the way, clubbing the face on the mantelpiece. But when she finally got to translating the letter, it wasn't like that. Her cousin had moved his office to another section. "From the best neighborhood to a ghetto. I know the street." And his wife and he had decided to divorce, she taking the child. "He's doing it to save his daughter, so they won't know what she is." But the revealing sentence was at the end.

"I wish I could visit you," it said, "because I want to see you again before I die."

It was this sentence that produced the tears, and Tyler couldn't quarrel with Mrs. Swerdlov's interpretation of it.

"He's asking me for help," she said. "He's begging me to get him out of there before they kill him. But where can I get the money? Not from that greenhorn!"

"That greenhorn" was *Mr.* Swerdlov. Most of the year he was glimpsed only early in the morning and from the back, a short plodding figure in a long black coat and black fedora hat on his way to the streetcar stop. But on summer Sundays he'd work on his miserable little lawn, unshaved and shirtless, his grisly chest one of his many sources of embarrassment to his wife.

Mrs. Swerdlov always seemed to be apologizing for him, for his appearance, for his being at work whenever they went downstairs to visit, for his ignoring them when they did happen to pass on the street because he couldn't see a foot in front of his nose and wouldn't wear glasses outside. Sometimes she'd weave insults into the apologies, about how ignorant and crude and miserly he was, like when she said he knew practically no English, just how to count. And once, when she thought Tyler was out of earshot, she confided to his mother that Mr. Swerdlov was so repulsive to her that they'd slept in different rooms since she knew she was going to have Eunice. As if Tyler hadn't figured out who slept in each of the three bedrooms below.

But in spite of how she felt about him, Mr. Swerdlov was insanely jealous where she was concerned. He bought an expensive Philco radio because she played Russ Columbo records on their victrola one whole Sunday. And she got the first Kelvinator in the neighborhood out of him just by mentioning how good-looking Grady, the iceman, was. Mrs. Swerdlov tried to think of something like this to make him cough up the money to bring her cousin over. But as Eunice Swerdlov explained it, her father's jealousy only led to tangible things like Philcos and Kelvinators. Humanitarianism was something beyond the peasant mentality. Still, Mrs. Swerdlov tried—arguing and threatening and, most of the time, just plain screaming.

The battle was always carried out late at night in the bedroom below Tyler's, Mr. Swerdlov's bedroom, when he got home from work. Tyler, awakened, would lie listening for the slightest waver in the noises Mr. Swerdlov made, any sign that she was making headway. But Mr. Swerdlov's grunts became, if anything, more sullen, driving Mrs. Swerdlov's shrieks higher and higher until she sounded like Jessica Dragonette being goosed.

One night that January, her screaming filibuster never stopped, and she was still going strong the next morning when Tyler and Ross got ready for school. They could hear the battle below shifting from room to room as Mr. Swerdlov was obviously trying to wash and eat and get dressed. Then, just after Tyler and Ross went down the front steps, taking them slowly because of the snow and ice, Mr. Swerdlov came scooting out. Tyler called to him to be careful, but Mr. Swerdlov had never been more surefooted, waddling down the steps in five choppy, Charlie Chaplin strides. Mrs. Swerdlov, slippers clacking, red flannel robe billowing in the wind, was two paces behind.

"*Goniff! Shtunk!*" The second name was called in mid-air for she'd taken off from the top step as if it was a ski jump. Tyler winced as she landed. Luckily, she fell in a sitting position, and the snow was a foot deep. Still the whole neighborhood shook. But Mr. Swerdlov, skidding on his right foot and pivoting left where the sidewalk had been shoveled clear, didn't even look back.

"Morris!" she screamed, scooping up a handful of snow and heaving it toward him. But it fell apart like granulated sugar, most of it drifting back on her. She rolled to her hands and knees, as if on the mark for a hundred-yard dash. Then she threw her slippers at him, the second one missing him only by inches as he churned out of range.

The street, which had been deserted a minute before, suddenly sprouted people. Tyler counted eight of them, inching out of doors and driveways and delivery trucks to get a better view of Mrs. Swerdlov pushing herself to her feet. Then she stood in the snow, barefoot, appealing to all the women in sight.

"He's got money in twenty banks, and he won't spend a few dollars to save a life. Don't you buy a fur coat from him, you hear? You can live without Persian lamb!"

When Tyler got home from school that afternoon, his mother was just taking some hot soup downstairs. He went with her to find Mrs. Swerdlov on her couch, the colored pillows supporting her like life preservers. She was sniffing desperately, already sure she'd caught pneumonia and blaming her husband. But as she ate the soup, she became quiet and resigned.

"Thank God," she said, "I still have my ace in the hole."

Being only fourteen then and still naïve, he didn't know what she meant. And it was about a week before it dawned on him that no one was sleeping in the bedroom below his. It'd been repulsive to think about, enough to make him want to be a monk. He hadn't known then that marriage was just legal prostitution.

But even if the God Mrs. Swerdlov was always thanking did exist, he sure wasn't listening to her. When she wrote her cousin inviting him to visit and saying she'd buy his steamship ticket, there was no reply. She waited another two months before getting in touch with some organization that got Jews out of Germany. More waiting, more cursing her husband and Hitler with alternate breaths. Then the organization reported that Dr. Axelrod was no longer in Düsseldorf. In fact, there was no trace of him at all. Mr. Swerdlov moved back to his own bedroom. That had been more than two years ago.

It was the morning after Dr. Lessing chiseled the cast off Tyler's wrist that the letter came from England. He was still hypnotized by the pale pulpy skin and worried if this arm would ever again look like the other one. But Dr. Lessing had told him not to favor it, so he was helping dry the breakfast dishes when Mrs. Swerdlov lurched in without knocking, clutching her heart and waving off the chair his mother offered. Instead she grabbed Tyler's face with both hands, twisting it to meet her own and puffing fumes of cigarettes and pickled herring up his nose as she kissed him. Then she did the same to his

mother and to Ross, who wiped off the kiss as soon as she finished. And in between her loud, sucking smacks she waved the
letter in that same slanted handwriting and let them know that
the Dentist of Düsseldorf was on his way.

Part Two

I

SOME Rubicon.

Dr. Axelrod had expected the gangplank to provide a long descent, a descent he would make slowly, girdling himself with an imperious air and setting firmly and for all time on his face the expression of strength that he would present not only to his cousins, the Swerdlovs, but to all America.

He had been determined on just such a metamorphosis when he'd boarded the *Queen Boadicea* at Liverpool. And those first hours alone in his stateroom, he'd been confident that all he despised about himself had been left on the dock—like a sloughed snake's skin, Goethe would say. But the Harvard hoodlums soon spoiled that. Irony had followed him to sea. Four passengers on the freighter, and the other three had to be university adolescents, cavorting throughout the nine-day voyage like caged baboons, unable to sit quietly and read or converse, always throwing a ball back and forth or pummeling one another or strumming a ukulele and trying to sing in harmony— incredible songs about moonlight on a river or victory on a field.

Or they would extemporize their own, as when he was introduced to them by Mr. Young, the purser, at the first meal in the small claustrophobic dining room. He was still trying to sort them out, to link names with faces, when the pimpled one (was he Leroy?) shouted, "Axelrod!" Then he seized the ukulele beside his chair, struck a chord, and the three of them sang;

"Axelrod, Axelrod,
Won't you be my Axelrod?"

It was a test and he surmounted it with a withering stare. He would completely ignore them, turning a visage of stone toward any overtures they made. And if absolutely necessary to speak, he would impale them on laconic replies.

There were six at the table: Captain Plummer, Mr. Young, the three hoodlums, and himself. It seemed to be the purser's task to conduct conversation, and this Mr. Young did quite effortlessly, asking each of the hoodlums which city he was from and then mentioning a landmark of that vicinity familiar to him. But to Dr. Axelrod's "Düsseldorf" he merely said, "Is that so?" Two years ago that would have astounded Dr. Axelrod. But he'd met many people in England who didn't know where Heinrich Heine was born.

Captain Plummer hardly spoke, which was as it should be. Sociability would undermine his authority. Dr. Axelrod doubled his determination to avoid his former mistake of talking too much. He also tried emulating the way the captain peered up from under his eyebrows at whoever was talking and his manner of smiling faintly at the hoodlums' attempts at humor. The smile was always delayed, reflective—playing the moon to Mr. Young's sunny laughter. Dr. Axelrod decided that the captain wasn't listening to the table conversation at all. Several times he was certain he saw worry deepen the lines in his forehead and around the eyes. But if they were headed into a gale their first night out or toward icebergs, it didn't affect Captain Plummer's digestion.

After the coffee, the captain took out a pipe. Then, sucking a match flame into the bowl and getting it smoking properly, he suddenly became talkative. A mistake, thought Dr. Axelrod, especially so early in the voyage. But the hoodlums showed no disrespect. The pipe could explain that. To the young it symbolized thought and maturity, a conditioned reaction which undoubtedly had tribal origins. What was the word—a calumet.

The captain feigned interest in what the hoodlums were studying at Harvard. The short overweight one who would lose his hair at an early age said that he was majoring in political science.

"Politics is a science?"

Dr. Axelrod blurted it without thinking, and when they all looked at him, he reached for the silver coffeepot as if he hadn't spoken. Would he never learn? Must he cut out his tongue?

Fortunately they did not pursue his question. Instead the captain turned to the earnest-looking one, the most acceptable of the three in appearance. Dick, he was called and he kept referring to liberal arts. Dr. Axelrod tried to fathom the term. In what way could art not be liberal?

Leroy, he with the skin condition, claimed he was not pursuing anything special. He was in his third year, he said, and had tried everything from economics to chemistry.

"But what interests you most?" asked Mr. Young.

"Basketball and boobs," said Leroy.

"Boobs? What are boobs?" There could be no harm in his asking that.

"Wouldn't do you any good, Doc." Leroy had a stallion's mouth—the lips loose, the teeth protruding, and the gums fully visible when he guffawed, which was often. Also the skin condition was revolting, not the blemishes of youth, but something requiring a dermatologist.

Dr. Axelrod was suddenly aware that they all were looking at him again. He must have been asked a question.

"I beg your pardon," he said.

It was the one with the thinning hair, Russell, who apparently had addressed him.

"I asked if you have the same curriculum in Germany."

"It has been almost thirty years since I was in the university," said Dr. Axelrod. "Since then I have confined my studies to the problems of being."

"What's the diff' what you study?" said Leroy.

"Your studies lead to the work you do," said Dr. Axelrod.

"And your work determines your character." A simple statement, he thought, simple and incontrovertible. But not at Harvard. Dick insisted on clarification.

"We have the whole voyage," said Dr. Axelrod. "We will
have plenty of time to discuss."

"Put up or shut up," said the pimpled Leroy.

The room was stifling. Or was it only from the attention
focused on him? Attention generated heat. "As Lamarck
proved," he said, "the environment creates the organ."

"Lamarck?" queried Russell.

"Left tackle for Georgia Tech," said Leroy.

"A man's occupation determines his character," repeated Dr.
Axelrod. He looked around the table for an example. He could
not use himself, so he was left with the purser or the captain.
"Captain Plummer, for instance, reflects his position."

He had meant it as praise, but the captain tapped the ashes
out of his pipe with annoyance. "In other words," he said, "I
look like I belong on this stinking little tub instead of the
Queen Mary."

"No, no," said Dr. Axelrod hastily. "I was referring to your
composure, your obvious confidence and capability. These are
characteristics of a man who deals with the elements of nature
and has responsibility for the lives of others."

"Aren't you being too pragmatic?" asked Dick. From the way
he said the word, he was not sure of its meaning.

"Pragmatism does not enter in," snapped Dr. Axelrod. He
said it with finality and could feel the others aligning themselves with the earnest young man.

"I think it's the other way around," said Mr. Young, placat-
ingly. "I think the kind of person you are determines the kind
of work you do."

"Then Leroy's going to be the doorman of a cathouse," said
Russell, and they all laughed.

Typical, thought Dr. Axelrod. As soon as thought gets close
to truth, laughter is the escape. But he stood and pushed back
his chair as the others did, trying to appear to have forgotten
the conversation as easily as they had. Still, some good came of

it. The hoodlums were careful not to engage him in serious talk again. Having discovered his strength, they kept out of range and resorted to thinly disguised insults. Like counting in cadence in what was supposed to pass for German as he took his morning constitutional up and down the small deck. He met this with silence—cold, contemptuous silence. But they mistook this for inarticulateness, and their remarks became braver, the pimpled Leroy who seemed always to wear a nubbly red sweater with a big white *H* finally having the audacity to refer to him as Schicklgruber.

He should have faced him with a retort equally crude. "And what does your *H* stand for, Hitler or Himmler?" Or even better, a direct confrontation on the most elementary level. "Why did you call me that? By what right?" But he had said neither, and after the crucial moment had passed, it was too late to assert himself. Once a relationship is established it *is* impossible to change it.

He'd known this much when he went to London two years ago. But time after time there he'd still made the same mistake. In the dental laboratory where he labored, making prosthetics unfit even for Goebbels' mouth, his position as the butt of all jokes and target of bad tempers was quickly established. He had done it himself, refusing to confine his words to the work at hand, discussing his opinions openly as if the others carving and molding at the long bench were on his intellectual level. Like the morning after he'd attended the meeting of the Fabian Society, when he'd come in and repeated the speaker's "Any man over forty is a scoundrel." Mr. Trueman, who owned the laboratory, often boasted of having all his own teeth at sixty-two. No one around the bench was less than fifty. And like all those who lived in terror of possibility, they regarded every new-stated truth as a threat to their inconsequential selves. How they ridiculed him that day!

Multiplied by two years, this had been his nightmare, made all the more fiendish by the stench of baking plastic and the shelves of disembodied mouths which also seemed to be mocking him. As for his hours free from work, most were spent alone

in his small room off the Edgware Road, reading, learning, thinking. And there had been the organizations—the Secular Union
on Ebury Street, the Goethe Society, the Anti-Vaccination
League, the Tottenham Court Ethical Club. He'd approached
each reborn, not from the reasons of loneliness that prompted
so many members, but because of a sincere belief. New shabby
rooms, new shouting posters on the walls, new faces. Each time
he was greeted as a friend, thumped on the back as he quoted
Lucretius on the evils of religion or voiced his admiration for
Goethe or the dangers of smallpox inoculation or his feelings
about the responsibility of man. Small dissensions came later, a
difference of interpretation, a preference for Burckhardt over
Nietzsche, a conflicting cartography of the boundaries of moral-
ity. At first he had handled them clumsily, still trying to endear
himself, his vocabulary small. But even later, when he could
overwhelm them with their own language, he'd wound up
shunned, snickered at, his facts blunted by others' ignorance.
He hadn't yet learned that knowledge was sustenance, not am-
munition. Nor that all arguments, being basically battles of ego
and not information, were decided by force of personality. This
was the lesson hardest to learn because it was so repugnant to
the intelligent mind. But finally he faced it and began to sculpt
himself again, chipping arrogance from pride and disdain from
contempt. Then, just when he thought he had it perfected, the
Harvard hoodlums had to enter his life. But his mistake with
them was obvious. His timing was at fault. He had failed to
take the initiative from the very beginning. But, after all, this
had been his first encounter with the pampered barbarism of
American youth. He couldn't blame himself too much for expecting them to behave like young people elsewhere. Never
mind. May all divinities have mercy on the next one who
aroused his temper.

Meanwhile, the true test awaited him. Sunning in his deck
chair, lying in his creaking bunk at night, he struggled to avoid
thinking about it. He had made up his mind before leaving
England, adamant then. But the rhythmic, lapping water lulled

him. Was it worth taking a stand? Dignity could be dissipated by a minor cause.

Overhearing the "Schicklgruber" decided him. Or, more accurately, his failure to contend with it. He was fifty-two years old. This was his last chance. Any backing down now would be the end, not of an isolated conviction, but of the totality of himself. From the moment he crossed the Rubicon from the *Queen Boadicea* to the dock of New York he must be completely the man he'd been so long fashioning; incapable of compromise, abrupt with nonsense, intolerant of frivolity, unmindful of the approval of others. Anticipating the encounter ahead would only unnerve him. Better to use the days and nights mulling over and dispersing the last remnants of memories. This he did, and the remainder of the voyage was a sluggish movement through time.

The gangplank should have been long and descending. But it was barely two feet wide and horizontal, with frayed ropes serving as railings. He traveled it in three strides, stopping momentarily midway to glance down at the slimy, acid yellow water in the narrow space between dock and ship. Some Rubicon.

The Harvard hoodlums had preceded him and waited restlessly on the dock with tennis rackets and ukuleles. The pimpled one saw him first and nudged the others. They had never seen him wearing spats, since there'd been no occasion on board to do so. Nor his Homburg, of course. No doubt, to American university students, these were sources of great mirth. But if they so much as commented, they would find that more had changed than his attire. Perhaps they sensed this. Perhaps a warning emanated from him. Or else it was the arrival of the immigration inspector that made them look away.

Dr. Axelrod turned to watch the inspector, too—this man who would prove his first test. Mr. Young was giving him a large Manila envelope, and the two men exchanged words as if long acquainted. The inspector seemed weary, disgruntled, certainly in no hurry to deal with the passengers. No older than

Dr. Axelrod, he was a man living by rote, his civil servant's face soft and nondescript. This would be a battle, not of personalities, but with protocol.

A small wooden table was set up inside the dock shed, just beyond the line of shade. And on this the inspector slowly arranged the tools of his trade—rubber stamps and booklets and forms and paper clips and pens—all removed from a small cardboard box with split seams. The inspector's uniform was as shabby as the box, frayed at the cuffs, a bud of threads indicating a missing button in front and the collar of the white shirt soiled. Some contrast between this and the appearance of a similar official in Germany or even England. But in one sense Dr. Axelrod was pleased. A man so careless about his appearance would not be too strict about other aspects of his work.

The small cardboard box was empty at last. Then the inspector sat down and pressed the nib of his pen with his fingertip to be sure the ink was flowing. Satisfied that it was, he beckoned to the closest of the hoodlums.

The three of them went through quickly. One look, a nod, a stamp, stamp, stamp, and "Welcome home." Why not? With those clothes and haircuts, they couldn't belong anywhere else. And all three had the little yellow card.

The pimpled one was last. Good riddance. But he couldn't just pick up his ukulele and go off like the others. He had to turn around and offer his hand.

"So long, Doc. I can't say it's been fun."

"I extend my deepest sympathy," said Dr. Axelrod, "to your parents and all those who must endure you."

It was a sentence he'd rehearsed for several days, ever since the Schicklgruber. And it had even more effect in reality than in his imagination. Even the pimples turned a deeper red.

"Yeah?" said the boy. But after that he mouthed only air, backing away until he turned and trotted after his two subhuman friends.

"Next!"

The immigration inspector waited. Certainly he had looked more pleasant when he'd greeted the others. No matter. The success of his retort to the pimpled one had buoyed Dr. Axelrod. He stepped up to the little table and thrust out his sheaf of documents. They'd been folded a long time, and some were on the tissue-weight paper that got crumpled. But this didn't necessitate the endless smoothing out that the inspector was doing. Then he held up the top form and studied it.

"Your first name is spelled with no *e*?"

"Yes," said Dr. Axelrod. "W-O-L-F."

"Sometimes they spell it with an *e*," said the inspector. His finger moved down the paper. "Your cousin's name ain't the same as yours."

"Her maiden name is," said Dr. Axelrod.

"But her married name is Swerdlov, right?" asked the inspector. He looked up and saw him nod, but waited until he said, "Yes," before continuing. "And this is her present address?"

"Yes."

"And she knows you're coming?"

"I wrote her, yes."

"How long are you going to stay, Mr. Axelrod?"

"Doctor." It was a petty correction, but it might prove valuable in a minute. The thought of another day flashed through his mind. At a labor exchange in London he'd insisted about being addressed as Doctor, not Mister, only to discover that dentists in Britain were never called Doctor. But this time he'd made sure in advance by asking Mr. Young, the purser.

"That's right," admitted the inspector. "Doctor. How long are you planning to be with us?"

"I don't know," shrugged Dr. Axelrod. "Perhaps for the remainder of my life. I have an immigration visa." He started to reach for his papers, to point out the visa, but the inspector's hand was on them.

"Then you're planning to become a citizen?"

"I understand that it is not a condition of entry."

"Uh-huh." The inspector seemed to lose interest in him, picking up one of the rubber stamps and pressing it hard into the ink pad between each impression on one of the papers. No questions about politics, about affiliations in Germany or money in his pocket. The man was incompetent. Enough so to overlook the yellow card, too? As if reading the thought, the inspector started searching quickly through the documents.

"Where's your vaccination certificate?" He looked up impatiently. "The yellow card."

"I do not have one."

"Nuts!" The inspector stood up and looked around as if for assistance. But the purser had gone back on the ship, and the only person in sight was the man at the customs end of the shed. The inspector turned back to him.

"Didn't they tell you to get vaccinated when you got your visa?"

"Yes," admitted Dr. Axelrod.

"Then why the hell didn't you? Now I gotta get a health officer. Screw up my whole day."

"I do not believe in smallpox inoculation," said Dr. Axelrod. But the inspector was rubbing his head and not listening. Then he scooped up all his paraphernalia into the box and handed Dr. Axelrod back his papers.

"You'll have to wait here until I get somebody."

"If you will just listen for one minute."

The inspector turned to him, ready for any solution. "Yeah? What?"

Dr. Axelrod had prepared the speech carefully in his mind. The important thing was to make it sound calm but impassioned, a statement of scientific logic, not of fanaticism. In other words to make it sound just what it was.

"Well?" The inspector was still waiting.

"The smallpox vaccination is stupid," said Dr. Axelrod. "For the past two years I have been only in London, England, where there has been no smallpox epidemic, so why must I be inoculated?"

"I don't make the laws," said the inspector. "You gotta be vaccinated within three years."

He walked away, as if that were the final word on the subject.

Dr. Axelrod wanted to summon him back, to quote the facts and statistics he'd memorized. But he waited too long.

The sun had moved so that the table was no longer in the shade. Empty now, just a simple scratched table without veneer, it remained a barrier. Beyond it was shade and, against one wall, a crate on which he might sit down. But he was afraid to go past the table or even to sit on the inspector's chair, unofficial as it looked. So he stood stiffly in the sun, the very hot July sun.

Needing something to concentrate on, he turned and looked at the *Queen Boadicea*. It seemed much larger here in dock than when one was aboard, its black and rusty hull curving away so he could not see the prow or the winch that he could hear turning somewhere forward. Then the heavy net rose and swung out toward the dock far up at the customs end. Three laborers stepped out seemingly from nowhere to guide it down and, once it went limp, to lift out its cargo of heavy wooden crates, steel-slatted and stenciled. Cargo was more easily admitted than humanity.

He considered moving the chair into the shade and sitting on it. And he'd almost massed up enough nerve to when he saw the inspector come out of an office and stand silhouetted at the far end of the dock shed. He was looking out, but he might turn around. Dr. Axelrod remained standing, feeling his feet swell and the perspiration ooze under the brim of his hat. He wanted to take the hat off, his coat, too. But the health officer might appear at any moment, and Dr. Axelrod didn't want to be found in shirt sleeves. As for the hat, it provided dignity, imperturbability. That was the purpose of a Homburg.

Dr. Axelrod assumed that a health officer would wear white. But the man with the inspector wore a suit, so he thought this was just another immigration official come to give argument. Then, as the two men neared him, he saw the small black case.

The health officer put this on the table without even looking at him. And he opened it and took out the vial before he said, "Roll up your sleeve."

"No," said Dr. Axelrod.

Both men stared dumbly at him.

"What is this?" asked the health officer, more of the immigration inspector than of him.

"Do you know what it is in that vial?" asked Dr. Axelrod. He rushed his words, tumbling them out. "That is cowpox, poison taken from infected cows. There is no relation between cowpox and smallpox. Have you ever seen the cattle they take that from, with their big open sores? That is what you are putting into people's bloodstreams."

The health officer and immigration inspector were still looking at each other. "One of those," said the health officer.

"I challenge you to look at the statistics," said Dr. Axelrod. "In the past ten years in Britain and Belgium and France and the Netherlands three times as many persons have died from smallpox vaccinations as from smallpox."

"You ain't gonna die," said the inspector.

"I guarantee you it don't hurt," added the health official.

"It is not a question of pain!" Dr. Axelrod almost shouted it. "Whenever a person takes a moral stand, he is accused of cowardice." He held out his hand. "Here, fracture my fingers as a substitute." They stared at his quivering hand until he lowered it. Then the immigration inspector took out a soiled handkerchief and mopped his forehead. This seemed to remind the health officer of the sun, and he moved his black case back onto the shaded part of the floor.

"Okay," he said. "If you refuse to be vaccinated, I've got to put you in quarantine."

"I agree," said Dr. Axelrod. His willingness made the officer uneasy.

"You're asking for it. They can keep you there ten days if they want."

"Yes," said Dr. Axelrod.

"Look," said the officer. "It's just a little scratch."

"No," said Dr. Axelrod.

"Can't they make him pay for the hospital room while he's

in isolation?" Dr. Axelrod caught the wink that went with the immigration inspector's question.

"Definitely," said the health officer.

"I have," said Dr. Axelrod, "exactly thirty-six of your dollars and fourteen cents."

This produced another exchange of looks. Then the men moved together, bowing their heads as they met and shielding their mouths from him with their hands. But some things were said deliberately loud for his ears.

"Then he goes back where he came from."

"When does this freighter sail?"

"I have a visa," said Dr. Axelrod, "and you stamped it." But the two men ignored him. "I have no money for a return passage," he added.

This made them turn and glare at him. Then the health officer came over and tried to smile.

"Look, Jack, it's no skin off my nose, but believe me—you don't want to spend ten days in an isolation ward at Bellevue."

"I am prepared for any eventuality," said Dr. Axelrod.

"You'll be sorry." The immigration inspector chimed the words.

"Why don't you just have the little scratch?" said the health officer.

"Because it is archaic, pagan, and mystical," said Dr. Axelrod. He'd left out the most important reason. "Because I am opposed to it," he added.

"Okay." The shrug that the health officer gave to the immigration inspector was helpless and resigned.

"I'll call the ambulance," said the inspector. He sauntered away slowly, stretching, looking up at the girders of the shed, taking maybe a dozen steps before looking back. Then, seeing that neither of them had moved, he turned and walked off quickly.

The health officer didn't acknowledge Dr. Axelrod again. He just concentrated on examining the contents of his little case, as if something precious might have been stolen while they were talking. Dr. Axelrod was sure he could step into the shade now. But they hadn't suggested it, and the sun had become part of his test. He would remain in its hot glare as long as necessary. As if in defeat, a cloud moved over it. And like a reward, the cool breeze reached him.

When the white ambulance appeared at the far end, the health officer motioned him toward it. Their footsteps on the splintered and sometimes loose floorboards of the shed rang hollow. The man of conscience and the man of duty. Of the two, whose tread was lighter, whose shoulders more erect? Triumph swelled in Dr. Axelrod; a fanfare throbbed in his brain. He had done it. He was a new and different man.

II

THEIR first guess was the *Queen Mary*, due Monday, July 17, with 1,926 passengers. Mrs. Swerdlov didn't move from the house on Monday and Tuesday. She didn't even do her laundry because she didn't want to be looking like a slob when her cousin arrived. On Wednesday they again checked the list of ship arrivals in the paper and decided he was on the new *Normandy*, which arrived the next day with 1,749 passengers. Saturday, Mrs. Swerdlov called the police and was told they had no jurisdiction over people arriving four hundred miles away. After that, she just waited for a telegram to arrive with some tragic news. And when Tyler predicted that Dr. Axelrod would be on the *Britannic* which was due the following Thursday, Mrs. Swerdlov just shrugged.

"What's the difference which boat? When you fall overboard, they're all the same."

The last day of July was a real scorcher. Mrs. Swerdlov, who'd resumed her Monday washday, was feeling faint from the heat and asked Tyler to help her take her clothes down off the lines. Then he went back upstairs to the porch and continued reading *In the Fog* by Richard Harding Davis.

Some kind of telepathy must have made him look over the railing. But by then the man was almost in front of the house. There was no resemblance to the face on the mantel. Not that there would be after about thirty years. But Tyler thought that after what Mrs. Swerdlov's cousin had been through, the change would be in the direction of death and decay. And the man below looked healthy and well fed. He wasn't tall, but he walked very straight, and this, combined with his portliness, made him seem big. The mustache in the photograph was missing and the face wasn't sad, just round and sweating. But there were still reasons to think it was him. The hat for one thing. Men here didn't wear that kind. And the spats. The suitcase, too—bulging brown and closed with heavy straps, it had tags and stickers on it that could be from an ocean voyage.

Tyler heard the downstairs bell ring. He heard Mrs. Swerdlov's thundering feet and her "Who's there?" He heard her open her front door. And from the scream that followed, it was obviously her cousin. Or else she was being raped.

After the scream, the man disappeared, swallowed up by the flat below as if he'd walked through the Sire de Maletroit's door. In fact, it was the next afternoon before Mrs. Swerdlov made an appearance, clumping up the backstairs to invite them to dinner Wednesday night to meet him.

"Ten days ago he should have been here," she said. "Ten days they kept him in quarantine, like he had lice. You'd think after everything else he's been through." Then the automatic afterthought. "It should only happen to that greenhorn."

"Does he think there'll be a war?" asked Tyler.

"He'll tell you himself," she said. "He learned good English in England. It's a pleasure to listen to him."

He looked forward to Wednesday night—to the conversation, not the food. But the meal would be a first, too. In the eleven years they'd lived there, soup had been exchanged, and homemade cake and dill pickles. But there'd never been an invitation to dinner. Not that they'd minded. Whenever the sweet and sour smells wafted up from the kitchen below, they had to open all the windows.

"Half past six," Mrs. Swerdlov had said. "So we can be all through in time for *One Man's Family*."

They were ready before six-thirty. But his mother made them wait. "And don't ask too many questions," she warned.

"Christ," he wailed, "I finally get a chance to meet somebody from outside this vacuum, and I'm restricted."

"Don't blaspheme," she said. She'd finally shed black. The

olive dress, her best dress, showed her collarbones. And she'd shaved her legs.

"He's only a dentist," said Tyler. "You know what a dentist is?" He waited for her to prompt him, but she didn't. "A dentist is a guy who flunks out of medical school."

"Where's that letter you had in the paper?" Talk about changing the subject.

"Why?"

"Eunice never saw it."

"It's way over her head."

But he got it out of his dresser drawer and gave it to her. Then, at twenty-five to seven, they went downstairs and rang the bell.

Eunice opened the door. She'd had her hair done in a beauty parlor and greeted Ross and him as if they were prospective husbands or something. She kept up the gushing after they sat down, making the room they'd been in so many times feel strange. But the only things different were the two plates that had been set out. One held still-wet radishes and stalks of celery, the other had crackers smeared with chopped liver, and Eunice made a big deal of passing both around. Then Mrs. Swerdlov made her entrance.

The way she swept aside the curtain of beads and stood there, Tyler expected to hear castanets. Her fat, pasty face, heavily rouged and powdered, peeked out through a lace shawl that hung all the way down the front of her black taffeta dress. And her eyebrows were gone, replaced by long, thin pencil lines. Marie Dressler with a little Bela Lugosi thrown in.

Mrs. Swerdlov greeted them just as phonily as Eunice had. "We're so glad you could join us." What was she talking about? "Unfortunately Mr. Swerdlov had to work this evening." This evening? What happened to "tonight"? What happened to "greenhorn"? But Mrs. Swerdlov, daintily and noisily munching a piece of celery, went blithely on, and his mother and Eunice joined in, arching their voices and using pear-shaped tones like it was an elocution class, and there was a lot of nothing talk

about how hot it had been and when was school starting and
how glad Eunice was that she'd quit teaching and taken up social work.

"Where is he?" asked Ross.

"Who?" smiled Mrs. Swerdlov.

"The Dentist of Düsseldorf."

Great! Even allowing for his age, the kid was backward.
Tyler had coined the title for Mrs. Swerdlov's cousin years
ago. But Ross had never said it until now. What timing! After
the first blink, though, Mrs. Swedlov's beaming composure was
unshaken.

"Dr. Axelrod will join us presently," she said. "Have a
radish."

Dr. Axelrod got off to a bad start. He tried to walk right
through the hanging beads instead of pushing them aside, so
his glasses were almost pulled off and he got all tangled up,
swiping away at the beads as if they were wasps until Mrs.
Swerdlov rescued him. Then, when introduced, he tried to kiss
their mother's hand, and she didn't know what he was up to
and pulled it away, and he wound up just bending over. He
didn't offer to shake hands with him or Ross, merely nodding
as they were named and pointed to. Then he sat stiffly in the big
purple easy chair as if the current was going to be turned on
any second.

The poor guy, being sized up like something on sale. Tyler
felt like walking over and patting the smooth, shiny head with
its horseshoe of hair. He didn't see how anybody could perse-
cute someone who looked so harmless. In fact, almost cherubic.
An old, melancholy cherub squinting over the bifocal disks in
his glasses at the celery and radishes and chopped liver as Eunice proffered them.

"No, thank you," he said. "But I would like an aperitif."

Mrs. Swerdlov recovered fast. "Didn't I tell you? Doesn't he
speak good English?"

"I've only spoken a few words."

"How many does it take?"

"I don't speak any of your language," gushed his mother.

"I do," said Ross. *"Gesundheit. Auf Wiedersehen."*

"Excuse me," said Mrs. Swerdlov. She stopped at the colored beads and motioned frantically for Tyler to follow her. He did, into the kitchen, where the cooking smells almost disintegrated him.

"Please," she said, shoving a dollar into his hand. "Run out to the liquor store, and get what he said."

The owners of the liquor stores in this neighborhood didn't know an aperitif from an enema. He went to three places, running all the way. The first two guys covered their ignorance by claiming they didn't sell to minors. And the only thing the third would let him have was blackberry brandy.

"Never mind," said Mrs. Swerdlov when he got back and plunked down the bottle. "It's almost done."

It was under the pot lids that she and Eunice kept lifting and sniffing. Something out of *Macbeth,* but more lethal. As he headed for the parlor to escape the smell, he heard Ross.

"The biggest word in the dictionary is antidisestablishmentarianism."

"I have not encountered that word," said Dr. Axelrod. "Please use it in a sentence."

Ross looked relieved to see Tyler. "I'll bet Tyler knows more words than you," he said.

"Yes?" Dr. Axelrod squinted an appraisal at him.

"Do you know what?" said his mother. "Dr. Axelrod learned a new word of English every day for the last two years."

"Good for Dr. Axelrod," wheezed Tyler, still out of breath from running.

"Tyler knows a million words," piped Ross.

"I did not know American youths were interested in etymology," said Dr. Axelrod. "I thought they were only interested in basketball and boobs."

What a lousy thing to say in front of his mother! Lucky she had a clean mind.

"I always encourage the boys to improve their vocabulary," she said.

"Anyway," said Tyler, "etymology is the origin of words,

not their definitions." The squinting eyes turned toward him, challenged. It was either a look of hate or cataracts. But he shouldn't have corrected him. All the poor guy had left was his pride.

"I told ya Tyler knew more," said Ross.

"Then maybe we have a little contest," said Dr. Axelrod. "Yes?"

"I'd rather discuss Europe," said Tyler.

"Ask me a word," said Dr. Axelrod. "Any word. But you must know the meaning yourself. Proceed."

"What for?"

"Proceed." Boy, once a German made up his mind to anything.

"Go on, Tyler," said his mother. "It's all in fun."

"Give him a tough one," said Ross.

What the hell. But he sighed openly first, to let them know he was doing it under duress. How about duress? No, something tougher.

"Idiosyncrasy," he said, and Dr. Axelrod jumped up as if a teacher'd called on him.

"Idiosyncrasy . . . a noun . . . like a peculiarity . . . like eccentric. Right?" It shot out, deadpan and staccato.

"That's right," said Tyler.

"One for Dr. Axelrod," chirped his mother.

"Now I ask you. Ah. . . ." Dr. Axelrod took off his glasses and started wiping them with a handkerchief. "Ushabti," he said.

"Huh?"

"U-S-H-A-B-T-I."

"You sure that's English?" asked Tyler.

"It is in the *Concise Oxford Dictionary*," said Dr. Axelrod. "Do you surrender?" Anybody but a German would say, "Give up." Ushabti? Jesus!

"Never heard of it."

"Ushabti," droned Dr. Axelrod. "Noun, meaning statuettes of servants deposited in the tomb of a mummy."

"Isn't that interesting?" cooed his mother.

"Imagine not knowing that," said Tyler.

"It's Tyler's turn," said Ross.

"Concomitant," he said. And Dr. Axelrod's face told him he'd picked the wrong one.

"Concomitant, adjective, to go with, to accompany like butter is the concomitant of bread, yes?"

"Yes," admitted Tyler.

"So I am three points ahead. Now I give you an easy one." He seemed to run down a mental list of words, then found one that made him beam. "Graminiferous," he said.

Graminiferous. Break it down. Gram—a unit of weight. An iferous unit of weight. Something that looked like a gram. The old bastard was still leering at him, still wiping his glasses, so pleased with himself. For what? Any bookworm could memorize a bunch of words.

"Maybe that is not easy enough," said Dr. Axelrod, turning the knife. "How about ontology?"

Ontology. That sounded familiar. One of those goddam words you keep seeing in books but never bother to look up.

"You don't know?" said Dr. Axelrod. "Then maybe you know praenomen."

Praenomen. Where the hell did he dig that up?

"It's from Latin," said Tyler.

"Obviously," admitted Dr. Axelrod. "But what does it mean?" He waited until Tyler shook his head. "You don't even know praenomen? Your praenomen is Tyler. See—your Christian name."

"Dr. Axelrod could improve your vocabulary," said his mother.

"How about adumbrate?" Dr. Axelrod rocked up onto the balls of his feet with each new word. "Or intumescence? Or nidificate?" No question about it. There was a key in his back, and he wouldn't shut up until it unwound. "How about simulacrum? Maybe clistogamy?"

"You must know what every word means," fawned his mother. Dr. Axelrod attempted a modest shrug. A modest shrug from a German was like a cartwheel from somebody in splints.

"Not every word," said Tyler.

"No?" Dr. Axelrod put his glasses back on and looked at him in amazement. "What word do you know that I don't? Tell me. Name one."

"Boobs," said Tyler. Let him get out of that.

"You are right," frowned Dr. Axelrod. "What is boobs?"

"Dinner is served!" called Mrs. Swerdlov, shoving her face through the strands of beads.

Ross ran for the dining room, and Tyler saw the helpless look his mother gave Dr. Axelrod, one of those "it's so hard to raise a boy without a father's guidance" looks. But it was wasted on Dr. Axelrod. He was still glued to Tyler.

"So tell me, what is boobs?" He honestly didn't know.

"It's a kind of ushabti," said Tyler and went into the dining room.

Mrs. Swerdlov made a big deal of seating them, Dr. Axelrod between his mother and Ross, Tyler next to Eunice. Then she hustled off to the kitchen. The chatter was bland again, the contest seemingly forgotten. Tyler tried to forget it, too, breathing deeply so the tremble in his throat would subside. What the hell. Let the guy have a little glory after what he'd been through.

"Words ain't everything," said Ross. "I'll bet we know things you don't."

"Drop it," said Tyler.

"Name the Four Horsemen of Notre Dame," said Ross. And when Dr. Axelrod stared at him vacantly, "Elmer Layden, Harry Stuhldreher, Sleepy Jim Crowley, and Don Miller." Ross looked round the table for congratulations.

"Shut up," hissed Tyler.

"Name Detroit's million-dollar infield," challenged Ross. Dr. Axelrod's stare turned into a scowl.

"That's enough, Ross," said his mother. But the dumb kid wasn't through.

"I'll bet you don't even know whose real name is Spangler Arlington Brugh."

"Robert Taylor," rasped Mrs. Swerdlov, bringing in the stinking food.

Pink and purple cabbage leaves wound around sweetened hamburger meat. Tyler toyed with his, struggling to get enough down to avoid attention. He watched Ross dig into his, go on to a second helping. Could he possibly like this crap, or was he having another competition with Dr. Axelrod?

Her cousin's appetite was obviously a great compliment to Mrs. Swerdlov. Okay, *chacun à son goût*. But the reason for this dinner wasn't just to stuff themselves with stuffed cabbage. He sneaked looks at Dr. Axelrod. The guy must realize he was their first contact with the outside world. He'd been there when the fire in Europe was starting. He'd left there just a little while ago. The least he could do was talk about what was going on. And, for Christ's sake, he could wipe the side of his mouth. A piece of cabbage had stuck there. Tyler made a big gesture out of raising his napkin to pat his own mouth. But Dr. Axelrod never looked up. He just sat there gorging himself.

Maybe he was making up for months in prison being starved. Tyler tried to feel compassion, but it didn't work. If only he'd wipe off that piece of cabbage. All hostility concentrated there. Tyler put down his knife and fork and stared at it. It almost worked. Dr. Axelrod's wet tongue emerged, wagged, licked. But it just missed. The offending speck of food got bigger, stretching Tyler's nerves. He tried to look away, but it magnetized him back. He knew in one more second he'd say something wrong. It would come out no matter how much he fought it. "Excuse me, Doctor, you have something right there." But it wouldn't sound as polite in the air as in his brain. So what?

"Excuse me," said Tyler. But the Prussian tongue licked again, the speck was gone. Still his words had stopped the clinking of silverware, and the women were looking at him, waiting. "What's it like over there?" he asked.

Dr. Axelrod took another mouthful. Then, aware of the silence, his eyes circled the table and ended on Tyler.

"Er fragt Sie wie sieht aus drüben," said Mrs. Swerdlov.

"We are in America where English is spoken," said Eunice.

"Only in North America," said Ross.

"He asked you what it's like over there," said Mrs. Swerdlov.

"My hearing is perfect, thank you," said Dr. Axelrod.

"So, what's it like?" persisted Tyler.

"In Germany?"

"Yes."

"I have not been in Germany in more than two years."

"Then, what was it like two years ago?"

Dr. Axelrod put down his knife and fork as if they were impeding his memory. "Two years ago," he said distantly. "Let's see, two years ago the violinists were temperamental, the landlords were ruthless, the butchers were thieves, the paupers were humble, and most people were dunces. In other words, it was exactly like any other country at any other time."

"Isn't that being kind of superficial?" said Eunice, porkily.

"Superficial?" he practically shouted it, and Eunice blushed and bristled. But Mrs. Swerdlov broke it up.

"It's almost eight," she said. "We'll have dessert and coffee later."

She led the way back to the parlor and switched on the radio. As it tuned in, the familiar theme music was beginning.

"One Man's Family," said the announcer. "Dedicated to the mothers and fathers of the younger generation and their bewildering offspring."

Then they all sat and listened to another episode in the life of the Barbour family, real corn with the father handing out advice that would screw up anybody. Mrs. Swerdlov hung on every word, letting out a long *oooh* at the parts that were supposed to be dramatic. His mother was engrossed, too. But not Eunice. She was still burning from the conversation at the dinner table. Dr. Axelrod sat forward in his chair, frowning at the tapestried speaker of the radio. He looked up at the others several times. And each time he did, Tyler twisted his face in disgust, so it would be obvious that he didn't go for this mush.

Mrs. Swerdlov waited until the last note of the theme music before turning it off.

"It's my favorite program," she said.

"I never miss it," said his mother.

"Except when we're in mourning," added Tyler.

"That girl," said Dr. Axelrod. "Why was she crying?"

"Teddy," said Mrs. Swerdlov.

"Teddy is a girl?" Dr. Axelrod looked confused.

"Teddy is a jerk," said Ross.

"She isn't really one of the family," explained his mother.

"Paul is her guardian, you see?" Mrs. Swerdlov acted as if that made everything clear.

"I love his voice," said his mother.

"Paul's," agreed Mrs. Swerdlov. "He talks, I melt."

"So why was she crying?"

"Why do people cry?" Mrs. Swerdlov often answered a question with a question.

"I suppose young girls never cry in Düsseldorf," said Eunice, icily.

"Tears should have a reason," said Dr. Axelrod. "When the storm troopers come and drag a man from the house and load him onto a truck and his daughter cries, then she has a reason. But this girl was crying for nothing."

"If you have a toothache," said Eunice, "it doesn't hurt any less because somebody else has cancer."

"Never mind." It dropped out the corner of Mrs. Swerdlov's fixed smile. But Eunice wasn't finished.

"Ever since he's been here, none of *our* experiences are important."

"I said, never mind."

"Besides," said Eunice, turning on Dr. Axelrod, "you didn't see any men dragged away."

"How do you know what I have seen?"

"Because the pogrom didn't start until November of last year. And you were in England long before that."

"I apologize," said Dr. Axelrod. "I should have chosen an example simple enough for your mind to absorb."

"Does anyone understand what he's talking about?" Eunice appealed to all of them.

"Eunice!" The way Mrs. Swerdlov said the name promised a good clout later. "Bring the dessert and coffee."

Eunice went, leaving an embarrassed silence in her wake. With each passing second, it got harder to break into. Tyler watched them all trying to think of something innocuous to say. But no one could. Even Ross was stumped. Then his mother took out the newspaper clipping.

"I thought you might be interested in this, Dr. Axelrod."

"He isn't." Tyler jumped up, trying to intercept it. But too late.

"Tyler's very concerned about the world situation," she said. But Dr. Axelrod, already reading the letter, waved her quiet. Tyler watched him. With all his great knowledge of the *Concise Oxford Dictionary* he sure was a slow reader. Or else he was reading it more than once. Then he just grunted and looked up.

"It was in the newspaper here," said his mother, and got another grunt.

"Such a letter," said Mrs. Swerdlov.

"It is—" They all waited for Dr. Axelrod to find the word he was trying to think of. "It is . . . yes, callow."

"Callow," repeated Mrs. Swerdlov. "What's callow?"

Tyler didn't know either. He wasn't even sure if it was an insult or a compliment. But it didn't sound very complimentary.

"More than that," said Dr. Axelrod. "It is not sincere."

All the stuffed cabbage rose up to Tyler's windpipe, threatening to stay there until he broke something over that goddam big head.

"Oh, but it is sincere," argued his mother. Why didn't she just shut up? Why didn't she go help Eunice in the kitchen?

"No," said Axelrod firmly. "It is written not from deep feeling or belief. It is only an attempt to be clever."

"But, you see," said his mother, "they left out the last sentence."

"That would not alter what I object to."

They kept going, back and forth, as if he wasn't even there, as if the blood in his head wasn't going to burst out of his ears any minute.

"I just do not believe this," said Axelrod, handing the letter back. "It is not honest."

This time Tyler intercepted it, snatching the clipping away as their hands met. And he kept going, past Mrs. Swerdlov, past Eunice balancing the tray through the stupid colored beads, right to the front door.

"Tyler," called Mrs. Swerdlov. "Look—sponge cake."

"Fascists!" he yelled back, and slammed the door.

III

HE knew he'd wind up at a movie. But the Mercury was showing *Dodge City*. And even if it didn't have tragic associations, it wasn't good enough to sit through a third time. The only other movie within walking distance was the Liberty up on Monroe Street, the edge of what the bigots called Niggerland. Tyler hadn't been inside the Liberty for years, but he had to pass it on his way to high school, the posters outside always advertising pictures that had played at the Mercury a year before. This was one reason he'd stopped going there. The other was that the seats were *sans* cushions, as hard as those in the school auditorium. His not going there had nothing to do with the increasing numbers of Negroes in the audience.

The Liberty didn't have a marquee with what was showing in big letters like other movie houses had. So he'd have to go all the way up Monroe Street to see what was playing. Either that or *Dodge City*. He didn't have enough money on him to go downtown.

Monroe Street was the only street in the city which still had its streetcar tracks imbedded in cobblestones. They extended about a foot on each side of the rails, as if they'd been left by oversight and no one in the city administration knew how to authorize their being taken up. Tyler had often said that something should be done about this. He'd said it to Howie fifty times. The cobblestones widened the gulf down the middle of the street, keeping the races further apart. There was the "white" side of Monroe Street and the "black" side. And until the cobblestones were taken up, the twain would never meet.

His staying on the "white" side now was only because he'd

be able to make out the Liberty's posters half a block sooner. If anything, though the whole street was deserted, it was spookier on this side. All the shops here were closed and dark except for an occasional tube of red or blue neon that would glow all night. But across the street there was both light and sound—first, angry voices from one of the shacks with newspapers hanging over its windows, then the high, cackling laughter from the saloon. Its insides were blotted out by dark green plate glass. But as he got opposite it, he could see under its louvered half door—a spittoon and three pairs of legs that looked planted in the sawdust. Then one pair moved unsteadily, and the man stumbled out the door, his belly still shaking with laughter.

"You jis' wait, you mudda fukka!"

He hovered at the curb, his hand pawing at his fly. Then, seeing Tyler, he wheeled and went up against the saloon, leaning his chest on the plate glass as if being X-rayed.

The magazine shop on the next corner was also open. A hand-painted sign in the window said simply BACK ISSUES—2 CENTS. And behind it Tyler could see the heavy, dirty woman who always smelled like the musty pulp paper of *Dime Sports* and *Street & Smith's Western* and who always glared suspiciously at the two magazines he'd return in order to get one for nothing. But he hadn't been in the shop for a long time, ever since he'd stopped reading junk.

Seeing the woman sitting there now bothered him. She hated Negroes. Several times he'd heard her say she couldn't even look at them. Coons, she called them. But there she sat on the "black" side, imperviously picking up a Coke and drinking from the bottle, while he hovered over here on the "white" side. Never mind about saving half a block. He'd already been accused of insincerity once tonight. He went across the streetcar tracks to the other side and trudged on, hands in pockets, stepping on each crack that divided the pavement blocks, still fuming, still wanting to slug that goddam fat German face.

He saw the toes of the sneakers first, sticking out of the doorway; then a cigarette butt shot out in front of him, spewing sparks all the way to the curb. Tyler moved as far from the buildings as he could without making it too obvious and avoided looking at the doorway.

"Hey!"

He kept his face straight ahead. They could be talking to each other and might resent it if he assumed they meant him.

"Hey! You!"

He had to make a decision then, to break into a sprint, streaking as hard as he could for the lobby of the Liberty, still a block away, or to slow down and turn toward the voice. Not that the lobby of the Liberty was so safe. There'd been more than one fight there. Inside, too. He had a vague memory of a night long ago, when there were shouts from the balcony and a man came sailing out of it, his fall cushioned by the up-raised hands of the people sitting downstairs, and of his mother dragging Ross and him outside, so they never found out what happened. But safety wasn't the issue. The issue was what he believed in. Would he run like a nut if someone on Granite Street called, "Hey," to him? Was it the tone of the voice or the fact that it was calling from "Niggerland"? The guy probably only wanted a light anyway. Tyler stopped and turned.

There were three of them in the doorway. The one with the sneakers was grinning at him and getting to his feet.

"What's your hurry, white boy?"

"Yo' got fleas in yo' ass'ole?" added the one with a dirty undershirt hanging out over his pants. His eyes never left Tyler, even when he reached out and scratched a match on the wall to light another cigarette. Well, *that* wasn't why they'd stopped him. Maybe they wanted money. He had thirty-eight cents in his pocket. He didn't know whether to offer it or if that would make them mad, like they could be bought.

"Com'ere," said the sneakered one. "Wanna tell ya somethin'."

"I'm late," said Tyler backing away and drawling his words the way they did. "See ya on my way back."

But it wasn't going to work. They moved as if on springs, the sneakered one heading toward the curb. A flanking movement, and he was right smack in the middle. Which way now? He could turn and run, or he could try to dash between them and make it back to the magazine store. Maybe the woman there kept a gun.

But there was still one of them left in the doorway, probably figuring he might run that way. He was coming out now, a real giant, with a red and white striped polo shirt. Then the light caught him, and Tyler almost yelled his name.

"Richie. Hi'ya, Richie."

The other two turned to Big Richie as he emerged from the doorway, blinking and looking at Tyler puzzledly. Tyler wanted to supply credentials—algebra three years ago, study period last year, and the same gym class. I was on your side in a choose-up basketball game, remember? If only he would.

"Oh, yeah," said Big Richie, scratching his huge head. "Wha'-cha say, Moe?"

Moe? There wasn't any Moe at school. But Big Richie was giving a shake of his head to the others, and the flanker movement broke up. Good old Moe, whoever he was.

"See ya," waved Tyler and started off, trying to keep his strides normal.

The Liberty was showing *Rose Marie,* which he'd never wanted to see, plus a cheap second feature called *Berlin Bombshell.* Just what he needed tonight was something about Germany. Also, assorted short subjects. The woman in the box office looked at him as if he was a dope to go in, then tore a ticket off the roll hanging above her. The place hadn't even installed a push-button machine which shoved them up out of a slot. Then she tore the ticket in half, giving him his part and dropping the other into a paper bag, which meant the old man who used to be both ticket taker and usher was no longer there. Probably squashed dead by a body from the balcony.

Inside, the place smelled as if it had been dipped in popcorn butter. Tyler groped his way to an aisle seat at the side, and as he pushed it down, he felt the cluster of hard wads of gum that had accumulated underneath it for years. As his eyes got accustomed to the dark, he counted eleven people sitting downstairs, their race indistinguishable in the gloom except for the old colored couple directly in front of him. He still felt fluttery, the pounding in his chest still loud. Dr. Wolf Axelrod and what had just happened, in one night, were enough to kill anybody weaker. He tried to squeeze both episodes out of his mind and concentrate on the screen. It was as crummy as he'd always thought it would be, with Jeanette MacDonald prancing around in ruffles and ringlets and Nelson Eddy with a Mountie's hat glued on his head. And every time they looked at each other, they started harmonizing:

> *"When I'm calling youuu, ou-ou-ou, ou-ou-ou.*
> *Will you answer toooo, ou-ou-ou, ou-ou-ou."*

After about twenty minutes he got up and left. The woman in the box office didn't look surprised when he came out. She must have seen the picture.

He trotted back to Granite Street, keeping on the "white" side in case it dawned on Big Richie that he wasn't Moe. But he couldn't go home yet. It wasn't even ten thirty. If only Howie was in Pitkin's Drugstore.

He wasn't. Neither was anyone else, except Pitkin doing a crossword puzzle. The druggist looked up, expecting him to buy something. But Tyler just pointed to the phone booth and went in.

He deposited a nickel and dialed O.

"Operator, you gave me the wrong number. I want Granite three, four, seven, seven."

"Sorry, sir."

His nickel was returned and the number dialed for him. But it was busy. The old crone on Howie's party line could gab for hours. He looked down at the telephone directory on the shelf and started leafing through it. Keyhoe. Her father's first name was Rodney. Live and learn. Mr. Mulleavy, who he'd have for history this year, wasn't even in the book. Bishop. There was

no Tyler, but there was a T. R. on Utica Street. He wondered
if T. R. Bishop ever got any calls for him. He could phone him
and ask. But he had a better idea. Insincere, huh? He looked
up the number, inserted the nickel, and dialed O again.

"Operator, you gave me the wrong number. I want Main two,
two, one, nine."

"Sorry, sir."

It was answered on the first ring. Female. *"Evening News."*

"Could I speak to the editor, please?"

"Mr. Dobson?"

"The editor." He cleared his throat while the line buzzed.
"Yeah?"

"Is this the editor?"

"Who'd you want?"

"The editor."

"The night editor? The sports editor? Which editor?" The
guy sounded like he had a cigar in his mouth.

"If I was to write a letter to the editor, who would it go
to? I mean, to whom would it go?"

"What kind of letter?"

"Are you Mr. Dobson?" asked Tyler.

"Dobson's the editor in chief," said the man. "What kind
of letter?"

"I think Mr. Dobson's the one I should talk to."

"He ain't here at night," said the man, as if any dope should
know this. Then he called out, "Hey, Solly! I'm waiting for
that."

"Then could I leave a message?"

"Huh? What d'ya say?"

"Could I leave a message for Mr. Dobson?"

"Okay. What's the message?"

"Tell him he's got a great future in the Third Reich."

"The third what?"

But Tyler was already hanging up. When he left the booth,
Pitkin looked at him as if he'd had a girl in there or something.
He almost ordered a milk shake. But even dragging it out, the

drugstore closed at eleven, and he didn't want to go home before midnight. The only place that stayed open that late was Ryan's.

When he went in and ordered the beer, Ryan sized up the three other men at the bar more than him. Either he figured that none of them would report him or business was so slow that he decided to take a chance. As he bent over to get a beer glass, Tyler saw the photograph Scotch-taped to the mirror. He hadn't noticed it the day he came in looking for pallbearers. If he had, he wouldn't have come back tonight. He'd seen the lousy picture before—Roosevelt standing and throwing out the first ball, his cane hooked over the box-seat railing in front of him so the handle looked like a limp prick hanging out.

"It's not his fault he had infantile paralysis," said Tyler.

Ryan ignored him, waiting for him to pay. The beer was poured. Walking out now would make it Ryan's loss. He could threaten to unless Ryan tore up the picture. But where would he go? And how many battles could you fight in one day? Tyler put his dime on the wet bar and lifted the heavy glass. The nickelodeon was halfway through "South of the Border."

"I think you've got to be retarded to write popular songs," he said, and one of the men at the bar glanced at him.

Tyler sipped the beer and felt the foam cling to his chin. What little liquid he got into his mouth tasted more bitter than he remembered beer to be. It was going to be tough to get enough down to have any effect.

The song ended, and he turned to the nickelodeon, watching the record make its slow-motion trip from the turntable back to its slot in the rack. Then the machine clicked off, and none of the men made any motion to feed it. Tyler walked over and looked at the typewritten tabs abbreviating the titles and performers:

MUST BEAUT BABY
D. Powell

AURORA
Andr. Sis.

DEEP PURP.
T. Martin

Screw you, Dick Powell; screw you, LaVerne, Patti, and
Maxene. And Tony Martin, too. You're not getting a nickel out
of me. Instead he put it in the pay phone on the wall, dialed the
operator again and tried to sound as if he was running out of patience about getting the wrong number.

"I'm pooped," whined Howie, when he finally got him.
Then lowering his voice. "I just left Lois. Bro-ther!"

"Tell me about it over a beer."

"Now?"

"Now."

"I don't want any beer."

"If I don't talk to someone soon," said Tyler, "something's
gonna give."

He hung up and walked tensely back to the bar. Howie's
house was maybe five minutes' walk from the saloon. So the
next five minutes would tell how good a friend he was. Tyler
watched the electric clock over the bar, taking a sip of beer
each time the second hand reached the twelve. Five complete
revolutions, and no Howie. Six. Seven. Seven and a half, and he
came in the door.

"Took you long enough," groused Tyler.

"Jesus! I practically broke the world record."

"What you drinkin'?"

"Champagne," said Howie.

Tyler ordered him a beer, and Ryan served it up without
any hesitation at all. And Howie was six weeks younger than
him. Screw it. Screw everything that moved. He took his glass
to the table in the corner, and Howie followed.

"So what's gripin' you?"

Tyler just glared at him and took another drink of beer.
"Who's Lois?" he finally said.

"Somethin' I just met."

"Sounds like you did more than meet her."

"What a broad!" said Howie. "She's got hair all over her stomach."

"So's King Kong," said Tyler.

"But all the time her old man's snoring in the next room. So it wasn't very satisfactory."

"Keep it up," said Tyler. "Just keep it up."

"Why? What's the matter?"

"Nothing. Just keep it up, and I'll run out of here and rape Rowena."

"You and your Rowena," said Howie.

"You and your hairy-bellied broads," said Tyler.

"But don't think I forgot you," said Howie. "I asked Lois if she's got a friend."

"And?"

"She's gonna get somebody for you."

Tyler's head began to feel severed at the neck. He didn't know whether it was the beer or what Howie had just said.

"Who?" he asked.

"A girl," said Howie, "a fat, cross-eyed girl."

"And only a little bit pregnant," added Tyler. He took another drink. "So when?"

"Hold your horses," said Howie. "You don't set up an orgy just like that."

"An orgy would wake up her old man," said Tyler.

"It can't be at her house, jerk. We almost got caught tonight."

"So where?"

"She might baby-sit for somebody Saturday night," said Howie. "Just be patient. Soon you'll be a man."

"Yeah," said Tyler. His tongue felt swollen and heavy, and he didn't want to talk any more until he could maneuver it better. But Howie wasn't having any trouble He'd downed half his glass of beer, and his speech hadn't changed. Of course, Howie's diction always stunk. Stank? Hell with it! Howie was his pal. Howie had come to the funeral. Howie had been a pallbearer for his father. And now Howie was going to get him a great lay. Looking at Howie, he felt a greater friendship for him than ever before. He wanted Howie to know he regarded him more highly than anyone else in the world, that he trusted him completely, that he'd tell him things he'd never told anyone else. And he would, too.

"When you think about it," said Tyler, "what do you think?"

"When I think about what?" asked Howie.

"You know." Tyler winked. "The only thing you ever think about."

"Oh, that."

"When you think about it," said Tyler, "you picture somethin', don' you?"

"Not so loud," said Howie, looking over toward the bar.

"Don' you?" persisted Tyler.

"Yeah," said Howie. "I picture things."

"What?"

"What kinda question is that?"

"Don' be such a goddam puritan," said Tyler. "If we're pals, we can be honest with each other, can't we?"

"Who's lyin'?"

"I was just tryin' to find out if you think the same kind of things I do," said Tyler. "Or—" It was difficult to get out. "Or if there's somethin' wrong with me?"

"Like what?" Howie was looking at him suspiciously. Tyler wondered if he should drop it. But the die was cast.

"When you think about it, you see yourself in the act—right?"

"What else?" asked Howie.

"I don't," said Tyler. He sat back enigmatically and took a big gulp of beer.

"What do you see?" Howie looked intrigued now.

"Various things."

"Like what?" Howie waited. "For instance?"

"Sometimes," said Tyler, "I see myself as invisible."

"How can you see yourself if you're invisible?"

"You know," said Tyler. "Like Claude Rains."

"With the bandages?" Howie circled his hand around his head as if winding strips of gauze.

"Then I take off all my clothes," said Tyler. "And I sneak into places."

"What places?"

Tyler shrugged. "Like the showers in the girls' gym."

"That's kinda screwy," said Howie. He sat back a little as Tyler leaned toward him.

"And sometimes I think I'm a sadist."

"A what?"

"Christ!" said Tyler. "Haven't you ever heard of the Marquis de Sade?"

"Who?"

"Forget it."

But Howie didn't seem able to. He kept fidgeting, troubled.

"Listen," he finally said. "If Lois gets this other broad for you, you ain't gonna pull anything weird."

"Don't worry," said Tyler. "Nothing but the acceptable positions."

"Yeah. But there's forty-nine of them."

He took it slowly going up the front stairs. Not that one lousy glass of beer could make him drunk. The spinning in his head had to have another cause. Maybe a tumor budding on his brain. But he didn't want her to think he was sneaking in, so he switched on the lamp in the parlor for a few seconds, then kicked over the lopsided footstool Ross had made in manual training class.

She was standing in front of the medicine chest mirror in her nightgown, pushing her lip up and examining her teeth for cavities. Naturally.

"You want the bathroom?"

"No," he said, and his bladder ached in protest.

"You owe Mrs. Swerdlov an apology," she said, now searching her lower teeth.

"Yeah? Well, I think she owes me one. When I go to somebody's house for dinner, I don't expect them to have a Fascist there." She looked at him in amazement.

"Fascist?" She almost laughed it. Wasn't *she* in a good mood!

"He's a lousy Fascist."

"Is that what you said when you ran out—Fascist?"

"Didn't run."

"None of us could figure out what you'd said."

"Axelrod is a Fascist," he said stubbornly.

"*Dr.* Axelrod is a refugee."

"Who says?" He knew he should clamp his mouth closed and go to bed. But he couldn't leave this unfinished. "How do you know what he's doing here? Where was he those ten days?"

"Stop being silly."

"Sabotage," he said knowingly. And when she laughed again, he got mad. "You think saboteurs all go around looking like Bruce Cabot or Eduardo Cianelli?"

"Who?"

"Or Peter Lorre?" She seemed to recognize that one.

"Have you had something to drink?" She stepped forward sniffing, but he backed off.

"We'll see," he said. "Wait till the Curtiss-Wright plant gets blown up."

"You *have* been drinking. I can smell it."

"He's a Nazi."

"Tyler, he's *Jew*ish.'

"Half."

"I'm surprised at you."

"And which half?" he demanded. "Which genes dominate? You know anything about genes?"

"I never expected to hear you being anti-Semitic."

"His German genes are a lot stronger than his Jewish genes. A hell of a lot stronger."

"Stop swearing."

"He probably hasn't got a Jewish gene left. So how can it be anti-Semitic?" He stuck out his tongue to let her know what he thought of *that* accusation.

"All right. Go to bed." She turned off the bathroom light and gently pushed him aside as she came out.

"He can't even walk without goose-stepping," he said. "One . . . two. . . ."

He followed her down the hall, kicking his feet high and keeping his knees straight. But she didn't even look back.

As he lay in bed, a hundred fragments kept circling above him, all bad. Would he ever learn how to handle situations, to say just enough and always the right thing, to wither people with a look? He retraced the whole evening, trying to shift the inflections of what had been said so he'd come out aloof and sophisticated. But it didn't work. Now, hours too late, the right words came to him. To his mother just now, instead of looking like a jerk with that goose-stepping, he should just have said that Fascism was more subtle than she realized. That would have stumped her. And before leaving Mrs. Swerdlov's parlor, he should have stopped and leaned against the door casually and said something that would have given Axelrod a hemorrhage. He lay working on the phrasing. "By the way, Doctor, is it true that all dentists are sadists? . . . That all dentists are basically sadists? . . . That you have to be a sadist to be a dentist?" It still seemed juvenile. Was that what callow meant? He got up, put on the light and looked it up. *"Not covered with feathers"?* Did the word expert have the wrong word? *"Unfledged, unbearded; inexperienced; low-lying and liable to be submerged. An alluvial flat."* Okay, he was inexperienced. Admitted. And unless Howie and hairy-bellied Lois came through, he'd stay that way. But the bastard also said his letter was insincere and dishonest. If he'd stopped at callow, Tyler might have forgiven him. But nobody could call him insincere and dishonest and get away with it. Alluvial. What the hell was alluvial? He flipped the dictionary pages back toward *A;* but his eyelids were heavy, and his stomach felt sick, so he turned off the light and flopped back in bed.

Consanguinity! Why hadn't he asked Dr. Axelrod to define that? Bet that would have thrown him. He probably knew plenty of words that Dr. Axelrod didn't. But the word game didn't rankle any more. It was that reaction to his letter. After all the time he'd spent writing it, rephrasing it six different ways until it was perfect. Jealousy. That's all it was. Plus viciousness. Old men hated the young. Old men made the wars, and young men died in them. Goddam that beer. Ryan probably bought the cheapest kind. How could he go to sleep when he was so dizzy? He opened his eyes, and the darkness of the room writhed around him, his bed too, like a huge caterpillar.

He made plenty of noise going to the bathroom, but her door was still closed when he came back. No concern about how he was. No. She was probably dreaming about her Prince Charming with his shining head and bifocal glasses. Playing up to him the way she did. Defending *him*, instead of her own son. Then just going to sleep as if everything was all right. Well, there was something he could do about that. She wanted a singer in the family. She was so crazy about music. It was about time she was reminded of a few things.

He went right up to her door and sang out at the top of his lungs.

"I walk along the street of sorrow,
The Boulevard of Broken Dreams."

Part Three

I

CARRIE thought Nelson Eddy the handsomest of men. Even the way he stood. Whenever the boys slouched, she told them to notice Nelson Eddy's posture. She admired Jeanette MacDonald, too, particularly her neck. She had the loveliest neck.

The music raised Carrie's spirits. At first she'd felt guilty, but no matter how long she stayed in mourning, there'd probably be the same feeling of guilt when she first went to a movie or otherwise enjoyed herself. And she *was* enjoying herself, caught up in the story on the screen, transported to the Northwest wilderness with the snowcapped mountains and shimmering lakes as Nelson Eddy and Jeanette MacDonald blended their voices in the moonlight. It was all too beautiful.

Carrie glanced at Dr. Axelrod to see if he was enjoying it too. It was hard to tell. His face was so sternly set. But his head seemed to be nodding to the music, just slightly.

A girl giggled shrilly behind them, and Dr. Axelrod looked around. Carrie did, too. It was a young colored couple a few rows back, both slumped down with the boy's feet on the back of the seat in front of him.

The girl giggled again. But it was forced this time, as if in defiance of them. Cheap little thing. Carrie turned back to the screen. But the music and dancing had been spoiled for her. She felt Dr. Axelrod watching her and lifted her face so that her chin line would be straighter in profile, a smooth arc to her throat like Jeanette MacDonald's. Then Dr. Axelrod's hand reached toward her and proffered the box of chocolate-covered raisins he'd bought from the slot machine in the lobby.

He'd been waiting there when she arrived, never questioning why she'd asked him to meet her at the cinema, as he called it, when they were both leaving from the same house. Perhaps he suspected that Tyler was the reason. But he never indicated it. The whole thing had been so formal.

"Mrs. Bishop, it would be my pleasure if you would accompany me to the cinema Saturday evening."

This, after scaring her out of her wits, the way he leaped out the Swerdlovs' kitchen door while she was coming down the backstairs. And her standing there holding a bag of garbage and with runs in her stockings.

Maybe more dutiful than formal. Because Mrs. Swerdlov had obviously put him up to it. She'd been after Carrie to go out before then, to go downtown or to a beauty parlor, or to do anything except sit home and feel sorry for herself. Yes, Mrs. Swerdlov had asked him to take her out as a personal favor. She may even have given him the money for the tickets. And the chocolate raisins.

As for why she accepted—well, there were reasons. First of all, the anxious way he stood there. It had obviously taken him some effort to invite her. Then too, she'd been relieved because his asking her meant he hadn't overheard Tyler's ranting about Nazis and Fascists. Imagine equating those terrible bullnecked people with the apprehensive man saying it would be his pleasure if she'd go out with him. Besides, she hadn't really said she'd go. She probably would have said it, but he never gave her a chance. He just more or less assumed she'd accept. He'd been walking through the neighborhood, he said, and had passed two cinemas—the Mercury and the Liberty. So she had a choice of cowboys and Indians or a musical operetta. She chose the operetta without first asking which was playing where. And by the time she found out it was at the Liberty, they'd made the arrangement about meeting in the lobby at exactly eight o'clock. He was so precise about it all. She couldn't very well then say that she never went to the Liberty since she'd seen a man thrown out of the balcony there.

Several times she'd been at the point of going downstairs and calling it off. Not that there was anything wrong with sitting through a movie with him. But it meant she'd have to lie to Tyler, and she never lied to her sons, except maybe in little ways for their own good. But saying no to begin with was one thing. Calling it off after accepting was more delicate. Dr. Axelrod was bound to ask why she'd changed her mind. And she couldn't very well tell him how Tyler felt. That would just upset him unnecessarily. Besides it wasn't very likely that Tyler would ever find out where she'd been.

Of course, it would be tonight that he'd spend hours in the bathroom. He said he was going to Howie's. But from the way he was primping, a dance was more likely. He just didn't want to admit he had stopped mourning. She told him it was all right to enjoy himself again. She even told him she was going out, too. She had to tell him that to get him out of the bathroom. And she might have told him the truth if he hadn't looked at her so suspiciously when he asked her where.

"Mrs. Abromovitz is in the hospital," she said.

"What'd they take out this time?"

"It's not anything to make fun of."

She'd never said she was going to visit Mrs. Abromovitz. She hadn't actually lied. But tomorrow he'd undoubtedly ask her how Mrs. Abromovitz was. And that meant more oblique answers, more deception. Carrie put her hands to her head and almost groaned. What was she doing? Her husband dead only a little over a month, and she was sitting here in this shabby movie house with another man, taking sticky chocolate-covered raisins out of a box. She looked around at the couple three rows back. The boy was swarming over the girl now, her eyes staring absently at the screen through the crook of his neck and shoulder while he nuzzled her hair.

Then Carrie began to itch. The back of her knee, her left side, her head. The Liberty was supposed to have bugs. Mrs. Mintz said so. She claimed her little Harold had come home from there with them, and she had to sit him in a bathtubful of vinegar. The itching got worse, particularly under her knee. Carrie reached forward casually and rubbed a knuckle there. This, too, made her feel guilty. Every movement, every word did. If everything were as she claimed, if it all were so harmless, she would simply lean down and scratch her leg. But she couldn't.

She was a widow, a mature woman. And yet it was exactly as it had been twenty years before, this total awareness of men, these attempts to avoid all human gestures in their presence, even the slightest scratch or sneeze. She was back practicing that total deception she thought she'd rid herself of when she got married. When speaking to any single man, she heard her own voice sweetened; even asking someone as repulsive as Mr. Pitkin for some witch hazel. And when this man next to her was only being kind at the request of his cousin, she was afraid to scratch her leg. The other night, too. If Dr. Axelrod had been married, she wouldn't have been so upset at Tyler's taking a dislike to him. Here was this poor refugee, newly arrived, trying to get his bearings and she was—she was what?

Well, why not? Widows did remarry. And she *had* been thinking about it. Even when Frank was alive, she thought about it. That was his fault. Every time he had a twinge of pain or found a lump he hadn't noticed before he started talking about dying.

"And the next time, you marry a rich one."

He'd always said it as if making a sacrifice. And for a moment, before she shook them out of her head, there were wicked little thoughts—jigsaw pieces of a nicer home, another man.

The movie was ending, and Carrie realized her mind had drifted from the story. Now she'd never know how it all turned out. Not that it mattered. Nelson Eddy and Jeanette MacDonald were kissing as the final scene faded out. That was all that mattered. Carrie wondered if it ended then for them until they met to make their next motion picture or if they were in love offscreen, too. They weren't married, but that didn't matter in Hollywood.

The newsreel began, loud and abrasive. Carrie hoped there wouldn't be more scenes of people being pushed around and beaten on the streets in Germany. It upset her to see them, so she could imagine how they'd bother Dr. Axelrod. But the newsreel was an old one, and except for showing a terrible train wreck in Argentina, it was on the light side. There was a fashion show in Miami with the bathing suits very skimpy, and some roughnecks in the audience shouted and whistled. Then there was a tennis match in England and a loving cup being handed to a young man in white ducks named Bobby Riggs. Carrie, bored, glanced at Dr. Axelrod again. He was looking just as fixedly at the screen, his head still bobbing slightly. Then it wasn't the music.

The itching had stopped, but the hard wooden seat was getting more uncomfortable. Carrie wondered if Dr. Axelrod intended to sit through the whole of the second feature. Apparently. As it began, he still seemed engrossed. It was a shoddy little film. The walls of the rooms shook every time a door was closed, and the views out of the windows were so obviously painted. Carrie didn't recognize any of the actors either. And the story was silly. Something about a private detective getting a scientist out of Germany, where he was in prison.

And why shouldn't she get married again? The fact was she almost had to. She had two boys still in school and the grand sum of twelve hundred and eighty-six dollars. That's what Frank's insurance had come to after paying for the funeral. Luckily, the boys were old enough for her to go out to work. She would soon. Maybe Monday she'd go down to Mathiesson's. They were advertising for temporary help for their August sale. Two dollars and fifty cents a day. After carfare and lunches that wouldn't go very far. But it would get her used to working again—to being employed, that is. Then she'd look for something better. But even if she got a well-paying job, there still was the possibility she'd remarry. Not soon. But in a year or two, maybe—if she met the right kind of man. It might hap-

pen, and it might not. These things were all accidental. Like
the way she'd met Frank. Up until then she thought she'd marry
Ralph Hamer even though he was slightly crippled and walked
with a cane. Then she met Frank, on a park bench of all places.
He'd been in the Navy then, stationed in Baltimore. And he'd
just sat down next to her in Druid Hill Park and started making conversation.

Something funny was happening in the movie. The fat
woman in front of her was shrieking and quivering like she
couldn't catch her breath. Carrie tried to pick up the thread
of the humor. It was a chase, in and out of rooms, up and down
corridors with the German soldiers bumping into each other.
She looked around at the laughter behind her—row upon row
of white teeth gleaming from black faces. One man was half in
the aisle, his mouth slack, his hands holding his stomach.

"Disgusting!"

For a moment she thought it came from the movie. But it
was Dr. Axelrod who'd shouted it. The woman in front of them
looked around, still chuckling and shaking, as if asking them
to come on in and join the fun. Then Dr. Axelrod leaned right
into her face and pointed at the screen.

"You think that is funny? You can laugh at that?"

Carrie put a hand on his arm, but he pulled away and jumped
to his feet.

"Shame on you!" he yelled. Then, singling out the man
slouched in the aisle seat. "Especially you!" The laughter
dwindled as the rows of faces turned toward him. "You haven't
had enough of caricatures?" He asked this of the whole theater.

"It's all right." She tried to sound reassuring, as when her
children had hurt themselves and she'd had to comfort them
before locating the injury. She stood up and started edging
Dr. Axelrod toward the aisle. She didn't know what had upset
him, something in the film obviously. But she had to get him
out of there.

"They are ridiculing a whole people when they do this."

"G'wan!"

They were starting to answer back.

"Sit down, man!"

"Jack off outside!"

"Shut up, you ol' bastard!"

His head pivoted toward the last as if he'd been slapped. Clutching his arm, she could feel the fury swell in him.

"What about Leibnitz?" he shouted. "What about Goethe?"

"Please," she begged.

She kept saying this one word as the catcalls followed them out to the lobby. Then he exploded again. Two colored boys were just buying their tickets, and he shouted past them at the little woman in the box office.

"You have to show such filth?"

The woman looked frightened, the boys pleased. One elbowed the other expectantly, and they went in.

"Look," Dr. Axelrod demanded of the woman in the box office. "I am German. Do I strut when I walk?" He strode up and down the dirty tile floor of the lobby, watching her for an answer. Then he stopped and pointed to his left eye. "Do I wear a monocle?"

"Dr. Axelrod." Carrie took his arm again.

"Do I click my heels?" he yelled back at the woman as Carrie almost pulled him out to the street.

They walked several blocks in silence.

"I am sorry," he suddenly said. Breathing heavily, so obviously upset, he could still be apologetic to her.

"It's all right," she said.

"Not for what I did. But for making you a sinecure. No," he corrected himself. "Cynosure. I always confuse them. The center of uninvited attention."

They were walking toward Granite Street, and she wanted to bring up the subject of approaching the house separately. Then he stopped and turned to her.

"There is somewhere we can have coffee?"

"I don't know." She tried to think of a place. Of course, he was expecting her to say she'd make him some at home.

"In Düsseldorf," he said, "we have many coffeehouses."

Yunkes' Delicatessen would still be open, and there were two tables at the back. Or the diner that looked like a bus without wheels up on March Street. That would be safer.

"Guess who was sitting at the table next to me," he said. She must have looked puzzled. "Once in a coffeehouse. In Düsseldorf."

"Who?"

"Thomas Mann," he said. "At the very next table."

"Really?" She tried to look as if she knew the name. "There's a diner not too far," she said. "But it won't be very grand."

She was glad it was practically empty. Just an old man huddled on a counter stool, so they had their choice of the six tables. Carrie went to the one farthest from the counter and where the fluorescent ceiling lights didn't seem so bright. Dr. Axelrod scampered around behind her and held her chair. Another thing men here could learn from the Old World.

The counterman in his white cap came out of the kitchen and looked toward them. He was only about eighteen, with his sleeves rolled up high over muscular arms.

"Just coffee," she said. But Dr. Axelrod seemed waiting for the young man to come over and take their order. She hoped he wouldn't make another scene.

"We just call out what we want," she said. Then, turning to the counterman, "Two coffees, please."

The young man nodded and went to the urn. His movements were deliberate and surly. Perhaps he'd been ready to close up when they came in.

With the coffee before them, after passing back and forth the sugar container, while they both moved their spoons in slow circles, she suddenly had the sinking sensation that they had nothing to talk about. Ordinarily, it would be up to the man to make the conversation. During her courting days, she'd never taken the initiative with words. Frank had called her a counterpuncher, something to do with prizefighting, but he meant as a conversationalist. Still, when a man was newly arrived and he was so visibly upset, she should be able to think of something to say. But all she could manage to do was clear her throat.

"You understand my anger?"

"Naturally." She hoped he wouldn't ask her more specifically. She had a vague feeling that his outburst at the movie house had been justified. Not because of what he had shouted. She'd been too surprised and embarrassed to follow that. But because of the intensity of his behavior. After all, he was an educated man and very polite, so he wouldn't have lost his temper over nothing.

"The world is drowning in slogans," he said.

"That's true," she agreed.

"Everything is for the ignorant."

"Well—" She hoped her hesitancy showed an independence of thought. She didn't want to appear a parrot.

"It is," he insisted, and for a moment she thought he was going to start shouting at her.

"I suppose," she said.

He looked at her searchingly. Had he already noticed that one of her front teeth was a pivot? She pressed her lips together as if thinking.

"Always such compassion," he said.

"Pardon?"

"The way you speak to me. Always so gentle and sympathetic. You feel sorry for me, yes?"

"Of course, I do," she said, resting her cheek on the back of her hand.

"Why?"

"Really," she said, looking down at her coffee. "I'm not on the witness stand."

He frowned, then looked over at the counterman.

"You sure you would not like to eat something?"

"Quite sure, thank you."

"So why do you feel sorry for me?"

"You *are* persistent, aren't you?" She tried to make it light and lilting, but it had a defensive note.

"There is something wrong with my question?"

"No."

"Then why do you feel sorry for me?"

"Because," she said, groping for diplomacy, "because it all must be so new to you. And I'm sure you went through a great deal over there."

"Because I've lost everything?" he prompted.

"Well, a great deal."

"Because I have no family, no home?"

"Yes," she said.

"St. Augustine told us to purge our hearts of all affection for home and parents."

"Did he?" She couldn't stop there. "Then I don't agree with him."

"I secured the divorce from my wife," he said. "Not vice versa."

"Oh."

"Believe me. It was not a loss."

"But your daughter."

"She was five years old at the time," he said. "And a man's parental feelings last only four years."

Carrie wondered if it were some kind of European joke. But no. He was completely serious.

"You do have unusual ideas," she said. And this made him smile, a self-satisfied smile.

"Everyone is so quick to pity," he said. "It does not occur to them that there is freedom in having nothing. When you have only one suitcase, what can you lose?"

"One suitcase," she said.

"Exactly!" He roared it with approval. "And as for being in a new place, what is so terrible? If one has the willpower to free himself from memory, it is like being born again. Only full-sized. No teething, no wetting, none of the horrors of childhood."

"That's a very interesting way to look at it," she said. "I mean, so optimistic."

"I am an incurable optimist." He drank down his coffee. "Cold!" He snapped his fingers at the counterman. "More coffee," he called gaily as if ordering champagne.

The counterman seemed even more surly when he brought

it, almost rude. He probably objected to the finger snapping. But he might not if he knew he was waiting on a professional man.

"Where do you think you'll open your office, *Doctor?*" It worked magic. The counterman put the cups down gently and went to get them clean spoons.

"Nowhere," said Dr. Axelrod, and she tried to remember her question. Something about his office.

"We could use a good dentist in this neighborhood," she said. "Dr. Lazaar is just terrible. The number of mouths he's ruined." At home now in gossip, she talked easily, almost excitedly. "Mrs. Hapke was going to sue him for what he did to her. Some kind of crown he put in that was apparently very painful. And how long do you think it lasted?" She waited, but he made no attempt to guess. "Three days," she announced. "Then it crumpled like sand, and she had to have all the teeth he'd drilled into out. They were just shells." Dr. Axelrod looked impatient, and she wondered if there were something unethical in his listening to complaints about another dentist. "I think he drinks heavily," she said, dispensing with Dr. Lazaar. "And the only other dentist within blocks is Dr. Kyriakides on Monroe Street."

"Kyriakides," he repeated.

"He's Greek," she said, "originally." She lowered her voice. "His practice is almost all colored. The way he sells them on having gold fillings in front."

"I did not come all this way," said Dr. Axelrod, "just to resume dentistry." He seemed angry again.

"You didn't?" She tried to make it sound unimportant. After all, what did it matter to her?

"Do you know what they say in Germany?" he asked. "They say a dentist is a man who failed to pass his medical studies."

Carrie remembered Tyler telling her the same joke. Only Dr. Axelrod wasn't joking. "We have a different saying here." Carrie waited for him to frown before telling him what it was. "We say that you never see a dentist on relief."

"Relief?"

"Charity," she explained. "From the city."

He looked as if expecting more, then shrugged.

"The slate is clean," he said. "Why should I draw old pictures on it?"

She couldn't think of any reason. She could only think of a blackboard that her mother had once sent Tyler and that was later passed on to Ross. She saw them both printing first, clumsy letters on it, the chalk screeching. And she felt very empty and depressed.

"What are you going to do then?"

"I don't know yet."

He didn't know, and she didn't care. What difference did it make to her what he did? Let him dig ditches.

"Of this much I am certain. The only purpose of life is to affect the purpose of life."

"One has to make a living," she said, applying it to herself.

"Let me ask you, Mrs. Bishop." He leaned forward, pointing a stubby finger at her, and his accent suddenly sounded very German. "When I say Spinoza, do you think lens grinder?"

"Lens grinder?"

"Spinoza ground lenses," he said. "You didn't know?"

"I'm afraid not," she said, still trying to remember where she'd heard the name Spinoza. Was he one of those men they executed in Boston?

"It does not matter." He brushed aside his previous question and substituted another. "What I am asking is, when someday someone says, 'Wolf Axelrod,' will they think of only a dentist, or will they think something more?"

"What something more?"

"That we will see." He sat back in his chair and slapped himself on the ribs. "Now that I am born again, there is no telling what I may accomplish. It does not matter that I have started late. As Nietzsche said, 'Some are born posthumously.' It is merely a question of when the time is right."

"I suppose it's very exciting for you." She tried to say it with finality. She wanted to end the conversation and go home.

For all she knew he was prepared to stay here all night drinking coffee and talking about himself.

"It is more than exciting," he said. "It is of great consequence. What I am doing can prove that Spengler is wrong."

"I see," she said.

"I am determined to shape my own destiny," he said. "I am reforging myself according to my own images of admiration, not those which have been handed to me. If I cannot do this, then Spengler is right and I am only another carcass on the conveyor hook of historic necessity."

"It's getting late," she said, but he ignored it.

"Describe me," he said.

"What?"

"You have seen me twice. Describe me."

"Well, you must be about five feet ten."

"Not my appearance," he snapped. "My character."

"You're very intelligent," she said, and he nodded. "And very . . . nice."

"Nice?" He looked hurt. "How can you say that? I offended your son the other night. Tonight I embarrassed you. Is that nice?"

"I suppose not," she said and put her fingers over her mouth to cover a yawn.

"I'm aggressive, you would say?"

"A little," admitted Carrie.

"And dominating?"

"Yes, you are."

"I am a man who suffers no nonsense?"

"Definitely."

"Good," he said.

"I must get home." She started to stand up, but his hand pressed down on hers.

"Not yet," he said. "Let us talk a few minutes more." She hesitated. "Unless I am boring you."

"All right." She relaxed and withdrew her hand. "Just a few minutes."

"As Goethe told us," he said, "nature has no system, it has

only life. The system is up to us. But so far man has produced only childish hopes to sustain himself—that the next hill will glitter with gold, the next shell contain a pearl."

"Do you know what?" she broke in.

"What?"

"My husband saw McKinley shot," she said. "President McKinley."

"So?" He scowled impatiently. "How does that apply?"

"It was right downtown in front of City Hall. My husband was in this long line waiting to shake the President's hand. Of course, he was very young. He was with his uncle. But they were only about ten places behind this man with his hand bandaged. Czolgosz his name was." Dr. Axelrod was staring at her pivot tooth, ready to interrupt, but she wasn't giving him a chance. Why shouldn't they talk about Frank for a change, instead of him? "Then he stepped up to President McKinley, Czolgosz did, and he had a gun inside this bandage, and—"

The counterman had come out with a mop and bucket and started noisily sluicing water on the floor.

"I think he's giving us a hint," she said.

This time he wasn't reluctant to leave, getting up when she did.

"I'll go on ahead," she said.

"No, no. We will walk together."

"Just partway," she conceded.

"Why?" He left three pennies' tip on the table, then turned to her. "Are you ashamed to be seen with me?"

"No," she said flatly. "But my older son objects."

They walked several blocks before he spoke again.

"I am escorting you right to the door," he said. And she knew there was no point in arguing.

II

"ALL I know," said Howie, "is her name's Margaret."

"Did you tell Lois I'm partial to nymphomaniacs?"

Instead of answering him, Howie just looked back at the prescription counter. Pitkin was still waiting on the tall man in the wrinkled suit. "What's that guy buying so long?"

"A jockstrap for his face," said Tyler.

Howie turned back and sucked at his soda straw. There was only a drop left in the bottom of the glass so all he got was a slurping sound.

"You sure she's sixteen?" asked Tyler.

"I'm not sure of nothin'." Howie looked around again. The man was about to pay Pitkin, then remembered something else. "Jeez, he's buyin' out the whole store."

"A hypochondriac," said Tyler.

"A what?"

"Somebody who imagines they're always sick." He remembered his father. "And sometimes they are," he said.

Howie concentrated on his straw, pinching and folding it until it looked like a tapeworm. "Look, Ty," he said. "I'm telling you this as a pal, okay?"

"Okay," said Tyler, his mouth feeling stiff.

"I mean, like you said that time, since we're pals, we can be honest with each other."

"That's right." He tried to anticipate what was coming. BO maybe.

"So, I'm tellin' you as a pal, lay off the big words tonight."

"What's the matter?" asked Tyler, only partly relieved. "They give you an inferiority complex?"

"See? That's what I mean—inferiority complex."

"You've made your point," said Tyler.

"You're not sore."

"No. From now on, nothing more than two syllables."

"There you go again," groaned Howie. "Syllables! These broads don't know what syllables is. They go to vocational school."

"Coast is clear," said Tyler. It wasn't quite, but Pitkin was giving the tall man his change.

"Go ahead," said Howie.

"I thought you were gonna get them."

They both just sat there, watching the tall man go out.

"Hurry up," said Howie, "before somebody else comes in."

"You've never bought any," said Tyler. "All this time you've been bullin' me."

"Okay." Howie got up. "Then we'll both get them."

"Good enough." They walked back to the prescription counter, each trying to shoulder the other forward.

"Twenty cents," said Pitkin, thinking they came to pay for the sodas.

"My treat," said Howie, laying a dime and two nickels on the counter. "And ah—" He nudged Tyler, but Tyler stared straight ahead.

"And what?" asked Pitkin.

"And some spearmint gum," said Howie.

"Anything else?" Pitkin took the additional nickel.

"Ummm," Howie looked around as if trying to remember. "Oh, yeah," he said offhandedly. "And a package of safeties."

"Safeties," said Pitkin. "What's safeties?"

"You know," said Howie, suddenly hoarse.

But it was possible that Pitkin didn't know. It was about time Howie found out that a vocabulary had advantages.

"Contraceptives," said Tyler. "A package of contraceptives."

"Oh." Pitkin turned to him. "Something for the sinuses."

"Come on, Mr. Pitkin," said Howie. "Stop monkeying around."

"Who's monkeying?" Pitkin spread his hands and raised his shoulders.

"Condoms," said Tyler. "Rubbers."

"Rubbers!" Pitkin's face lit up. "Why didn't you say so?" He leaned over the counter and beckoned them with a wagging finger. "It couldn't be that you boys are gonna get a little nookie tonight."

"You never know," said Howie.

"And who are the lucky girls?"

"Look, Mr. Pitkin," said Tyler, "just give us a package of safeties and go mix your prescriptions."

"You boys know how to put them on?" Pitkin's tongue kept flicking out to lick his lips, keeping his grin wet.

"We know," said Howie.

"And you know what to do after you've got them on?"

"How come you're not married?" asked Tyler. He made the question sound innocent, but it wiped off the wet grin.

"Bright boy," Pitkin said. "And you ain't even been tipped off."

"Come on," said Tyler, poking Howie's arm. "We'll buy them at Rexall's."

"Easy, easy," soothed Pitkin. "What's the matter—you can't take a joke?" He opened a drawer under the counter and came out with a small packet, palming it. "You didn't tell me what size," he said.

"Let's go." Tyler took a step toward the door, but Howie didn't follow.

"You have to have the right size," said Pitkin. "You don't want it to fall off."

"Come on, Howie."

"How many inches is yours?" asked Pitkin. "Three, four?"

"Nine," said Howie. "After I've finished."

"Your girl's gonna like you." Pitkin smirked.

"You selling us those or not?" Tyler went back to the counter.

"Of course." The shoulders lifted again. "But I gotta know the size."

"Look, the joke's over."

"I'll get a ruler. Just take them out and—" Pitkin looked past them and suddenly stopped. Then he slid the packet toward Howie, who pocketed it just before Mrs. Mintz got there.

"Thirty-five cents," said Pitkin, all businesslike.

"You were going to get a ruler," said Tyler, reaching for his fly.

"All right boys, no horseplay in here," said Pitkin.

"But how do we know you gave us the right size?" asked Tyler.

"Yes, Mrs. Mintz?" said Pitkin, one eye on the coins Howie was counting out.

"I only got thirty-three cents," said Howie.

"Thirty-five," said Pitkin.

"I'll have to owe it to you," said Howie.

"I still want to be measured," said Tyler.

"Some Sal Hepatica," said Mrs. Mintz.

"Sal Hepatica!" echoed Tyler, and she looked at him, startled.

"Good old Sal Hepatica!" chortled Howie. Then they leaned their heads together and tried to harmonize.

"My gal, Sal . . .
He-pat-i-caaa. . . ."

It faded away, off-key and terrible. Snickering, bumping together, they headed for the door.

"Have a good time, boys," called Pitkin.

The girls were baby-sitting up on Maryland Street, where the houses were one-family and well spaced. This one had just been repainted, blue and cream, and the sidewalk up to the front door was flanked by evenly clipped bushes.

"At least the neighbors are too far away to hear them scream," said Tyler.

Howie gave him a funny look. "Lois said not to ring the bell." He rapped on the front door. "Don't wanna wake the brats."

There was a lot to take in all at once as they went inside—
Lois, Margaret, the furniture, and one of the brats running
around like a Comanche, half the buttons off his pajamas and
his dong hanging out. Tyler tried to sneak looks at Margaret.
But the kid chose his leg for a punching bag, slugging away
like Henry Armstrong at one spot just above his knee until Lois
managed to drag him off and upstairs to bed. A great beginning. He grabbed another look at Margaret while walking non-
chalantly across to the bookcase, then examined the titles there.
A hell of a lot of Zane Grey and Fannie Hurst.

Not bad. That was his first impression of Margaret. Tall
enough for him and not fat and with a Betty Boop mouth.
Then, when he sat down and looked at her openly, he probed
for imperfections. The beauty spot on her left cheek was one.
Tyler hated beauty spots—nothing but black, permanent pimples. Margaret had a few of the red kind, too, glazed over with
makeup. Her blouse was loose-fitting, so he couldn't tell about
her bust. It was probably pendulous. And she was sort of
gangly—the basketball type. Tyler guessed it before she said
so. But she sure didn't waste any time bringing it up. Just because Howie offered her a cigarette.

"I don't smoke," she said. "It shorts my wind."

"What d'you do?" asked Howie. "Play a tuba?"

"Tuba!" she snorted.

"Okay—French horn."

"Basketball," said Margaret with a so-there inflection.

"Margaret O. is on the basketball team," verified Lois, coming into the room. "She scored fourteen points against Hub-
bard High last year."

"Sixteen," corrected Margaret, looking at her lap modestly.

"Still," said Howie, blowing out smoke, "who plays basketball in summer?"

"I gotta keep in training, don't I?" She said it fiercely. He
would get a fierce one.

"You look in *perfect* shape," said Howie, roving his eyes
over her deliberately.

"One-track mind," said Lois, shoving him off-balance. She

was stumpy with piano legs, and her anthropoid features explained the undergrowth on her stomach.

So far the conversation had been kept to the three of them,
as if he wasn't even there. If he didn't barge into it pretty
soon, Howie would wind up with a *ménage à trois*.

"Lois called you Margaret O.," he said. "Why the *O?*"

"There's another Margaret Jones at school," she said. "Margaret L." She said it as if it was a heavy burden.

"Still," said Tyler. "A rose by any other name." She stared
at him blankly, and Howie gave him a warning look. "It must
get confusing," he added quickly.

"Yeah," said Margaret O.

"You could get the wrong marks by mistake," said Howie.

"And lots of other things," said Tyler. She looked at him,
worried.

"What things?"

He tried to think of some, but couldn't. Then Howie came
to the rescue.

"This other Margaret. She on the basketball team, too?"

"Naw."

"S'too bad," said Howie. "That would really louse up the
other side, with two of you."

"Margaret Jones passes to Margaret Jones," said Tyler.

"Who passes back to Margaret Jones," rasped Howie, trying
to sound like Graham McNamee.

"Who dribbles under the basket—" Tyler picked it up.

"And fouls the left guard right in the—"

"Two free throws!" broke in Tyler. At least Lois laughed.

"Margaret L.'s a drip," said Margaret O. "She wears stockings
every day and lives with her aunt."

"A real drip," agreed Tyler.

"Well," said Howie, rubbing his hands together. "Let's liven
up the party, huh?"

"We can't dance," said Lois. "The music will wake the kids."

"Who wants to dance?" Howie gave her a big wink, and
she giggled. "They got any cards in this dump?" He started
opening drawers.

"Don't touch anything," shrieked Lois.

"He's not contaminated," said Tyler, and again Howie threw him a warning look.

"I only know how to play casino," said Margaret O.

"You mean you've never played poker?" She shook her head, all innocent. And while Howie convinced her she'd pick it up in no time, Lois found a deck of cards, and Tyler dragged another chair over to the coffee table so they could sit in a circle.

"Now remember," he said to Margaret O. as Howie started dealing. "You want two or three of a kind, or all of one suit, or a straight like eight, nine, ten, jack, queen."

"How about four of a kind?"

"See!" said Howie. "I told ya she'd learn fast."

They picked up their cards and studied them.

"You can replace up to three of the ones you've got," said Lois.

"And everybody except the winner has to take off something," added Howie.

They all looked at Margaret O., but she was still frowning at her cards. Then Howie's words sunk in, and her face came up horrified.

"What d'ya mean?" She started pushing herself up from the chair.

"You know how to play poker?" asked Howie.

"No."

"Then sit down and learn."

"It's all in fun," Tyler assured her, trying not to look at her blouse and skirt, wondering if she was wearing a slip.

"As I was saying," said Howie.

"Before he was so rudely interrupted," said Tyler.

"Yeah," said Howie. "So after each hand the three losers take off something. And none of this hairpin and earring stuff. It's gotta be clothes."

"That's strip poker!" yelped Margaret O., jumping up again.

"I said it was pinochle?"

"I'm not playing that." Margaret O. backed away.

"Me neither," said Lois, trying to sound equally indignant. Girls never admitted to each other that they put out.

"What's the matter with you two?" Now it was Howie's turn to act insulted. "You got something to hide?"

"Wouldn't you like to know?" said Margaret O., sitting down haughtily across the room and taking a *Ladies Home Journal* from the table.

"I thought you said she was a good sport." Howie turned to Lois accusingly, but she just shrugged.

"You might win every hand," said Tyler.

"Sure," echoed Howie. "Beginner's luck."

"I have no desire to see either of you without clothes on," said Margaret O., burying her face in the magazine.

"The feeling is not mutual," said Howie.

"Maybe we oughta get a horse," said Tyler, "and paint it red, white, and blue." Lois giggled. So Howie had told her the joke, too.

"Okay," sighed Howie, putting the cards back in their box. "Then we'll have to play one, two, three. You know how to play that, Margaret?"

"I'm reading," she said.

"Say, Tyler's a big reader, too. What was that book you were reading the other day, Ty?" Howie signaled him with an exaggerated wink. "You know, the open something?"

"The Open Kimono," said Tyler, his throat dry. "By Seymour Hairs."

Lois and Howie let out big laughs. But Margaret O. just turned the page.

"I liked that Russian book better," said Howie. "What was it called?" He snapped his fingers twice. "Oh, yeah." He looked right at Margaret's blouse as he said it. "The Flat Chest by Ivan Bittertitsoff."

"You!" Lois punctuated her shriek with an elbow in his ribs.

"Dirty minds," said Margaret O.

"Aw, relax," said Howie.

"Yes," agreed Lois. "Don't be like that, Margaret O."

"What time is it?" asked Margaret O.

"Twenty to ten," said Tyler, subtracting half an hour from what his watch said. But she still put down the magazine.

"I gotta go home soon," she said. "I go to summer school."

"It's early," said Tyler.

"I got studying to do."

"In vocational school?"

"Yes, in vocational school! It ain't all sewin' and cookin', ya know."

"He didn't say it was," said Howie, but she wouldn't be pacified.

"I take English and introduction to business and typing."

"How can you study typing?" asked Tyler.

"Ty." Howie was motioning him out to the hall. "Listen," he said when Tyler joined him there. "You want to lay her, or you want to debate?"

"It's the girl who lays," corrected Tyler. "We *get* laid."

"Jeez, you can be exasperatin'."

"Now who's using the big words?"

"What'd you have to go and make her mad for?"

"Never mind," grumbled Tyler. "You use your technique, and I'll use mine."

"Some technique," said Howie.

"We'll see."

"You want to flip for the bedroom?"

"You can have it," said Tyler. "I'm a couch man myself."

"Meeting over?" asked Lois coyly when they came back in. Margaret O.'s face was back in the *Ladies Home Journal*.

"I'm all yours," said Howie. He marched right up and kissed her, just like that. Then he whispered something in her ear that made her giggle some more and squirm. Tyler wondered if it was something to do with him. He was about to dare Howie to repeat it out loud. But Lois was drifting toward the stairs.

"I'd better see if they're sleeping," she said, and went up. And two seconds later Howie went right after her. Tyler was sure that behind her magazine Margaret O. knew exactly what was going on.

"Is it that interesting?" he asked.

"Huh?" She peeked over the cover.

"What you reading?"

"It's a story."

"Who by?"

She had to turn back the page to find out.

"W. Somerset Mawg-ham."

He didn't correct her pronunciation. "What's it about?"

She shrugged. "I can't tell yet."

Again she pretended to read. Tyler sat down on the sofa, spread his arms across the back of it, and stared at her seductively, moving his eyes languidly over the bare mottled shins above her ankle socks, over the creases of her skirt and the folds of her blouse, up the stalk of her neck.

"Wha'cha lookin' at?"

"You."

"Well, look somewhere else." She lifted the magazine to put a wall between them.

Tyler let his head droop, slumping into wistfulness, waiting for her to notice and ask him what was wrong. But she didn't. Even when he coughed, the magazine stayed put.

"What do you think about the situation in Europe?" He waited. "Oh, Margaret O." Singing her name did it. The *Ladies Home Journal* bit the dust.

"Huh?" She really had a stupid stare.

"The situation in Europe. What do you think about it?"

"Awful."

"I'm violently anti-Fascist," he said. She seemed to be trying to figure out whether this was good or bad. Like people who couldn't tell which side was which in Spain. "I might join up," he added.

"Join up what?"

"The RCAF. I'll be seventeen in October. If there's a war by then I'll hitchhike to Toronto and join up."

"What's the RCAF?"

"The Royal Canadian Air Force." Didn't she know anything? "I'm going to be a fighter pilot," he said.

"Maybe there won't be any war," she said.

"Of course, there will," he snapped back. "You're as bad as Senator Borah."

Her face went like a pickled beet. "What do ya mean?"

"I meant that speech he made last week." She still looked stormy. "No offense," he said lightly.

"What speech?" she demanded.

"You know, when he said war isn't as imminent as Roosevelt and Garner think."

"So what's that got to do with me?"

"Nothing," he admitted. Boy, never talk politics with a basketball player. "Anyway," he said, trying to look doomed, "I expect to get killed."

"That's silly."

"Why is it silly?"

"Talking like that."

"I'm merely being realistic," he said. "The cycle of war comes around every quarter of a century, and I just happen to be the right age for this one. So don't call me silly."

"Okay," she shrugged.

"I don't expect to ever be twenty-one," he said.

"My brother's twenty-one."

Tyler wondered what her brother was like, probably a weight lifter or something. What would he do to him for knocking up his kid sister?

"He'll probably be killed, too."

She jumped up. "Quit talkin' like that."

"Why?" He didn't back down. "Why pretend? The important thing is to face facts. If my life's going to be short, I've got to cram as many experiences into it as I can, *while* I can." He patted the couch cushion next to him. "Sit over here."

She didn't move, but he kept patting the cushion like a tom-tom.

"You sure are gloomy," she said.

"Come on. Sit over here."

"What for?"

"So we don't have to yell. We'll wake the baby."

That was the kind of reasoning she understood. But she took

her time, trailing a finger behind, over the top of a lampshade, the back of a chair, the very space between them, until finally lowering herself down to the opposite corner of the couch.

He inched toward her, imperceptibly at first as if she were a sparrow on a branch. A direct move would send her flying back to goddam W. Somerset Maugham, so he had to close the gap between them by shifting his position and pretending to tug up his pants legs, all the time chattering decoys about basketball being the toughest sport and requiring the most skill. Then, within arm's length, he made the mistake of reaching out to touch her hair, and she bounced up as if he'd released some coils. She must be murder on rebounds from the backboard. But he caught her arm and held on until she relaxed and sat back down. More squirming. Then his hipbone was against hers, both of them still facing straight ahead as if crowded together on bleacher seats. The next move was the tricky one—to turn off the lamp next to her.

"It's like an operating table," he said, leaning across.

"Leave it on!"

Hell! When would he learn to take action without commenting first? If he'd just turned it off, she probably wouldn't have protested. That's why he still hadn't had any. Howie was right. He talked too goddam much. Maybe Howie was right about girls in every way. No time like the present to find out.

He grabbed her chin, pulled her face around, and lunged.

"Stop it!"

She puffed it at him just before he landed, her breath flavored with spinach. But she didn't seem to be struggling very hard. He couldn't tell if she was kissing him back or if he was doing all the work. She got an arm loose, and he opened one eye to follow it, expecting her fingers to settle in his hair and pull his head backward. But she was reaching in the other direction, and the lamp suddenly went out. Then she went wild, her mouth wide open and sucking at him until he shoved out his tongue.

His boner was so big he had to push it down and cross his

legs. Still kissing as if starved for saliva, dueling his tongue with hers, he worked his hand up the back of her blouse and around to the front, rubbing her slip gently and, when she didn't resist, grabbing her left breast and squeezing and pushing until it lost its excitement. Then he crawled his fingers up to the straps and tried to reach down inside.

"Wha'cha doing?" She tore her lips away and leaned back to look at him.

"I love you," he purred. "I love you, I love you." He French-kissed her again, extricating his hand and starting it up the inside of her skirt. Her thigh was smooth and firm, unbearably smooth on the inside. She quivered as he stroked it. She was hot. She wanted it, too. Her response worked him up even more. His fingers reached the elastic leg band of her pants, snaked inside, touched hair! He was there! It was going to happen! He swarmed over her, pressing her flat, mumbling, "Sorry," without unprying his lips when his belt buckle caught on a button of her blouse. Then he was flat on top, his legs between hers. And he remembered that Howie had all the safeties.

"Stay there," he said, clambering off her. "I'll be right back." He stopped at the foot of the stairs and called back. "I love you. Stay right there."

Some moron had turned off the light on the upstairs landing, so he could hardly see. There were four doors, all closed.

"Howie?" He called it softly, urgently. Then louder. But the doors stood mute. He opened the first and got a noseful of baby smell. He should have known enough to retreat, but his mind was still on the couch downstairs. So he went in, calling Howie's name again, and the baby started screaming. Then Lois was bustling past him, straightening her clothes, and a rumpled Howie was yanking him out to the landing, ready to sock him.

"What the hell you doin'?"

"The safeties," he stammered.

"I was almost there," growled Howie.

"So was I," said Tyler. "For chrissake give me a safety."
It finally dawned on Howie, and he took out the packet.
"There's three. Want to flip for the extra one?"

"Later." Tyler grabbed one of the oval foils. The baby was bawling louder, and the older kid was coming sleepily out of his room, still unbuttoned. They were Howie's problems. Tyler ran downstairs and bounded toward the couch. But the lamp was on and she was back in the chair with the magazine.

Nothing worked. He tried nuzzling her neck but she straight-armed him away. Attempting to kiss her was like bobbing for apples, and he kept landing on her head and chin. He flattered her with words she could understand, words like pretty and gorgeous and swell. When she still sat there like something waxed, he resorted to begging, a "please" with each lunge or grab. But she parried all of them, suddenly having more hands than him. He called on the RCAF again, trying to make her dull eyes see him spiraling down in flames with no pleasures to remember in his last seconds. But she didn't even blink.

It had gone quiet upstairs, and the vision of what Howie was doing right now made everything worse.

"Please, Margaret O. Don't be like that."

"Leave me alone."

"I love you, Margaret O."

"Well, I don't love you."

This was getting nowhere. It was bad enough being turned down. But to humble himself to an idiot and still not get any.

"You're frigid," he said. He walked over to the couch, sprawled on it and looked at her with disdain. "I assure you that you would have enjoyed it more than me."

"Hah-hah," she said.

"I hope you'll be proud of yourself when you see my name on the casualty list."

"Will you please tell Lois that I have to go home?"

"Lois is very busy."

"Then I'll tell her myself."

He got up to head her off as she started for the stairs. Then the pain hit him, and he fell back. It was just like the two times he'd been kneed, in a collision at second base and a pileup in a game of tackle. Both times it had been the same, rocking in agony on the ground, skewered from groin to throat, his eyes bulging past the grinning faces of the other players to the sky. But the pain in his groin now was even more agonizing. And instead of easing after the first cramp, it was getting worse. He tested it by moving his legs and almost screamed. Even his shorts touching him was unbearable. So he lay rigid, taking in quick sips of breath, charting the mounting pain. He wondered if he'd still be lying there when the people who owned the house came in and how Lois would explain him. He wondered if they could get a stretcher somewhere to carry him away.

"Lois!" Margaret O. was at the foot of the stairs. "Lois, I'm going!" Then she was standing over him. "You don't have to play sick," she said. "I don't want you to walk me home."

"I'm not playing," he gasped, but she wasn't listening.

"Low-issss!"

Empty-headed, spinach-eating CT. Howie had really fixed him up good. Tyler tied the pain between his legs to both of them, hating them, hating everybody.

"Hey, what's with you?" Howie's face above him looked genuinely concerned.

"I can't move."

"What d'ya mean?"

"I mean I can't move."

"Sure ya can. Try."

"I can't, I tell ya."

"Come on. Sit up."

Howie grabbed him under the arms and pulled. Like eggs being smashed by a sledgehammer. Sweat broke out all over him. "Donnnnn't!"

"What's the matter with him?" Lois was peering over Howie's shoulder.

"Nuthin'. He'll be okay."

"Good night, Lois." Margaret O. was standing indignantly at the door.

"Wait a sec'," said Lois. "Tyler will walk you home."

"How can he walk her home?" asked Howie. "He can't even stand up."

"Nobody has to walk me home," said Margaret O.

"He can't stay here," hissed Lois.

"Okay, okay," comforted Howie.

The front door slammed. Margaret O., insulted and ignored, had left, her parting gesture waking up the goddam baby. Lois cocked her head toward the wailing from above, then looked at Tyler as if trying to decide who was more bother. The baby made up her mind for her. What a pair of lungs!

"Do something," she ordered Howie, then ran upstairs.

"Lean on me, Ty." Howie shifted himself into different positions, trying to give him leverage. But when he tried to pull himself up, the pain was too much. "You can do it," said Howie. "No matter how much it hurts, keep going."

"Thanks."

"I'm trying to help, ain't I?"

"Yeah," said Tyler. "You're about as useful as a nun's tits. Fixing me up with that kangaroo." The wave of light washing across the room showed Howie grinning. "What's so goddam funny?"

A car motor explained the lights. Then Lois came flying down. "They're back!" she squeaked. "Quick!"

Howie jerked him to his feet so fast there was no time to yell. Tyler swayed, legs apart to protect the pain, while Howie and Lois peeked out the curtains to gauge which door the people would come in. First, they thought it was the back one and hustled Tyler toward the front. Then, when the shadows of the man and woman appeared outside the glazed glass panel of the door, Howie grabbed him and propelled him through the dining room and kitchen. With each stiff-legged stride, Tyler let out a groan. Then they were in the back hall, and the five steps loomed before him.

"I'll never make it," he said.

"Here." Howie hunched two steps below, bracing himself. Tyler threw himself forward, an arm around Howie's throat.

They bounced against the wall, then the cellar door—noises Lois would have to blame on giant mice. He heard Howie choking and tried to change his grip but couldn't. The piggyback ride got slower as Howie lurched along the grass bordering the driveway. Then they crashed through the bushes onto the lawn of the next house, and he fell off.

"Jesus!" croaked Howie, massaging his throat.

Tyler started crawling on his hands and knees. This hurt a little less. But Howie was still determined to get him on his feet.

"Take off," said Tyler. "I'll manage."

"Nothing doing." Howie pulled him up and half dragged him along until they were well up the block. Then he let go and started laughing.

"What's so hysterical?"

"The way you're walkin'. Frankenstein himself."

"I'm glad you're having a good time," said Tyler. Then the pain struck again and he grabbed for the lamppost. "Christ! I must have a triple rupture."

"The Ruptured Chinaman," said Howie. "By One Hung-Lo."

"Honest. I've never hurt so much."

"I know."

"A lot you know."

"I've had them, too," said Howie defensively.

"Had what?"

"What you got."

"For cryin' out loud," he wailed. "What *have* I got?"

"They've turned blue, buddy."

So this was what it was like. They'd kidded about blue balls often enough. But he didn't think it hurt this much.

"How long till it goes away?"

"Couple days," said Howie.

All hope collapsed. How could he hide it? Or explain it? If he said he'd fallen down, his mother would want to see the bruises.

"Come on," said Howie. "Just take it slow."

"No, I'll sprint."

"Make like you're on snowshoes."

"Snowshoes in August." He kept grumbling as he waddled up the street.

"How'd you make out?" asked Howie, one step behind.

"What d'ya mean, how'd I make out? Look at me."

"I thought you were getting in when you came up and woke the kids."

"I would've, if I'd been equipped."

"My fault," acknowledged Howie. "I should've divvied them up when we left Pitkin's."

"That does me a lot of good now."

"Still," said Howie, "you don't have to worry about a dose or anything."

"Talk about Pollyannas."

"Polly who?"

"Forget it," said Tyler.

"Anyway," said Howie, "I didn't enjoy it tonight. I hate quickies. You know what a quickie is?"

"I know."

"What?"

"A guy who double-parks in front of a whorehouse."

"Yeah." Howie was deflated. "How'd you know?"

"I read it in the *Ladies Home Journal*."

"Figures," said Howie.

"Boy, one thing I hate is a broad that smells of spinach."

He continued the grousing, but he was grateful to Howie for sticking with him. Howie could have been home and sleeping by the time it took them to get to Tyler's house.

"Can you make it upstairs by yourself?"

"I guess so."

Howie threw him a parting salute. "Screw everything that moves."

"Except Margaret O. Jones," said Tyler.

The house was completely dark, upstairs and down. He looked at it, debating which way to go—front steps or back. That had been his problem all night. He wondered how Lois had explained the racket in the back hall. Front steps or back?

There were the same number to climb either way. The main thing was not to wake his mother. He didn't want her hovering around him, asking why he was walking like a duck. Not that she probably wouldn't know as soon as she looked at him. Women inherited an instinct about these things.

He was bound to make some noise. So the front way, being farther from her bedroom, was better. Decision made, he took the porch steps one at a time, throwing out his right leg as if it was in splints, then hopping on his left. But no matter how careful he was, the dangling pain got hit occasionally, and he'd double over. Once inside the front door he sank to hands and knees and crawled up the varnished stairs. This cut down the sway of the pendulum. Elementary physics. Not only did it hurt less, but his journey was soundless. Success. Still on all fours, he started across the parlor. The moonlight outlining the furniture wasn't necessary. He could crawl through this room blind. But something was new—a garter, a patch of white.

Conscience! The guilt over what he'd done or tried to do wasn't content to turn his nuts blue. Now it was haunting him, like drunkards saw snakes coming out of walls. For the next couple of days, wherever he looked, he'd see ghosts of himself wrestling with that lanky broad, lying into her teeth about loving her.

"Tyler?"

It had to come from the bedroom. He was losing his sense of direction, too. Crawling took too long. He had to run for it. He lurched to his feet; but the first stride was too big, and the pain flared up again, making him stifle a cry.

"Tyler?" She said the name as if it were impossible to believe. Then the clump of shadows unwound, and the lamp came on, blinding him. He threw his arm before his eyes and staggered back toward his room. But not in time. He'd seen the white pulpy flesh above her stockings before she pulled down her dress. He'd seen the goddam blinking Dr. Axelrod.

III

I F he hadn't given up letter writing he might have sent one to the American Medical Association.

> *Dear Sirs:*
> *I have reason to believe that the cure for blue balls is for the patient to see his mother seduced by a Nazi dentist.*

Either that or he had amazing powers of recovery, for when he got up Sunday the excruciating pain was down to a dull, morning-after ache. He could almost walk normally. Not that he had to worry about her noticing a limp. She never even looked in his direction. Talk about strained atmosphere.

He should have forced a showdown then, but he hadn't yet figured out exactly what to say. Then on Monday she grabbed the chance to get away from him, going downtown to Mathiesson's to look for a job. And Monday night Ross didn't leave them alone for a minute. But at least the stupe didn't want to come along when Tyler asked her to have lunch with him Tuesday. She wasn't too crazy about the idea either.

"It's my first day at work."

"Still, you gotta eat something."

He watched her trying to think of another excuse. "All right," she finally said. "It's a date."

"On me," he insisted. It meant most of his last two bucks. But he couldn't very well lay down the law to her if she was treating him.

Mathiesson's was the oldest department store in town, squat-

ting over a full block and five stories high. There was a paint-
ing between the rest rooms on the third floor showing how it
looked when it was built in 1881, with horse-drawn carriages
and streamers across the muddy street and a brass band with
handlebar mustaches and what was supposed to be Mr. Mathiesson (a portrait of him also hung there) breaking a bottle of
champagne against the cornerstone. The store probably im-
pressed people then. But now it was just one of many big ugly
rectangles, pulsed by cash registers. So much for posterity.

Tyler got there early. But she was already waiting outside
the main entrance, where they'd arranged to meet.

"Where should we go?" She looked as grim as he felt. Everybody going in and coming out of the store seemed to bounce
off them. "Make up your mind," she said, "before we get trampled to death."

"How about Nero's? They've got booths so we can talk in
private." That made it clear that he had something on his
mind besides eating.

They got the back booth. She ordered a fruit salad with cot-
tage cheese, as usual. He chose a western omelet. Then, waiting for their food, they both kept giving dirty looks to the waitresses banging in and out of the swinging door to the kitchen,
as if daring them to spill something their way.

"How'd it go?" She jumped when he spoke. "The job," he
said.

"So-so." She gave him the brave gallows smile.

How to begin? He'd been rehearsing the scene for two days,
thinking up all kinds of brilliant things to say. Once he got
started, he'd be all right.

"It's too soon," he said.

"What is?"

"You know."

The waitress brought their plates of food, and they leaned
back like oarsmen while she plunked them down. Then his
mother's fork had something sticky on it, and getting a new
one took another valuable minute. He asked her when she had

to be back to the store, and she said there was plenty of time. Yes, for her, but not for everything he had to say. They poked at their food.

"I thought we might go out to the cemetery next Sunday," she said.

"Isn't that kind of hypocritical?"

That was one of the lines he'd rehearsed, but in answer to something else. It should have shaken her, but it didn't.

"You read all those books," she said. "What do you think happens after you're dead?"

"Nothing," he said.

"There has to be something."

"There isn't. You just rot."

"You're cruel," she said. "You have a cruel streak in you." Then she started to bawl, fumbling a handkerchief out of her handbag and pressing it to one eye at a time.

"Don't, Mom," he begged. Then, hardening. "Aw, for chrissake!"

When she finally took the handkerchief away, her face had gone all red.

"Mathiesson's don't like their help to cry," he said, keeping it flippant.

"I'm not going back."

He tried not to look surprised. "How come?"

"They put me in the cheap dress section," she said. "In the basement. Cotton print dresses for a dollar forty-nine."

"Real Hattie Carnegie, huh?"

"It's so oppressive down there," she said. "No ventilation at all. Everyone's breath smells so sour. And I'm supposed to stand there and lie about those dresses."

"So don't."

"I didn't!" She looked indignant. "If someone came up to me with one, I made out the sales slip and took the money, that's all. I told Mr. Eidelgeorge. I told him it would take a lot more than two dollars and fifty cents a day to make me tell people that those dresses would wash well."

"Who's Mr. Eidelgeorge?"

"He's in charge of the department."

"And what did he say when you told him?"

"He said they could get along without me."

It didn't immediately sink in that she'd been fired. Not until the tears started flowing again.

"Mathiesson's has junk," he said.

"I'll never keep a job."

"You're trying to do everything too soon," he said. Then he realized the double entendre. It was a perfect opening—but not while she was sobbing away. One of the waitresses going by gave him a "you brute" look. "Dad wouldn't want you to bawl like this," he said. Sentimental slop, but it calmed her down. The sobs turned into sniffs.

"We got along pretty well," she said. "Considering." A little laugh got lost in the sniffling. "Except for your name. What a time we had over that!"

"So I heard," he said. Jesus, did he have to listen to all that again?

"I was determined to call you Woodrow," she said. "After President Wilson. But he hated President Wilson."

"President Wilson always spoke well of him," said Tyler. But it didn't register.

"Your father used to say I have an obsession about the White House."

"You have."

"It's perfectly natural," she said. "Every woman wants her son to be President."

"Then there sure must be a lot of disappointed women."

"I remember figuring it out once," she said. She was gabbing away now, Mathiesson's basement and Mr. Eidelgeorge forgotten. "If every President served two terms and if you were elected at the age of forty-nine, you'd be the thirty-seventh President."

"I've got news for you, Mom. I'm not gonna make it."

"Woodrow Bishop," she said. "I still think it has a good ring. But he wouldn't have it. So I started thinking of other Presidents to name you after. You could have been called

Grover or Rutherford, after Rutherford B. Hayes. Or even
Gamaliel. That was Warren Harding's middle name."

"Ross looks more like a Gamaliel."

"Your father said that if I called you Rutherford, I might
as well have you grow pigtails."

"Uh-huh."

"Then I remembered John Tyler."

"Mom, you've told me this three hundred and eighty-four
times."

But he couldn't head her off. She was determined to give
him the whole load. So he tried to look interested while she
went on about his father's agreeing to call him Tyler because he
thought people would shorten it to Ty.

"He was a great admirer of Ty Cobb," she said.

"Ty Cobb's name is Tyrus," he told her for the three hundred and eighty-fifth time.

"Your friends do call you Ty, don't they?"

"Most of them," he said. Now how was he going to get from
Ty Cobb to Dr. Wolf Axelrod?

"Why do they call Ross Crisco?" The sudden question
caught him flat-footed.

"It's just a nickname," he said.

"But why Crisco?"

"They don't call him that any more. I told the kids not to."

"But why Crisco?" This could go on all day.

" 'Cause Crisco is fat," he said. "And it comes in a can." She
still didn't get it. "Ross is fat in the can, see?"

"Children are so vicious," she said.

"Yeah," he agreed. "Now can we talk about something more
important?"

"Like what?"

"You know."

"No, I don't know."

"Yes, you do."

"Now stop talking riddles," she said.

"I'm talking about Saturday night."

"What about it?" She looked innocent. She actually looked innocent.

"I don't want to sound like a puritan," he said. "But—"

"But what?"

"I object to what's been going on. That's what."

"Nothing's been going on."

"Aw, come on," he said. "Can't we be honest for once?"

"Nothing has been going on." She enunciated each word as if talking to a child.

"I see," he said. "Then are there going to be wrestling matches in the parlor every Saturday night?"

"If you're referring to Dr. Axelrod, we were just talking."

"With all the lights out?"

"The people across the street can see through our curtains when the lights are on."

"So what, if you were just talking?"

"We were just talking." Her voice was getting shrill.

"It looked like wrestling to me."

"Stop it, Tyler."

"Strangler Lewis and Man-Mountain Dean for the championship of the world."

"I said, stop it."

"That's what it looked like."

"Shut up! Shut up!" She covered her ears and looked ready to scream if he said one more word.

"You want any dessert?" It was the waitress, all sweaty under the armpits, standing there as if it was perfectly natural for a customer to sit holding her ears.

"Just the check," said Tyler, and the waitress mumbled numbers while she added it up. Then she slapped it down on the table and flounced away, and his mother let go of one ear to reach for her handbag.

"I told you it was on me," he said. But she was only getting out her compact.

"I can't go back there looking like this," she whispered.

"I thought you weren't going back."

"I have to see the cashier." She powdered the redness around her eyes. "They owe me for two hours and twenty minutes."

He picked up the check and went over the addition. A buck fifteen down the drain. If only once, just once, his perform-ance would live up to the rehearsal in his brain.

"Look," he said. "I know something about biology. I real-ize that middle-aged people still have . . . certain needs."

"What on earth are you talking about now?" But she didn't wait for him to answer. She didn't even wait for him to pay the check, and when he got outside, he had to run to catch up with her. Then she kept her face averted from him, so she didn't see the burlesque show coming up. Usually she crossed the street to avoid being contaminated by it.

Tyler kept looking straight ahead at the lighted dancing girl on the marquee. A missing bulb made her look like an amputee. Then, as they got in front of the lobby, his eyes rolled to the left. Georgia Sothern was playing this week. And as an extra added attraction—Gladys Foxx. Both beckoned from their huge, tinted photographs, the feathered fans just managing to cover their strategic places. But the big guy in the wrinkled tux was standing next to the box office, the same ape who'd refused to let Howie and him buy tickets the three times they'd tried.

He heard his mother snort disapproval and felt like ask-ing her if she was in any position to pass judgment on Georgia Sothern. But no matter how he worded it in his mind, it still sounded priggish. So he just stayed in step with her until they were back in front of Mathiesson's.

"Don't bother waiting," she said. "It may take awhile."

"I just wanted you to know where I stand," he said.

"So now I know."

"Our place isn't big enough for both him and me." Of all the crummy lines from all the crummy movies. He started to salvage it. "If he comes upstairs again—"

"Thanks for the lunch." She pecked him on the cheek and went into the store, leaving him standing there with his threat unfinished. Some woman's heavy shopping bag clipped him as she went by. Another jerk stepped on his foot. He moved out of the herd of shoppers to the first display window.

Three manikins stared back at him. One's nostrils were daubed unevenly; one had a chip in her ankle bone. They all looked about as interested in what he thought as his mother had. What griped him most was that she hadn't even acknowledged that there was anything to discuss. Nothing had happened, she said. Not much. In nine months he'd probably have a kid brother named Woodrow Rutherford Gamaliel.

Unless he was the one who was being thickheaded. Maybe her saying that *nothing* happened was her way of letting him know that *it* hadn't happened, that he'd arrived in the nick of time. Okay, so Wandering-Hand-Trouble Axelrod had been temporarily thwarted. So he wouldn't score until the next time. What did that solve? Besides, that wasn't even the problem. As he'd tried to explain to her, the issue wasn't sexual. It was political and ethical.

Except, of course, there didn't have to be a next time. If his presence had stopped the old lecher once, why couldn't it stop him all the time? Plainly and simply, it could. The idea made Tyler smile for the first time in days. Dr. Axelrod was about to develop a shadow, a callow permanent shadow. It would mean giving up lots of things himself—no movies, no hanging around with Howie, no chances with girls. Good enough. It would be a contest of celibacy. And if experience meant anything, he was a sure winner. As of right now, Dr. Axelrod had better find himself another woman to make.

Well, not quite right now. Unless they were having a rendezvous in the cashier's office at Mathiesson's, nothing was going to happen for the next couple of hours. Time for one last try.

He should have gone right up to the box office instead of wandering back and forth. When he finally did march up and plunk down his fifty cents, the peroxided old bag in the booth just looked at the guy in the tux. Then he came over, picked up the two quarters and handed them back to Tyler.

"Not today, sonny."

"Why not?"

"Come back next year."

"Hell, you gotta bring a birth certificate to see a show?"

"You do."

"Georgia Sothern happens to be my aunt," he said and walked away hunched over, like the men always did when they came out.

IV

Dr. AXELROD wasn't hard to keep track of. Most of the time he was on the Swerdlovs' porch, reading. And when he wasn't, he left a trail of high blood pressure through the neighborhood.

Of course, if his mother was home, there was no point following him. So Tyler wasn't around when Dr. Axelrod told off Mr. Dalesandro or when he tangled with Mr. Fedorchak. He had a legitimate gripe about the barber. When Dalesandro got through with the little hair he had left, Dr. Axelrod looked more like Erich von Stroheim than ever. But Tyler never found out what started the argument with Fedorchak. Howie, who'd been going by on his bike, only heard the last part—when Dr. Axelrod came out of the grocery store and Fedorchak chased after him, brandishing the knife he cut cheese with.

"What does patronizing mean?" asked Howie.

Tyler couldn't think of a synonym, so he stalled. "Why do you want to know?"

" 'Cause that's what your buddy said Fedorchak was doing."

"Don't call him my buddy."

"I'm only kiddin'."

"It's not a laughing matter."

"Okay, so he ain't your buddy."

"I hate his guts."

"Then why do you want to know every word he said?"

"I have my reasons." For a second he almost told Howie the whole story. But there was no saying how Howie would react. He might even laugh. It was better to look enigmatic.

159

"So you want to know what he said or don't you?"

"Go ahead."

"Now I've forgotten," said Howie.

"Try thinking for a change."

He got the argument in pieces. It didn't sound much like an argument, more like a speech by Dr. Axelrod. Howie acted part of it out, shoving a fist up in the air, wagging a finger in Tyler's nose, starting to march away, then turning around, and dancing back with another insult.

"Fool! Look at you. Twenty years ago you had a little shop in Prague."

"Prahg," corrected Tyler.

"Who?"

"If you mean the capital of Czechoslovakia, it's pronounced Prahg."

"I know how to pronounce it," said Howie. "I'm imitating him."

"Keep going."

"Where was I?"

"Twenty years ago I had a little shop, et cetera," said Tyler.

"Okay." Howie puffed himself up again. "Then you came here and you labored and you skimped and you saved until you had blue balls."

"Quit crappin' around, will ya?"

"You didn't have blue balls?" Howie tried to sound like Baron Munchausen.

"You're gonna have no balls in a minute."

"I'm tellin' you exactly what he said." Howie grinned.

"Come on," said Tyler. "This is important to me."

"Okay." Howie waited until he could keep his face straight. "What he meant was that Fedorchak had the same kind of shop here that he had over there."

"So? What's so awful about saying that?"

"Wait! Wait!" Howie wagged a finger at him again. "Never mind that in twenty years you haven't enough brains to learn correct grammar. You were nothing over there, and you are nothing here, and you think that makes you an authority on everything. Fool!"

"Then what?"

"That was it," said Howie. "I thought they were gonna fight, or I wouldn't a' hung around. But they're both wind."

What happened in the library was more intriguing, and at least he heard it firsthand. He'd followed Dr. Axelrod there, keeping a half block behind as usual. But he decided that going in after him would be too obvious, so he hung around outside. Later he realized that he should have known something was wrong when Dr. Axelrod came out without any books. But at the time he didn't even notice this. He just shadowed Dr. Axelrod again until he went into the bakery on Virgil Street. This was something he'd done many times before when Tyler was following him. And just as before, he came out with about a nickel's worth of broken doughnuts in a bag. Then on to Humber Parkway. He had a favorite tree he sat under there, gorging himself and throwing only a few crumbs to some pigeons when the bag was practically empty. But after crumpling it up and throwing it away, he made no sign of leaving. In fact, after a while, he made no sign at all. Tyler decided to walk right by the tree and see if he was sleeping. He was.

He had to pass the library again on his way home. And this time he went in. But the old woman with the goiter at the front table was hogging the new issues of every magazine except *Fortune*. He sat down across from her, tapping his fingers impatiently. But he couldn't look at the goiter. It seemed as if the skin of her neck would burst any second and a big blue egg would fall out. He turned away and stared at the set of encyclopedias nearby. A to BAG, BAG to CED, CED to DOD, DOD to—

He went over and pulled out Volume IV.

DÜSSELDORF: Capital of North Rhenish-Westphalia. (1934 pop. 411,809) Industrial and commercial city at the junction of Rhine and Düssel rivers. Home of Goethe museum, Jagerhof Castle. Picturesque parks. Church of St. Andrew, built

in 1630. Equestrian statue of John William II. Town Hall,
circa 1570. Benrath castle is one of the best examples of Ro-
coco building in Europe.

There was a lot more, about its history and products and how
its streets were laid out. The place sounded about as exciting
as Cincinnati. But there was one thing.

Birthplace of the poet Heinrich Heine.

He looked on the shelves of the poetry section, but the
names on the bindings jumped from Thomas Hardy to W. E.
Henley. And there wasn't any Heine in the card catalog. So he
went up to the librarian's desk. In all the years he'd been coming here, he'd never found out her name. She wore pince-nez
glasses, and ever since she'd tried to dye her gray hair, it had
been part purple.

"Excuse me," he said. "Do you know anything about Heinrich Heine?"

She gave him a weird look. "Is he German?"

"Yes."

"Now don't *you* start." Her voice was permanently muted
from working around silence signs.

"Start what?"

"I've had enough about German writers for one day."

It didn't take much encouragement to get her to whisper
what had happened. A man she'd seen in there several times
before had suddenly come up to her and asked for a book by
somebody named Karl Kraus. And when she said she'd never
heard of him, the man started yelling.

"I reminded him this was a library, but he became absolutely abusive. How could we call ourselves a library, he said,
when we have nothing by Karl Kraus? He said the exclusion
of books was as bad as the burning of books. Imagine."

"Imagine," echoed Tyler.

"I called the main branch after he left," said the librarian.
"They have a book by Karl Kraus there. *The Last Days of Man-
kind* or something like that."

"Never heard of it," said Tyler.

"They said he's an obscure German writer." The librarian was still smarting. "After all, a neighborhood branch can't carry everything."

"The guy sounds like a loony," said Tyler.

"He was." She leaned forward confidingly. "He wore spats." As if he didn't know.

Then there was the afternoon the Ferrara kid was practicing his accordion. When he started "Dark Eyes" for the eight hundredth time, Dr. Axelrod marched over and yelled into the Ferraras' front window. "By what right do you torture a whole street? Not to mention what you are doing to music. Read Schopenhauer on noise. Learn something!"

But when Mrs. Swerdlov went out and dragged him back, "Dark Eyes" was still going on.

After that, nothing. Shadowing Dr. Axelrod had become a big bore. And with less than two weeks of freedom before school started, the prospect of spending the time watching him eating doughnuts wasn't exactly thrilling. Besides, it was plain that nothing more was going on with his mother. Maybe what he'd said at lunch that day registered more than he thought. Maybe he *had* sounded mature and matter-of-fact. Or maybe she had other reasons for dropping Dr. Axelrod. In any case, she hadn't even breathed in his direction. And Dr. Axelrod hadn't jumped any fences to get at her. Keeping tabs on him was just a waste of time.

So the vigil ended, and it was completely accidental that he was sitting in the drugstore when it happened. He hadn't even noticed Dr. Axelrod come in. He just heard the guttural accent asking Mr. Pitkin for shaving cream. Tyler managed to concentrate on his hot fudge sundae instead of trying to hear what they were muttering about. Then Pitkin raised his voice.

"They should wipe it off the map," he said. "Every morning we should thank God we're here and not there."

"There is no God," said Dr. Axelrod.

"That's your opinion," Pitkin granted, wrapping up a jar of Palmolive. "In this country you can say anything you like."

"As long as it isn't meaningful."

"I beg your pardon?"

"If you must speak slogans," said Dr. Axelrod, "please do not include me in them."

"What slogans? You don't think you're better off over here?" Dr. Axelrod shrugged.

"How can you say such a thing?" demanded Pitkin.

"There I am persecuted for being something I am not," said Dr. Axelrod. "And here I am accepted if I deny what I am." He looked down at the palms of his hands as if they held alternatives. "One does more harm to the body; the other is worse for the spirit."

"Then go back to Germany," said Pitkin, getting red in the face. "If it's so good for your spirit, go back there!"

"Don't tell me what to do," warned Dr. Axelrod. His face was equally red.

"This is my place of business! I'll do anything I want!"

"More slogans," exploded Dr. Axelrod. "You gramophone!"

"Who?"

"You! Ignorance in action! As Goethe said, nothing is more terrible."

"Get out!" screamed Pitkin, tearing off the green paper he'd wrapped the shaving cream in. "I don't sell to people like you." He put the jar back on the shelf, then swung around and made a shooing motion with his hand. "Go on! Go back where you came from! Go to a concentration camp!" He waited until Dr. Axelrod was almost to the door, then pointed an accusing finger at him. "You can defend those swine after what they've done to the Jews?"

Dr. Axelrod stopped as if something had hit him in the back. Then he turned around slowly.

"If we must generalize," he said, "then the Jews are all cowards and Shylocks. They deserve everything that happens to them." He took his time walking out, but he was still gone before Pitkin recovered his voice.

"Did you hear?" he gasped to Tyler. "Is it possible . . . in my own store?"

"I knew he was a Nazi," said Tyler.

That was Thursday afternoon. And at dawn on Friday the German troops invaded Poland. He thought that was why Mrs. Swerdlov had come upstairs, moaning away. But then he heard her mention her cousin. He tried to listen to both things at once, to what Raymond Gram Swing was saying on the radio and what Mrs. Swerdlov was telling his mother in the kitchen. Lord Halifax had been officially notified of the invasion by the Polish ambassador in London. Sir Nevile Henderson was trying to see Hitler in Berlin. France was drafting more men into the Army. The British Fleet was massed in the Skagerrak. And Pitkin had told Mrs. Swerdlov what her cousin said.

Tyler went into the kitchen for a glass of water he didn't want.

"If the greenhorn finds out," said Mrs. Swerdlov, "he'll throw him into the street." She closed her eyes and shook her head as if refusing to look at what she visualized. "He's mad enough already because Wolf just sits. Listen, you can't just read and *stopf* yourself. *Oy,* can he eat!"

His mother kept sending signals like a third-base coach, but Mrs. Swerdlov was too worked up to notice.

"I told him I heard that Dr. Kyriakides wants to sell his practice and move to Florida. So do you think he's interested?"

"Tyler," said his mother, "are you going to stand there all day?"

"If he just didn't want to fix *Schwartze* teeth, I could understand it," said Mrs. Swerdlov. "But he won't fix any teeth."

"It looks like they'll declare war any minute," said Tyler.

"That's another thing," groaned Mrs. Swerdlov.

He went back to the parlor; but the news broadcast was over, and a soap opera was on. Will Veronica's period turn out to be a backed-up nosebleed? Tune in tomorrow. He tried the other station.

> *"Hold tight, hold tight,*
> *Foo-ra-de-ack-a-sa-ki,*
> *Want some seafood, mama. . . ."*

While the world went up in smoke. Nero had nothing on the National Broadcasting Company.

*"When I come home from work at night
I get my favorite dish. Fish!"*

Tyler turned it off. He could hear Mrs. Swerdlov still going on.

"We have a word for it. Apikoros—somebody who turns against his own religion." Her sigh was heavy and long. "Nothing is worse than to have an apikoros in the family."

Nothing worse? He felt like going back to the kitchen and telling Mrs. Swerdlov that having an apikoros in the family wasn't nearly as bad as having a Nazi in the family. But the hell with it. It would take hours to explain to her, and he had better things to do.

For the rest of the day and the next he stayed practically glued to the radio because they kept interrupting programs with news flashes. Sometimes, like when the bomb shelters were delivered to Buckingham Palace, a world war seemed a sure thing. Then the French Assembly or British Parliament would have an emergency meeting, and it looked as if Poland would be sold down the river. A lot of experts were predicting another compromise, like Munich. They kept predicting it right until Chamberlain sent Hitler the ultimatum. The Germans had until eleven o'clock Sunday morning to withdraw from Poland. This time Chamberlain meant it. Otherwise, why were they taking the stained-glass windows out of Canterbury Cathedral? This was it.

No one reminded him there was a five-hour time difference. So when he put on the radio at ten thirty Sunday morning, the war had already started. The biggest moment in his whole life, and he slept through it. But at least they'd made a record of Chamberlain's speech and played it later: "I have to tell you now that no such undertaking has been received and that, consequently, this country is at war with Germany." Still, it wasn't the same as hearing it when it was actually said. Something else bothered him. How could an undertaking have been received? Shouldn't the Prime Minister have said, "No *report of* such an undertaking has been received"? Chamberlain sounded calm. But he must have been pretty upset to leave out words in such an important speech.

Naturally, this would be the day when Ross' scout troop was having its annual picnic for parents. While getting ready, his mother kept popping into the parlor, listening to snatches of news and making little clucking sounds. Ross' total response was "Gee!" The first air-raid sirens had gone off in London. Kids like Ross were being evacuated. And all he could say was "Gee!" Tyler was glad when they left for the goddam picnic.

He'd read somewhere that King George stuttered. But when the king came on to address his people, he spoke slowly and precisely. Some contrast with the hysterical broadcasters who were trying to make it sound as if major battles were already taking place. The first air raid in London turned out to be a false alarm. By noon, when France also declared war, it was obvious that no shots had been fired yet. But the war had begun, and there was no turning back.

He went out on the veranda. It was as pleasant a Sunday as the summer had offered, the trees at their fullest, the lawns a deep green. Bare-chested Mr. Swerdlov was hosing his. The radio was on downstairs, but with his limited English there was no point in his listening to the news. Farther down the block, Mr. Green was polishing his car, and two girls were chalking a tennis court on the street. Otherwise, it was deserted, two placid facing rows of double-storied houses distinguishable from one another only because they were painted different colors or the patterns of the lace curtains in the windows weren't exactly the same. Inside each, people were eating or looking at the Sunday paper; parents were arguing; babies were crying. And none of them knew that everything was different now. Except maybe Dr. Axelrod. He probably knew. But he'd be looking at it from the German side.

Tyler had to talk about it to someone. He went over to Howie's. But Howie's mother said he was still sleeping, and she made no offer to wake him up.

"Tell him there's a war on," he said.

"Isn't it terrible?"

Howie's mother worked in a beauty shop and was always changing her hair to some screwy color. This week it was orange. He wasn't discussing the war on her level.

"If he ever gets up, tell him I was here."

He walked down to the intersection. Pitkin had a card in his window saying he was closed for lunch until two o'clock. It was only five to. Tyler went across to Mrs. Mintz's candy store. There were just the regular Sunday papers in the rack by the door. Not even an extra out yet.

"Six weeks," Eddie Dembo was saying. "I give them six weeks at the most."

Eddie Dembo had the Socony station on Monroe Street. He was holding the edges of the pinball machine, swaying his whole body as the ball bumped down and the lights lit up. He was talking to Blacky Roche.

"They'll never get me in the sonofabitchin' Army," said Blacky.

"Don't worry," comforted Eddie Dembo. "That English Navy will take care of 'em. They'll just blockade 'em and starve 'em out." He swayed an inch too far, and the tilt sign lit up. "Shit!" He put in another nickel and turned to Blacky. "You'll see, six weeks."

"It won't be that easy," said Tyler.

They both looked around at him. He waited for a flicker of recognition from Blacky. But the bookie stayed dead-panned.

"Who asked you?" said Eddie Dembo.

"Nobody."

"Then shut up."

They turned back to the pinball machine. Tyler bought a frozen Milky Way from Mrs. Mintz and went to the magazine rack. Rosalind Russell was on the cover of *Life*. Well, that was consistent. So was the article he happened to open to: TIGHT CORSET THREAT SPURS U. S. WOMEN TO NEW EXERCISES FOR WAIST CONTROL. He flipped the pages. LIFE GOES TO MARINELAND—ST. AUGUSTINE, FLORIDA. If religion was the opium of the people, what was *Life* magazine? Ether. Laughing gas. Pick your own anesthetic.

When he came out, Pitkin was shoving open the trellis gate across his door. Tyler saw him wave to someone, a "come over here" wave. The only other person in sight was Mr. Swerdlov, with a shirt on, walking toward the corner. Mr. Swerdlov pointed to himself, a "you mean me?" point. Then, looking suspicious, he changed his direction toward the drugstore.

Tyler walked back home. It might be possible to discuss the world situation with Eunice. But there was no sign of her, or Mrs. Swerdlov, or the storm trooper. He went upstairs, put the half of the Milky Way that was left in the icebox, then switched the radio back on. The keepers of the London Zoo were being given guns so they could kill any wild animals that might escape if the place was bombed. The Louvre Museum in Paris was closed and packing up all its paintings and statues.

Howie never showed up. Probably out with old hairy belly. Tyler stretched out face down on the parlor rug and did twenty push-ups. If this was the most crucial day of his life, it was also the longest. And his mother and Ross wouldn't be home until late because the outing included a moonlight wiener roast. That's what boy scouts were taught to do in the moonlight— roast wieners.

Tyler went to his bedroom and took down *Naked Beauties of the World*. Opening it to those pages now gave him about as much thrill as *Life* going to Marineland. What a dope he'd been! Instead of wasting the three dollars on this crap, he should have sent away for the book on hypnotism that was advertised in the same magazine. He could have practiced on Ross until he was able to put people in a trance just by looking at them. Then, when Rowena had stopped in front of the house, he would just have gazed into her eyes and planted some post-hypnotic suggestions. What suggestions?

Back in the parlor, sprawled on the davenport, he worked them out. The first one would have been not to go to Alexandria, Virginia. But the main one would have been that he was irresistible to her. When he was in sight, she'd hardly be able to control herself. Right now, knowing he was home alone, she'd be over in a flash, tearing off her clothes—

The thumping below almost shook him off the couch. It sounded like the Swerdlovs were moving all their furniture. But the thumping only punctuated what the voices were shouting. Tyler pressed his ear to the floor but still couldn't make out any words. The only thing he could tell was that Mr. Swerdlov was doing most of the yelling.

Tyler went to the icebox and got out the plate of chicken and potato salad covered in waxed paper that his mother had left. As if following him, the racket below moved to the kitchen, too. He went out to the back hall, where it sounded even louder. Then, daring himself to peek through the Swerdlovs' keyhole, he crept down the stairs.

He was almost at their door when something thudded against it from inside. He jumped back into the corner and just in time. The door flew open as if dynamited, framing Dr. Axelrod, his back toward Tyler. He was almost close enough to touch and gradually getting closer as Mr. Swerdlov shoved against him. The two men struggled without words, just making growls of exertion in their throats. But Mrs. Swerdlov, hanging on her husband's back, never shut up.

"You have to believe everything a druggist says? Whatever he is, he's my own flesh and blood."

She worked her hand under Mr. Swerdlov's chin and tried to lift it right off his neck. But he was a match for both of them. Slowly, but surely, Dr. Axelrod was being shoved toward the edge of the landing.

"Morris!" She shifted her grip to his right ear and pulled. "Morris, let him pack! Let him walk out like a *Mensch!*"

What she said made Mr. Swerdlov stop pushing and turn to her. Either that or because his ear was being stretched about six inches. And with Dr. Axelrod still pushing so hard, the three of them suddenly went sailing back into the kitchen, clutching wildly at walls, shelves, chairs. Then one of them kicked the door closed.

It was quiet again. Tyler sneaked to the keyhole, but it just gave a perfect view of the pipes under the kitchen sink. It served him right. War declared, and he was eavesdropping on a family argument. He was almost as bad as everybody else around here.

He went back upstairs, ate the cold chicken and potato salad, and tried not to think about what he'd just seen, the veins standing out in Dr. Axelrod's neck, the way both men had tried to shift their grips and feet for leverage. Looking through the rotogravure section of the paper, he came to an article about the types of planes in the Royal Air Force. Memorizing them would come in handy when he joined the RCAF. There was the Vickers Wellington heavy bomber, the Hawker light bomber, the Hurricane and the Spitfire which were both interceptors, the Handley Page Hampton medium bomber—

The knocking on the kitchen door startled him. He hadn't heard anyone come up the stairs.

"Who is it?"

The knocking was repeated. Just Howie crapping around. He opened the door, braced for some kind of gag, ready for anything but the suitcase and spats.

"May I speak to Mrs. Bishop, please?"

"She isn't here."

"Then may I wait until she returns?" Dr. Axelrod took off his hat. His hand was trembling as much as his voice. . .

"She won't be home till late," said Tyler. His voice wasn't exactly rock-steady, either.

"I have time," said Dr. Axelrod. He looked at Tyler's arm blocking the doorway. "May I wait inside?"

"What do you want from my mother?" Tyler kept his hand on the doorframe.

"I wish to ask a favor."

"What favor?"

Dr. Axelrod hesitated before deciding to tell him.

"I have nowhere to stay tonight. So I wondered—"

"You can't stay here," interrupted Tyler.

"I am perfectly willing to sleep on the sofa."

"No," muttered Tyler. He could have said something sarcastic about Dr. Axelrod's wanting to return to the scene of his latest conquest, meaning the sofa. "People around here have big mouths," he said.

"Yes?" Dr. Axelrod waited for a better reason.

"Besides, bigots aren't any more welcome up here than they are downstairs." Dr. Axelrod still stood staring at him. "My father's only been dead two months," said Tyler. "Why don't you leave her alone?"

Dr. Axelrod raised a hand to rub his scalp. "I see." He put his hat back on and started to pick up the suitcase. But a piece of striped pajamas was sticking out one side. Tyler waited until he fixed it before closing the door.

Back in the parlor, the radio was still on. He went to the front window and looked down at the sidewalk below.

"Many famous people have hurried to volunteer," said the news commentator. "The record-holding racing driver Sir Malcolm Campbell and boxer Tommy Farr in Britain, and former world heavyweight champion Georges Carpentier in Paris. Here at home, singer Grace Moore says she is canceling all her concert engagements to go to France and drive an ambulance."

Dr. Axelrod came into view below. He stopped to tighten one of the straps of his suitcase another notch. Then, without looking back, he walked away.

"And in New York," said the news commentator, "twenty midgets from the World's Fair have registered for military duty with the German consulate."

V

THE first day of school Mr. Mulleavy introduced himself by writing his name on the blackboard and making everyone repeat it after him.

"Mull-ee-vee," he kept saying in a high, hoarse voice, tapping out the syllables with a pointer. And the American history class echoed him.

Mr. Mulleavy was a thickset man, who walked lightly on crepe-soled shoes. He had pale blue eyes, a wide pug nose, and a jutting jaw. His hair at the sides and back of his head was curly and thick, but only a few strands remained on top, like broken banjo strings.

When he was finally satisfied with their pronunciation, Mr. Mulleavy made the announcement that he was famous for.

"There are two things that you boys in class want to remember," he said. "First, when I was at the University of Michigan, I was light heavyweight champion of the Big Ten. And second, anybody that steps out of line is going to be invited to put on the gloves with me after school in the gym."

He said it so melodramatically that Tyler could hardly keep a straight face. Shielding it with his hand, he sneaked a look at Rowena in the third aisle. Mental telepathy. She looked over at him.

"I'm speaking," said Mr. Mulleavy. He'd caught their exchange and stared at Tyler for what seemed minutes before giving the class its first assignment.

There were all kinds of stories about times in the past when Mr. Mulleavy's invitation to the gym had been accepted. One student was supposed to have hovered on the brink of death for a week after Mr. Mulleavy got through with him. Another time, no one was sure exactly when, Mr. Mulleavy had taken on the whole first-string football team, one at a time. Eleven knockouts in a row. And once, his right arm in a sling from a skiing accident, he'd still left-jabbed the toughest kid in school into a bloody pulp.

It was undoubtedly a lot of bull, but Ross believed every word of it. No matter what Tyler said, Ross still swallowed all the school rumors, like about Mr. Hackendorf, the chemistry teacher, having poisoned his wife and Miss Lockridge being a Lesbian.

On the way home from school the first day Tyler imitated Mr. Mulleavy making his announcement.

"Remember, I was the light heavyweight craphead of the Big Ten."

"He didn't threaten my class," said Ross. He had Mr. Mulleavy for ancient history.

"He doesn't have to threaten anemic little sophomores," said Tyler.

"Big Richie's in my class," said Ross. "And he ain't anemic." Tyler wondered what an anemic Negro would look like. "If he ever threatened Big Richie—" Ross wound up and delivered an uppercut at nothing. "Pow!"

Tyler thought of the night he'd been waylaid on the way to the Liberty, of Big Richie coming out of that doorway. He'd never seen Big Richie in a fight. No one he knew had. But everyone in school conceded that Big Richie was invincible. Jolly Jellnick, the football coach, claimed that if Big Richie came out for the team, they'd win the city championship in a walk. But Big Richie wouldn't. He was just waiting until he was seventeen and could quit school. Then he'd probably get a job at Bethlehem Steel or some other plant, where he'd be paid for his strength and could marry Inez Jackson, who was a senior. Inez was a mulatto and one of the best lookers in school except when she smiled and showed the gold filling in her front tooth.

"Big Richie would kill him," said Ross.

"Maybe," said Tyler.

Mr. Mulleavy sure didn't waste any time extending invitations. In the first two weeks of school, several guys had close calls —Samuel Gonziger, and Tommy Ricco, and Ladislaus Polkawycz. Ladislaus came closest of all. When Mr. Mulleavy asked him who said, "Give me liberty or give me death," and Ladislaus answered, "George Washington," Mr. Mulleavy said it was amazing how little got into Ladislaus' head, considering the size of his ears.

"You got no right makin' fun'a how I look," protested Ladislaus.

"Are you telling me what I can and cannot do?" asked Mr. Mulleavy.

"I can't help my ears," said Ladislaus, "any more than you can help bein' bald."

"Either you apologize to me and the class," snapped Mr. Mulleavy, "or you'll meet me in the gym after school."

He held his big fist up to his mouth and blew on his knuckles as if to cool them. But Ladislaus still waited a good five seconds before he apologized.

There were compensations. Not only was it Tyler's only class with Rowena, but Mr. Mulleavy often told some funny jokes, usually risqué enough to make the girls blush. As a teacher, he wasn't too bad either, except when he got all gucky about the immigrants coming to America. Whenever he could, he'd refer to the poverty in Ireland and what a hard time his mother and father had in County Cork and how they'd come to the New World in steerage. The happy ending to his story was always how they sent him to the University of Michigan. There were practically tears in his eyes when he said it. Christ, imagine if they'd sent him to Princeton!

The day it happened was the day after the Warsaw radio went quiet. Up until then the beginning of Chopin's *Polonaise* was played every thirty seconds to show that Warsaw was still holding out. Then the music stopped, and it was obvious that General von Brauchitsch had won.

Tyler wasn't the only one who felt sick about it. Harriet Jaffe came into history class looking as if she'd been crying all night.

"Isn't it unbearable?" she said to Tyler.

"That's putting it mildly," he said.

"Did you see that picture in the paper of that dead girl in Warsaw?" Tyler nodded. "That proves they bombed civilians," she said.

"And Borah calls it a phony war," he said scathingly.

Then the bell rang, and they scrambled for their seats as Mr. Mulleavy came in. All the time he was taking the roll, Harriet still looked miserable. And after Mr. Mulleavy said, "Zwimmer," and Agatha Zwimmer said, "Present," Harriet raised her hand.

"All right," said Mr. Mulleavy. "We're still on Jefferson's administration." Then he saw her hand waving and looked annoyed. "What is it?"

"Mr. Mulleavy," said Harriet, "don't you think we should get into the war?"

"We?" he asked. "You mean, you and me?" That got a big laugh.

"I mean the United States," she said.

Mr. Mulleavy came around to the front of his desk and stood looking down at her—short, dumpy Harriet with her silver-rimmed glasses and frizzy hair and the little square of adhesive tape over the boil on her chin. Mr. Mulleavy's expression was meant to be impassive, but Tyler was sure he saw dislike in it. Maybe Harriet saw it, too, fidgeting in her seat until it squeaked.

"Don't you?" she whined.

"On which side?" asked Mr. Mulleavy.

Some jerk in the back chortled, but Tyler didn't turn around to see who. He was watching Harriet, his own face feeling as hot as hers looked. Not that he'd been too surprised. After all, he'd seen *The Informer* twice, so he knew how the Irish hated the British. He'd been on their side in the movie, too. But that all happened long ago. And no matter how much the Irish had

been pushed around, it was nothing compared to what was going on in Poland right now. Mayor Straczynzki, the mayor of
Warsaw, was out in the streets with his people, digging trenches.
He might be getting mowed down by a machine gun this very
minute. And there was Mr. Mulleavy, smiling and pulling at
his left ear, the slightly cauliflower one, and saying, "On which
side?"

"On the side of England and France, of course," said Tyler.

"Of course?" asked Mr. Mulleavy.

"Of course, of course," said Tyler, wishing somebody else
would join in. Out of the corner of his eye, he could see Rowena watching him.

Mr. Mulleavy hopped backward, his hands gripping the front
edge of his desk. Then he swung there, as if demonstrating
how strong his arms were. And all the time he kept looking at
Tyler.

"I think we'll spend today reviewing," he finally said. "Let's
see how much you remember about the Revolutionary War."

Still dangling from his arms, he called on everybody else—
firing questions about the Boston Tea Party and Saratoga and
Bunker Hill. Smart bastard. He was working up the whole class
against the British without once stepping outside the bounds
set by the Board of Education. And nobody objected. Tyler
looked around. Rowena was nibbling her thumbnail. Ladislaus
Polkawycz was doodling. Except maybe for Harriet Jaffe, they
all were letting Mr. Mulleavy get away with it. Tyler stood up.

"Yes?"

"Mr. Mulleavy," he said, "I move that this class send a letter
of encouragement to the British Army in Europe."

"Seconded," piped Harriet. "And the French Army, too."
Mr. Mulleavy motioned her to shut up.

"Tyler," he said, "suppose you tell us what you know about
the Battle of Yorktown."

"I've made a motion, and it's been seconded," insisted Tyler.

"Yorktown," repeated Mr. Mulleavy. "This happens to be
a history class."

"History is being made today on the Maginot Line," said Tyler.

Mr. Mulleavy swung himself out away from the desk and landed almost daintily at the head of the aisle. "For the last time," he said, "the Battle of Yorktown."

"Okay," said Tyler. "In the first place, the battle wasn't *in* Yorktown. It was on the plains outside." He intended to do the whole thing that way, factual and nonpartisan. But when he got to the battle itself, he started sounding like Gabriel Heatter broadcasting from the spot. He described the rank upon rank of tall, straight British soldiers in their bright red jackets, the roll of drums in the misty October morning air, and General Cornwallis moving his men forward. Then his voice quivered with shame as he reported them being mowed down from ambush by a bunch of hired Hessians and drunken Indians.

"You little traitor," said Mr. Mulleavy.

"I'm third-generation American," said Tyler. "What are you?"

For a second he was sure Mr. Mulleavy was going to come up the aisle and sock him right there. But then Mr. Mulleavy smiled.

"Answering back," he said. "*And* insulting your teacher. For that you'll meet me after school today." His mouth practically carved the next three words. "In the gym."

No one in the room was breathing. Out of the corner of his eye, Tyler could hazily see Rowena watching him.

"I'll be there." It was still Gabriel Heatter talking.

In the cafeteria during lunch period, sharing the peanut butter and jelly sandwiches with Ross, Tyler felt the news spreading around him and the eyes turning his way.

"Keep him off-balance with your left," said Ross for the third time.

Then Andy Lupke and goony Samuel Gonziger came up to the table and offered to be Tyler's seconds. Andy Lupke had made the All-High second team at right guard.

"Don't worry about nuthin'," he said. "The guy's a pushover."

"He weighs more'n Tyler," said Samuel.

"So what?" snapped Andy. "He's old, ain't he?"

"About thirty-five," guessed Samuel.

"That's what I mean," said Andy. "He's out of shape."

"But don't clinch with him," warned Samuel.

"I hope my wrist holds out," said Tyler. "I don't want to break it again."

Samuel leaned down to look at it. "It won't break," he said.

"He's got a pretty thick head," said Tyler.

"See you in the gym." Andy gave him a reassuring pat on the shoulder before they walked away.

Howie, waiting in the milk line, suddenly spun around toward Tyler in amazement. Whoever was in the line ahead of him must have just told him the news. Howie jumped the railing and hurried over.

"What're you, nuts or something?"

"It's a matter of principle," said Tyler.

"Principle, hell." Howie sat down. "You and your principles."

"Hey, don't you want that?" Ross was pointing to the sandwich he hadn't touched.

"I'm not hungry," said Tyler and slid it toward him.

"Mulleavy, of all people," groaned Howie.

"He's a Fascist," said Tyler.

"He also was the light heavyweight champion of—"

"I know," said Tyler.

"So why do you have to tangle with him?" asked Howie. "If you want to fight with a teacher, pick on Miss Lockridge."

"She's a Lesbian," said Ross, his teeth clogged with peanut butter.

"What the hell do you know about Lesbians?" snarled Howie. Ross looked hurt.

"I hope he doesn't gouge my eyes," said Tyler. "You gotta have twenty-twenty vision for the RCAF."

"When Mulleavy gets through with you," said Howie, "you won't have twenty-twenty nothing."

"Thanks for the encouragement," said Tyler.

"Look," said Howie. "Maybe if you apologize to him."

"No."

"If I was you," said Howie, "I'd get down on my hands and knees and kiss his ass."

"That's the difference between us," said Tyler.

"Tyler'll kill him," said Ross.

Three o'clock, when school would let out, still seemed far away. Before then he had a study period, solid geometry, and Latin. The study period was the worst, for there was nothing to distract him. Not that he shouldn't think about it. In fact, he had to. He had to figure out some strategy for the fight. Mr. Mulleavy would undoubtedly plow into him, so he'd have to backpedal. But should he circle to the right or left? And how about when Mr. Mulleavy cornered him? He imagined himself ducking under a haymaker, spinning Mr. Mulleavy around, then dancing out of range. Hitting Mr. Mulleavy was harder to imagine, and not only because Mr. Mulleavy knew how to box. He'd just never hit anybody except when he'd lost his temper. And he wasn't that mad at Mr. Mulleavy. The fact that Mr. Mulleavy was pro-German and a sadistic bully should have made him that mad. But it just didn't.

He remembered reading once how a fighter got himself into the right frame of mind for each bout by pretending his opponent was somebody else who he really hated. He wasn't sure which fighter it had been—Carnera or Braddock maybe. But it sounded like a good idea. The only problem was thinking of someone he really hated. Though there were plenty of people he didn't like, hate was something else. The only person who qualified for that was Dr. Axelrod.

Tyler thought of Dr. Axelrod's gloating face throwing words at him that he couldn't define and the way it looked when criticizing his letter. Then he peeled off this face and pasted it over Mr. Mulleavy's. But the bell rang and he had to go to solid geometry.

Miss Lockridge, who taught it, had her hair cut like Amelia Earhart's. That was one reason for the rumor about her being a Lesbian. Plus her never wearing makeup or high heels, and the force with which she wrote on the blackboard. She crumpled up about three pieces of chalk per theorem. Watching her now, Tyler remembered what Howie had said. Sure, pick a fight with Miss Lockridge instead. And what if she won? There were women who could beat up men. That would be even worse than what was going to happen to him.

He concentrated on Dr. Axelrod's face again. During the fight it was this face that he had to keep seeing and hitting. But the hatred didn't swell. Two weeks ago it would have. But he'd had some revenge, turning the guy away when he had no place to go. And for all he knew, Dr. Axelrod wasn't even alive. Mrs. Swerdlov was getting more and more hysterical about not hearing from him. And Eunice was using all her social work connections to find out where he was. But since Dr. Axelrod had walked away from the house, no one had laid eyes on him. It was very possible he was floating in the river. Or at the bottom of it, tied by a shoelace to his heavy suitcase. And though one could hate a dead man, there was something wrong about using his face for a target. The bell rang for the last period.

Miss Hall, the Latin teacher, was a fresh-air fiend. But even with all the windows wide open, the room felt stuffy. Tyler ran a hand across the back of his neck, and it came away wet.

"Old Wooden-Tit" Hall was the school joke. Not only was there her dubious left breast, but the hairnet she always wore over what had to be a wig because no real hair could look that fake, *and* the two long black dresses she alternated, *and* her old-fashioned buttoned shoes. Tyler had got more than one laugh at her expense. But now, as she corrected their readings of Caesar with eager little chirps, he suddenly realized that Miss Hall knew she was laughed at. She *knew*. Yet, day after day, year after year, she stood before them, refusing to change her appearance just to avoid ridicule. And he'd made fun of her. He deserved to get beaten up.

Miss Hall's eyes kept flicking up toward the wall clock. Tyler watched it, too. The Roman numerals of the clock seemed appropriate. This being a Latin class was also fitting. He was a Christian martyr waiting to be summoned to the arena. The lion waited. The bloodthirsty crowd waited. The double bell rang, signaling the end of school.

Bloodthirsty crowd was right, and all trying to get through the gym doors at once like it was bingo night. Some girls, too. He hadn't figured on that. And Rowena! He stopped. He couldn't go through with it if she was watching. Then Andy Lupke and Samuel Gonziger came out of nowhere to grab him by both arms.

"Gangway!" Andy yelled. "Make way for the new champeen!"

The crowd at the door parted, and they charged through. Rowena's face blurred by as they did. Her lips had moved, but he hadn't been able to make out what she'd said.

"No girls," he hissed at Andy and Samuel. "Get rid of the girls." But they didn't pay any attention. They just shoved ahead until they got him into the locker room. Then Samuel kept massaging his shoulders, and Andy was trying to unbutton his shirt. And suddenly Howie was there, too. And Ross was trying to squeeze in.

"Feel him out for the first round," said Andy.

"As soon as he lays a glove on you," said Howie, "fall down."

"Keep out of this, Howie," warned Andy.

"Beat it yourself, Lupke."

For a moment it looked like they were going to square off. Tyler broke free from Samuel Gonziger's massaging hands and got to the door.

"Where you goin'?" called Andy.

"I gotta take a leak." Tyler piled through the crowd in the gym. The mats were out at the center of the floor, and Rowena already had a ringside seat, ready for an uninterrupted view of his humiliation. She probably believed in fairy tales. She probably thought he'd win.

"Here you are."

Mr. Zachary, the gym teacher, stood in front of him, two pairs of maroon boxing gloves dangling from his shoulders.

"Be right back," mumbled Tyler and pushed past him.

He could hear voices in the lavatory, so he stayed out in the corridor and bent over the water fountain. The water was luke-warm, but he couldn't get enough of it. When he finally stopped, his stomach was a lead balloon.

Some kid he didn't remember ever seeing came out of the lavatory and spotted him. "Give him one for me," said the kid, feinting a short left hook.

Tyler smiled weakly and bent back over the water fountain. Tipping his head, he could see the door of the principal's office. He wondered if Mr. Llewellyn was inside and if he knew what was going on. Since Mr. Mulleavy had been beating up pupils for years, the principal must know about it. But he was prob-ably afraid of Mr. Mulleavy, too.

Then Tyler noticed that the door of the janitor's closet was open. The inside was stuffed full of mops and buckets and light bulbs and toilet paper, but there was still room. He sauntered toward it, looking up and down the corridor. The kid for whom he was supposed to give Mr. Mulleavy one was just turning the corner. The coast was clear. He ducked into the closet and shut the door.

He wasn't going to hide. He just needed a couple of minutes to sort out his thoughts. It was almost dark with the door closed. There was a small window high above, but it was dirty and crisscrossed with chicken wire. Something smelled moldy. The mop handles threatened to fall and give him away.

He had to figure things out logically. He wished he had a pen-cil and paper so he could make a list of pros and cons the way he often did when he had a decision to make. The thing he had to know was just what he'd be accomplishing by the fight. It wasn't a question of victory or defeat. He had no delusions about beating Mr. Mulleavy. What he had to figure out was what he'd be accomplishing by getting knocked out. Would that keep Mr. Mulleavy from making pro-Axis cracks in the future? No. Would it make him stop picking on other kids in the future? No. Then what was he doing it for? He couldn't go around fighting every Fascist. He couldn't go to New York and take on those twenty midgets who wanted to join the German Army. The important thing to remember was that wars were won on the battlefield, not in some liniment-stinking gym.

He had to decide where he'd be most valuable. That was boiling it down. Was he more valuable as a punching bag for Mr. Mulleavy or as a pilot for the RCAF? It was as simple as that. And what he'd said in the cafeteria about eye gouging was true. One thumb in the eye, and he'd flunk the physical. Or his nose. He was bound to catch a few punches on the nose that would mash up his nasal passages. You couldn't fly at high altitudes with mashed nasal passages.

Someone ran by in the corridor, and he held his breath. Then more footsteps, and he heard Ross' voice calling his name. He couldn't stay here much longer. One of them was bound to open the door. Or the janitor would come back. He wanted to remember the point he'd been making, but there wasn't time. The footsteps had receded, but they'd be back any second. They wanted their kill today. He looked up at the small window, gauging it in proportion to his shoulders. The shelves up one wall would serve as a ladder, but the window didn't seem wide enough.

He scrambled up, kicking things off the crowded shelves to wedge room. Something metal clanked against a bucket. A light bulb exploded. But his hand reached the window. It was stuck! It probably hadn't been opened since the goddam school was built. Shoving against it, trying to get leverage without toppling, he heard Ross again, getting closer. There wasn't time to plunge his fist through the glass and pull out the jagged edges before crawling through. He tried to think of an excuse for being up there. Then the window moved, reluctant, creaking. He punched at the frame wildly until it was fully open. His head was out, one arm, one shoulder. Halfway through, he was sure he was stuck. Then, twisting and slithering, his shirt ripping, he crawled clear. As he jumped to his feet, the door of the closet below was opening.

He ran, faster than he'd ever run before—down the sloped

grass, across the rutted practice field. His feet ate up the ground. His body felt light. A big puddle was ahead of him, but he couldn't be bothered to swerve around it, splashing through, welcoming the cold wetness seeping into his shoes and socks. He heard his name called far behind but didn't look back. Two girls walked ahead, arms wrapped around their schoolbooks. He scissored between them, heard one yipe, and saw a green algebra book flutter and fall like a dead bird.

And he ran. His lungs were full and easy. He could keep going like this all day. Houses blurred by, shops, vacant lots with blistered billboards. The traffic was with him as he crossed each corner. Only once did a car have to jam on its brakes to keep from hitting him. Ahead, on the next block, a woman leaned over a baby carriage. Not enough room to squeeze by. He cut across a lawn and ran on the street.

It all had been downhill so far, but now the street curved up. His wet shoes began to weigh heavy. The muscles of his legs got rubbery, and his chest caved in. He stumbled on. He was on Monroe Street, passing the Liberty, passing what looked like Spencer Tracy in cheap colored posters, but he didn't have the strength to turn his head to see which picture. A few yards more. He gasped painfully for air, almost tripped over broken pavement, pushed against the plate glass window of a store to propel himself farther.

Then, when he was sure he couldn't go one more step, he got his second wind. The rest was easy, a steady gait down Granite Street, past the intersection and toward home. Head up, shoulders back, he cadenced his stride. The house was the finish line. Mrs. Swerdlov, coming out of the driveway, waved to him as if she'd been clocking his run. But he trotted right past her to the back door, and took the hall steps two at a time until his legs gave out, then one at a time, then the door and into the kitchen, and he was safe.

"Mom!"

He floundered through the rooms, concocting explanations for her—why he was soaked with sweat, why he'd never set foot in that school again. But each room was empty, scrubbed and empty, until he came in and contaminated it. Jesus, he was thirsty.

The icebox yielded a milk bottle filled with Kool-Ade. Lime. He drank it out of the bottle, almost half the quart. He couldn't get enough. His whole insides seemed scorched. He wanted to go into the parlor and turn on the radio to find out if the *Polonaise* had been heard again. But instead he stumbled back to the big bedroom, *their* bedroom. She'd bought a new spread for the double bed—purple, with a pattern as if a wagon wheel had fallen on the thick, fluffy pile. Why purple? Why not yellow? This was the coward's bed, wasn't it? Tyler threw himself across it, his face on the same pillow his father had tried to hide in. What else had he inherited from him? How much else? The grenadiers on the wallpaper watched him stupidly. Everything was stupid. Right now he should be lying on a stained mat that smelled of sneaker soles, with blood dribbling from his mouth and Mr. Zachary counting over him. He shouldn't have run away. He should have gone through with it. It couldn't have hurt more than this. He bit into his father's pillow to keep from crying.

It had all been the girls' fault. If Rowena hadn't been there, he would have gone through with it. And if Harriet Jaffe hadn't opened her big mouth, there never would have been anything for him to go through. And the way they clustered around the gym door, all there to see him bloodied up, the same way they always squealed around a street fight or at a dance hall when two guys fought over one of them. He'd seen their faces—pretending to be horrified, but all the time gloating.

The hell with them. Let them laugh at him. More than one person had been condemned in his time only to be redeemed by history. They'd change their tune when he became a war ace with twenty or thirty German planes to his credit.

A chill racked his body. He shuddered and thrashed over onto his back, tenting his eyes with his elbow. His forehead was burning; all his skin was—a tight, steaming crust stretched over the cold, rotten stew of his insides.

The girls were to blame, the lousy sonofabitching girls.
They had a cinch. They never had to take a stand about anything. All they had to do was grow up and snag themselves
some poor sap for a husband. Especially the girls over here, like
that dumb cunt on *One Man's Family* having a nervous break-
down because somebody didn't remember her birthday or
something. Dr. Axelrod had been right about that. The girls
over here ought to get a taste of what others were getting. It
would be a good thing if they had their noses rubbed in a war,
if they did a little screaming because their fathers were dragged
away.

He projected the scene on the insides of his eyelids—the
narrow cobbled street, the black-shirted Gestapo, the frightened faces of the men being taken from their homes, the wives
grabbing after them with feeble hands, and the children crying.
Then he changed the street to his own. The ice truck was there,
the back of it crowded with men from the neighborhood. He
picked out some of those who had daughters in school—Shirley
MacLeod's father and Diane Puccinelli's and Harriet Jaffe's
and Rita Garth's. Rita had the best shape in the senior class,
but she was practically engaged to some guy who drove a taxi.
The back of the ice truck was crammed full. But it made another stop—in front of the Keyhoe house—and two Gestapo
men went in, both huge with shaved heads, emerging a second
later with a squirming little Mr. Keyhoe between them and
jamming him in the back of the truck with the others. Then
Rowena ran screaming from the house and tried to get in the
truck, too. But one of the guards pushed her away, and she fell
to the sidewalk, skinning her knees, sobbing, and begging them
to free her father.

The scene changed. He was in it now, wearing a fancy uniform in a big office guarded by heel-clicking soldiers. And by
the line of people waiting outside to see him, he was pretty
important. They all had the same sob story, trying to save a
husband or father or brother who'd been dragged away.

"Next," he said. And the guard showed in Rowena. Her eyes
were rimmed red, but otherwise she looked beautiful. "Sit

down, Rowena," he said gently, and she slumped into the chair facing his big mahogany desk. Then his phone rang, something about whether a certain prisoner was to be pardoned or executed, and he distinctly gave orders to let the man go, so Rowena would know he had that power.

"Now, Rowena," he said, "what seems to be the trouble?" And she told him how she'd never known until they'd come for her father that his great-great-grandmother had been Jewish.

"It's such a small proportion," she said.

"Still"—he tried to cushion the blow—"I'm afraid we have to go by percentages, no matter how small."

"But only a great-great-grandmother."

"There are those who think they deserve everything they get," he said. "I don't happen to agree." He watched the hope begin to glow in her face.

"Then will you save him?" she begged. "Please."

"That's up to you." Naturally, she pretended she didn't know what he meant. They all did at first. "I'm a very busy man," he said. "If you're willing to do anything to save your father's life, all right. Otherwise there are plenty of other girls waiting outside."

"What do you mean by anything?"

"You know what I mean."

The fear in her eyes made her even more desirable. Then her shoulders sagged, signifying agreement.

"Stand up," he ordered, and she got slowly to her feet. "Take off your clothes."

"All of them?"

"All of them."

She did, delicately, blushing, then drawing herself up and facing him defiantly, her body like Hedy Lamarr's in the picture in *Look,* the one where she was coming out of the lake after swimming naked in *Ecstasy.* Only Rowena was three-dimensional and closer, and he alone could see her as she stood with her breasts quivering with shame. He reached for them, and she stood perfectly still, letting him touch her and squeeze her without a murmur.

The excitement throbbing in him had reached its peak and began to subside. With it the scene before him started dissolving. He struggled to get it sharp again, to get the furniture back in the office and the line of people back outside the door. Harriet Jaffe was next, her face covered with little pieces of adhesive, and the guard told her to go in. But she came in laughing and waving a petition she wanted him to sign and suddenly Eunice Swerdlov was swinging through a forest of beaded strings and he rang for the guards but none came and dozens of flat-chested headless female bodies were floating in a lake and before he could get Harriet Jaffe to undress he sank into fevered sleep.

Part Four

I

AFTER looking for him in the lavatory, Ross walked clear around the corridor, opening every door and calling Tyler's name. Then he noticed the janitor's closet and went in there to find the window open. By the time he climbed up to see out, Tyler was halfway down the hill.

Ross went back to the gym. Four girls were jitterbugging to their own humming just inside the door. About fifty more kids were sprawled on the varnished floor around the mats, waiting for the fight to start. Everything was ready. Two stools from the shower room had been put in opposite corners, and Mr. Mulleavy already had his boxing gloves on, munching them together impatiently. He still wore his crepe-soled shoes and the navy blue pants from his suit. But above them was a T shirt with black tufts of hair sprouting from many holes. And it had been washed so much the UNIV. OF MICH. printed on the front was almost faded away.

Mr. Zachary sat on one of the stools, the other pair of gloves hanging around his neck by their laces. Ross wondered if Mr. Zachary would spar a few rounds with Mr. Mulleavy so the crowd wouldn't feel cheated. But Mr. Zachary was about sixty years old. He had pictures of his grandchildren in his little office.

"Did you find him?"

It was Andy Lupke. Ross, watching Mr. Mulleavy, could only shake his head. Mr. Mulleavy had started shadowboxing, doing little crisscross steps and snorting as he threw each punch. Even from this distance, Ross could hear the gloves whizzing through the air.

"What we gonna do?" wailed Andy.

Ross swallowed and walked out onto the mats and up to Mr. Mulleavy.

"My brother had to go on an important appointment," he said. "So I'll take his place."

"You?" Still doing the crisscross jig, Mr. Mulleavy made a full circle around him, sizing him up from every angle. Ross stood perfectly still, staring straight ahead.

"What's up?" called Mr. Zachary.

Mr. Mulleavy ignored him. He finished his circle and faced Ross again. Then he stopped prancing and lunged. "Hah!" he yelled and feinted with his left. "Hah!" He bobbed and weaved, his right high and cocked.

Ross backed away, but Mr. Mulleavy came after him, crouching and shifting, shoulders weaving. Ross backpedaled faster, stumbling off the mat and making a girl squeal as he stepped on some part of her. Then, trying to get back on the mat, he tripped over the empty stool, and voices taunted him to stop running and mix it up.

They went past Mr. Zachary, Ross skidding backward and Mr. Mulleavy pounding after him and going, "Hah!"

"He's the wrong brother," said Mr. Zachary, but Mr. Mulleavy didn't stop. Then Ross' right shoe caught against his left ankle, and he sat down hard.

As he waited there for Mr. Mulleavy to go to a neutral corner, the laughter pressed on him. Ross looked at where it came from, at the cavities and sticky hair and the dandruff on the sweaters. He got to one knee. Then Mr. Mulleavy, motioning with his gloves, hushed the place down.

"It seems Tyler Bishop doesn't have the courage of his convictions," he said. "He sent his little brother to do his fighting. And I'm no match for *him*."

As his voice went up on the "him," he rumpled the top of Ross's hair with the palm of his boxing glove. He did it hard enough to make the laces hurt. But it looked like a gesture of sportsmanship, so the kids cheered him.

"Anyone else want a little workout?" challenged Mr. Mulleavy. But no one stepped forward, so he started untying his gloves with his teeth, and there was a stampede for the door. Mr. Zachary collared the last four boys, one of whom was Ross, and made them hang the mats back on the wall pegs.

All Ross knew was that he didn't want to go home. So he went to the cinder lot and got into a choose-up game of two-handed touch. The players started peeling off about six o'clock. Then the kid who owned the football had to go. Ross stood alone seeing how far across the lot he could throw pebbles. One skipped out into the street and clanked against a new car. He ran.

He took the last few blocks heel to toe, counting how many shoe lengths from corner to corner. It came to a different total for each block. Whoever'd laid out the city couldn't even read a ruler.

Halfway up the backstairs he heard a man's voice in the kitchen. Then his mother's. As he came in, she was handing Dr. Lessing a teaspoon. Dr. Lessing looked guiltily at Ross.

"I forgot my spatula," he muttered and hurried back toward the bedrooms. Then his mother started on Ross, wanting to know where he'd been when his brother was so sick. Before he could say anything, she went after Dr. Lessing. Ross followed her to her bedroom where Dr. Lessing had the spoon handle in Tyler's mouth, pressing down his tongue. Tyler looked awful. His head was rolling, and he was mumbling crazy sounds, his face full of purple blotches. Ross wondered if he'd swallowed some talcum powder again. That was what they'd both done in their mutual suicide pact about five years ago. Ross had thought they should take iodine, but Tyler said it would burn too much and that talcum powder would work just as good. It didn't. Maybe this time Tyler had taken the iodine.

Ross planned the announcement he'd make in school tomorrow.

"My brother has lateral sclerosis, just like Lou Gehrig. And even if he don't die, he'll never get out of a wheelchair. That's why he didn't show up yesterday."

It wasn't lateral sclerosis. When they were back in the kitchen, Dr. Lessing said it was just a collapse from studying too hard. He left some white pills and said Tyler had to have lots of liquids and absolute quiet.

The next day Mr. Mulleavy started picking on Ross. And every day after. Ross dreaded eleven o'clock when he had to go to ancient history. He decided to save up enough to write away to Charles Atlas for the course on dynamic tension, so he could develop muscles like Big Richie's. Mr. Mulleavy never picked on Big Richie. He just let him sit at the back of the room and sleep.

Big Richie was back there sound asleep when Mr. Mulleavy told the joke about the moron who couldn't think about anything except sex. Even with the whole class laughing. Big Richie's big head stayed cradled in his folded arms.

"At least some people might call him a moron," said Mr. Mulleavy, as the laughter started to die out. "I'm not so sure myself."

This doubled everybody up more than ever, including Ross, even though Mr. Mulleavy had been picking on him two minutes before for not knowing where the Hanging Gardens were. Even the girls were hysterical. Everybody in the room was, except Mr. Mulleavy and Big Richie.

"All right," said Mr. Mulleavy. "That's enough." But though a few kids stopped laughing, most of them couldn't. "I'm going to clap my hands together," warned Mr. Mulleavy. "And any boy who makes a sound after that will meet me in the gym after school. I don't care how many of you there are."

He spread his arms, then brought his hands together with a loud smack, and the laughing stopped like he'd slammed a soundproof door. Mr. Mulleavy stood there, moving his eyes back and forth across the rows, waiting for the slightest sound, the leak of a giggle, a nervous cough. But no one made any, not even one of the girls, as if his threat included them. Still

Mr. Mulleavy waited, leaning slightly forward to hear better.

Then Big Richie woke up. It was as if an invisible derrick was slowly lifting his head. He stretched lazily, eyelids drooping, fat lips hanging open. Then he let out a fart that would fill a Zeppelin.

The girls stiffened or fussed with their hairpins. The boys stopped inhaling. Mr. Mulleavy's mouth twitched. But he just said, "That's more like it," and started talking about Nebuchadnezzar.

One night the following week, while his mother was taking a bath, Ross sneaked into Tyler's bedroom. Tyler was curled up, facing the wall. But when Ross circled the bed, he saw that his eyes were open.

"Tyler," he whispered, "you gotta quit it." When Tyler didn't even blink, he shook his arm. "Quit it, will ya?" Tyler's head turned in slow motion until his eyes were staring at him. "Everybody's forgotten about the fight," said Ross. "Honest, even Mr. Mulleavy. He won't say nuthin' if you come back."

Tyler was trying to tell him something. But his mouth just opened and closed like a goldfish's. Then Ross heard the bath water gurgling down the drain and beat it back to his own room.

That same night he got the idea and wrote the note.

"I think you should know. . . ." Ross printed it with his left hand in case it was turned over to a handwriting expert.

The next day he trailed Big Richie out of the cafeteria to make sure which locker was his. And after school he went back and stuck the note through one of the vents in it. Big Richie cut school on Wednesday and Thursday, and by that time Ross was trying to figure out how to get the note back. Then on Friday, Big Richie showed up.

Big Richie always had a smoke in the lavatory between classes and would come in about five minutes late to take his seat in the back row. But on Friday he was sitting there before Mr. Mulleavy came in and wrote Claudius Ptolemaeus on the blackboard. After taking roll call, Mr. Mulleavy asked who could tell him what the Ptolemaic system was. And he looked like he was seeing things when one of the three hands raised was Big Richie's.

"Suppose we let Richard tell us," he said to the other volunteers.

Big Richie stood up.

"Go ahead, Richard," encouraged Mr. Mulleavy.

"Who you callin' a black bastard?" growled Big Richie.

"Huh?"

"Who's a black bastard?"

"I think you misunderstood the question," said Mr. Mulleavy. "I asked for an explanation of the Ptolemaic—"

"I'll knock you on your fat ass," said Big Richie.

"Now just a minute," said Mr. Mulleavy firmly. He took the hooked stick that he used to pull down maps and held it like Robin Hood. "Who do you think you're talking to, young man?"

"You," said Big Richie.

"Fight, fight," chanted Ross, but none of the others picked it up.

"I think you'd better go down to the principal's office, Richard," said Mr. Mulleavy.

"I ain't goin' nowhere," said Big Richie.

The veins on Mr. Mulleavy's neck and forehead bulged. "Then sit down," he ordered.

Big Richie swayed slightly, and for a moment looked about to obey. Ross, three desks away, cupped his hand over his mouth.

"The gym," he chirped. "After school."

Big Richie gave him a dumb look. Ross made fists and revolved them in short, pecking, little punches.

"Either sit down or leave the room," said Mr. Mulleavy.

"In the gym after school," said Big Richie, finally catching on. "I'll show you who's a black bastard."

"You'll stop using foul language in my classroom," said Mr. Mulleavy.

"You gonna fight me or not?"

"I've no reason for fighting you."

"Yella! Yella!" prompted Ross.

"You're yella!" said Big Richie. "You pick on little kids okay, but you're skeered of someone big as you. What you skeered'a? I'm only a black bastard."

"Once more," said Mr. Mulleavy, struggling to control his temper, "sit down or get out!"

Big Richie stuck his tongue out and blew.

"Another sound out of you," warned Mr. Mulleavy, "and we *will* meet in the gym after school."

There was a long silence with everybody in the class looking from Big Richie to Mr. Mulleavy and back to Big Richie. It was his move.

"Irish cocksuckah," he said.

Half the school showed up. The partition between the boys' and girls' gym had to be opened up to make room, and the kids at the back perched on the leather horses and parallel bars so they'd be able to see. Some climbed the wall ladders, and two guys managed to get up on the rings hanging from the ceiling and sat up there with their legs through them like jockeys in mid-air.

Ross was one of the first there and squatted Indian-style at the edge of the mats. Mr. Zachary, with his yoke of boxing gloves, got more and more nervous as the place filled up. He kept walking to the different corners of the mats, holding up his hands to press down the noise and yelling, "Put that out," every time he spotted a cigarette.

The colored kids had formed their own section. And when Big Richie's girl friend, Inez Jackson, came in they made a special space for her. Inez looked sick.

Then some rhythmic applause started, and Mr. Zachary couldn't stop it. So he tightroped his way to where Janet Rattazi sat next to Sally Doherty. And after he got everyone around them to swear that their places would be saved, Janet and Sally followed him back to the mats and led the victory yell.

*"What does rhyme with Hickock High?
V, I, C, T, O, R, Y . . .*

That's what rhymes with Hickock High.
Rah! Rah! Rah!"

The two girls didn't have their cheerleading skirts on. So when they jumped up on the final "Rah!" Ross could see their garters.

Miss Lockridge peeked in the door as if wondering what was going on. Then Jolly Jellnick came up behind her, and the coach seemed to be inviting her to come in with him. Whatever he was saying was drowned out when the roar went up. Andy Lupke and Samuel Gonziger were pushing a wedge through the crowd for Big Richie coming behind them. Big Richie still had his striped shirt on, but he'd rolled the sleeves up as far as they'd go, so his muscles looked bigger than ever. He didn't have sneakers, though, and Mr. Zachary wouldn't let him walk on the mats with his Cuban heels. Andy Lupke gave Mr. Zachary an argument. But Big Richie still had to take off his shoes. He had a hole in his left sock, and the toenail sticking through was so pink it looked painted.

There was a commotion in the colored section, but it was just Inez Jackson coming out. She tightroped around the edge of the mats as if afraid to step on them, calling out to Big Richie. Then he went over and listened to her. And when Andy Lupke tried to get between them and take Big Richie to his corner, Big Richie shoved him away. But he wasn't agreeing with what Inez was saying. He just kept shaking his head and pointing for her to go back to the colored section.

When she finally did, Mr. Zachary gave Big Richie one of the pairs of boxing gloves. It took a lot of pulling and pushing by Andy Lupke and Samuel Gonziger to get them on Big Richie's fists. Then Mr. Zachary assigned Big Richie to his corner and Janet and Sally led the locomotive cheer, except instead of ending, "YAYYYY, TEAM!" they ended, "YAYYYY, RICHIE!"

When Mr. Mulleavy came in, the cheer was given for him, too, but it was only half as loud. Mr. Mulleavy wore the same torn T shirt with UNIV. OF MICH. on it, but he had new Keds, instead of the crepe-soled shoes, and some orange shorts. Even though he was smaller and older than Big Richie, he looked in just as good condition.

But he wasn't as relaxed. Mr. Mulleavy kept jogging up and down as Mr. Zachary helped him on with his gloves. And he never once looked toward the opposite corner, as if he didn't want to know who was there. It was just like lots of fighters had been when they got in the ring with Joe Louis. Ross had seen the films of most of his fights. And Max Baer and Kingfish Levinsky and Paulino Uzcudun and Charley Retzlaff all had looked as scared as Mr. Mulleavy did now.

"Make room!" It was Jolly Jellnick, with Miss Lockridge in tow and carrying a folding chair with his other hand. They were squeezing past the front row that Ross was in. And it was right in front of Ross that Jolly Jellnick opened the chair.

"Come on. Move back!"

They were like sardines already. But somehow more room was made, and Miss Lockridge sat down on the chair with Jolly Jellnick kneeling next to her. Miss Lockridge was embarrassed by sitting up higher than the rest, and she kept looking down and putting her hand over her face. Then Mr. Zachary came across and handed Jolly Jellnick the stopwatch.

"Two-minute rounds," he said.

"Can't you stop them?" Miss Lockridge asked. But Jolly Jellnick was studying the stopwatch, and Mr. Zachary just went back to the middle of the mats and summoned Big Richie and Mr. Mulleavy to join him.

As Mr. Zachary gave them instructions, Mr. Mulleavy kept raising the heels of his sneakers one at a time and flopping his arms loosely. But Big Richie just stood there staring at him, waiting to get his revenge. Mr. Zachary finally finished and pointed to the two corners, and they went back to them. Then the gym became quiet for the first time, so quiet that the only noise was from Andy Lupke and Samuel Gonziger patting Big Richie on the back.

"Time!" called Jolly Jellnick, clicking the stopwatch.

Big Richie lumbered out of his corner, and Mr. Mulleavy

danced out of his, and all the girls started squealing the same high note, and the boys were all yelling advice to Big Richie about what to do with his left hand and his right hand and his feet.

No one offered advice to Mr. Mulleavy, but he didn't need any. After touching Big Richie's gloves, he just turned into a perpetual-motion machine. There was a one-two-three shuffle of his feet, followed by a one-two combination of punches, each blow thumping home with all the power of Mr. Mulleavy's hunched shoulders behind it. And home was Big Richie's face.

Ross couldn't take his eyes off it. Every few seconds, as one of Mr. Mulleavy's gloves landed, Big Richie's nose seemed to go deep between his cheeks, and his lips would flap apart to bare his huge white teeth. Then these would open and snap back together as if trying to bite the glove that was punishing them. But the glove would always be gone too soon, and Big Richie's nose would just manage to ooze back to normal before the next punch landed.

"Cover up!" yelled Jolly Jellnick. "Use your elbows!"

He appealed to Miss Lockridge. "Look, he ain't even guarding himself."

As if everybody couldn't see that. Big Richie's fists were held so low that he was an open target. All he did was keep pivoting so that Mr. Mulleavy stayed in front of him. But just when it seemed Big Richie might finally throw a punch, Mr. Mulleavy would move in with his fast one-two and knock him off-balance again.

Then the blood began to trickle out of Big Richie's nose, from both nostrils at the same time. Big Richie started sniffing, trying to suck the blood back out of sight, but it moved on in separate trails down over his lips and toward his chin like two red fangs. One trail was slightly ahead of the other until Mr. Mulleavy landed again, smearing both into a ragged blotch and bringing a gasp from those closest to the mats.

Big Richie turned helplessly toward the sound. There were specks of blood in his eyes and hair and, as Mr. Mulleavy hit him again, spraying the front of his shirt. Then Big Richie started backing away, and Mr. Mulleavy went after him, flat-footed now, rocking him with lefts and rights, and everybody was screaming. Big Richie was looking toward Inez Jackson, but her eyes were blindfolded in her hands, so he turned back toward Mr. Mulleavy just in time to get another left in the face. Miss Lockridge was jumping up and down now, shrieking, "Kill him! Kill him!" and Ross couldn't see past her. Jolly Jellnick was yelling his head off, too, and Ross was sure he'd forgotten about the time. It had to be more than two minutes since the fight started. Ross tried to see what the stopwatch said, but Jolly Jellnick kept waving the hand that held it. Ross tapped him on the back.

"Mr. Jellnick," he called. "The time! The time!" And when Jolly Jellnick still didn't pay any attention, Ross socked him on the shoulder.

He didn't mean to do it so hard, and it must have hurt because Jolly Jellnick swung around and grabbed him by the collar and pulled him until the tips of their noses were almost touching.

"What the hell you think you're doing?" yelled Jolly Jellnick.

Then the crack was heard, like a rifle shot, and the whole gym went quiet. Jolly Jellnick let go, and Ross was able to turn toward the mats just in time to see Mr. Mulleavy travel across them. Mr. Mulleavy was leaning backward, his legs churning in reverse, like he was riding a bicycle down a steep hill and the brakes were busted. The heels of his sneakers jammed into the mats, leaving imprints all the way from where Big Richie stood to the other side. Then Mr. Mulleavy left the mats and flopped into the first three rows of kids.

The ones he landed on were afraid to move until Mr. Zachary counted to ten, even Harriet Jaffe who had Mr. Mulleavy's head in her lap. She just kept staring at him, fascinated by the way his jaw was wagging loosely. And all the time Jolly Jellnick kept turning to everybody around him, asking, "What happened? What happened?" He grabbed Miss Lockridge and asked her, too, but she looked too weak to talk. Then Mr. Zachary got to ten, and everybody was rushing Big Richie, congratulating him, pummeling him, trying to hoist him on their shoulders.

"What a right!" someone said. "Right up from the floor."

Jolly Jellnick heard this, and it satisfied him enough to let go of Miss Lockridge. But she didn't let go of him, and as the crowd carried Ross away from them, Jolly Jellnick was looking worried.

Mr. Zachary could have counted to about ninety-eight by the time Mr. Mulleavy finally struggled to his feet. At first he wanted to fight everybody within range. Then he stopped and moved his loose jaw back and forth between the thumbs of his boxing gloves, and his face went all funny.

When Ross got home, his mother looked as if she'd been crying, and Dr. Lessing was there, so for a second he thought what he'd done was too late. But Dr. Lessing said the crisis was passed, and now it was just a matter of letting time take its course. In the bedroom Tyler was awake and his head propped up. But he still looked in pretty bad shape, so Ross didn't tell him the news.

He waited until Monday, until after the rumor about Mr. Mulleavy's jaw being broken was verified by the substitute history teacher. Then he just told Tyler that much, without saying how it happened.

It was another week before he told him everything. Tyler was able to sit up in the parlor for the first time, and there was enough room in there to demonstrate the whole fight. So as soon as his mother went out shopping, Ross started right in, beginning with how he wrote the anonymous note to Big Richie.

The way Tyler watched him made him uneasy. But he kept going, acting out Big Richie's uppercut, then swinging around and becoming Mr. Mulleavy churning backward and falling.

"And that's how his jaw got busted," finished Ross, getting up off the floor.

"You dope," said Tyler. "You stupid dope."

"Huh?"

"Did you have to get a Negro to do my fighting? Aren't they exploited enough?"

"I did it for you," said Ross.

"For me?" Tyler was trying to yell, but he was still too weak. "Did I ever ask you to do anything for me? Did I? Did I? Did I?"

He kept asking the same question over and over, even though Ross was shaking his head. Ross couldn't figure out what he was so mad about. All he knew was that he had to change the subject and calm him down before his mother got back. So even though she'd sworn him to secrecy, he told Tyler that she was going to marry Dr. Axelrod.

II

ᴇACH to his own conspiracy.

He had nothing to do but rest and watch theirs unravel. His mother had got a job sewing buttonholes in a clothing factory. She'd sew up the Mississippi if it would buy dental supplies. But with her out working, Mrs. Swerdlov had to come up every day to make Tyler lunch. And while he ate it, she'd give him another installment in "The Breathtaking Adventures of Wolf Axelrod, DDS."

CHAPTER ONE—How Wolf, turned out in the dead of night by a greenhorn, walked the streets until he came to a lighted bakery where he'd sometimes bought doughnuts and went inside and offered to do any kind of work in exchange for a roof over his head.

CHAPTER TWO—How Eunice, better known as Bulldog Swerdlov, organized a posse of social workers to track him down, which they still took weeks to do.

CHAPTER THREE—How Mrs. Swerdlov, finding out that Dr. Kyriakides definitely wanted to sell his practice, went to the bakery and told her cousin what seeing a man with his profession in such surroundings did to her. But he refused to leave the place where he was sleeping in the cellar with so many cockroaches she'd never eat bread again.

CHAPTER FOUR—How Eunice threatened the owner of the bakery that she'd have the board of health close it down if he didn't make Dr. Axelrod leave, and he said things that Mrs. Swerdlov couldn't repeat. *Meanwhile,* back at Dr. Kyriakides' office, that Greek *goniff* was trying to get away with highway robbery.

"Two thousand he wanted," she said. "Can you imagine? Two thousand dollars for a *Schwartze* practice."

"Negro," said Tyler automatically.

"But we got him down to a lot less."

"We?" he asked, and she got flustered like she always did when he pointed out loopholes in her serial. And when he asked her where the money was coming from, she just shrugged.

"Listen," she said. "God always provides."

God had obviously returned to earth as the Metropolitan Life Insurance Company. Tyler never did find out the exact price of Dr. Kyriakides' practice. But it must have taken just about all the insurance money. Otherwise, his mother wouldn't have gone to work while he was still convalescing. There were spasms of indignation. The insurance money wasn't hers alone. The least she could do was tell him how she'd spent it. But that would also mean telling him about the *big* day which, according to Ross, was going to be early in January. And she wasn't in any hurry to break the news. Instead she resorted to innuendo, calling on some invisible crystal ball where she was getting bleak pictures of his and Ross' futures because of her inability to send them to college. One night when she was going on this way, Tyler almost made it easy for her. He almost said, "Gee, if only we had a dentist for a father, we'd be okay." But he'd started taking a fiendish pleasure in watching her squirm. Why not? She'd waited until he was in a coma before making her bargain. Not that he really cared about that anymore. He had his own conspiracy to worry about.

Day by day, Tyler felt the strength seeping back into him. He was able to sit up for longer stretches in the parlor. And as November faded the lawns and emptied the trees, he started going outside. Short, wobbly walks gradually firmed and lengthened. Soon he'd have to return to school. And once he went back, he'd be tempted to stick it out until June and graduate. That meant living in the same rooms as Dr. Axelrod, having him as a stepfather. But impossible as this prospect was, something else made it even more important that he leave soon. No matter how delirious he'd been that day, his excuse for running away from the fight with Mr. Mulleavy had been to save himself for the RCAF. Six weeks had now passed since his seventeenth birthday. He was eligible. He'd made a pact with his conscience, and it was time to pay off.

But the mimeographed letter from the Royal Canadian Air Force said that the physical and mental examinations in Toronto extended over five days and that no funds could be advanced to applicants for their lodgings and meals during this period. According to the letter he would need a minimum of ten dollars to cover this. And he had exactly forty-five cents.

Only two people could make up the difference. Howie and his mother. But after a few awkward visits a month ago, Howie had made himself scarce. And he'd be damned if he'd ask her. Not that she wouldn't refuse him if he did. From now on every penny went for Novocain. Tyler's one remaining hope was in the classified ads in the paper.

These didn't take long to comb. Most of the "Help Wanted —Male" ads eliminated him with their first words—BOOK-KEEPER, ELECTRICIAN, METALLURGIST. Others specified a minimum age of twenty-one or said that being married or having a car was essential. So that left the few ads that began YOUNG MEN or BOYS. And these were always for peddling *Collier's* or the *Saturday Evening Post* door to door, which was a good way to make about eleven cents a year.

The long walks turned into dogtrots. Tyler also increased the number of push-ups each day, and by Thanksgiving he was up to forty-two. He was sure he could now pass the toughest physical. The following Monday the ad was in the paper.

YOUNG MEN WANTED. *Well dressed, intelligent, ambitious. Fifteen dollars for five days' work. Apply Mr. Forbes, Hotel Saracen, Tuesday.*

It seemed made to order. As long as Forbes didn't turn out to be a nom de plume for Mulleavy, the Royal Canadian Air Force was less than a week away.

There was a slight hitch Tuesday morning. He'd planned to go down to the Hotel Saracen as soon as his mother left for work and Ross went off to school. But Ross woke up with a stomach-ache and was staying home. If the dope saw him going out all slicked up, there'd be questions. So Tyler said he was going for a walk, slammed the door, then tiptoed back to his room to change into his good suit. He did it all without a sound. His bedroom door didn't even creak when he opened it. Neither did Ross', and they both stood there staring at each other. Ross had his suit on, too, and he'd glued his hair down.

"I thought you had a stomach-ache," said Tyler.

"I thought you went for a walk," countered Ross.

"I've got an important appointment."

"So have I."

Tyler leaned closer and smelled him. "What the hell you got on?"

"Brilliantine."

"Besides the brilliantine."

"After-shave lotion."

"Christ," said Tyler. "You smell like a whorehouse on Saturday night." He went to the back door, but Ross came right after him. "I'm going downtown," he said.

"Me, too," said Ross. "To the Hotel Saracen."

It took him awhile to realize that Ross had seen the same ad. Then he did his best to talk him out of it.

"You're not a young man. You're a boy. You're a half-witted little boy."

"I need the money just as much as you do," said Ross stubbornly. And while Tyler tried to figure out how to get rid of him, Ross kept going on about a wedding present. That was why he wanted to earn some money, and he assumed that Tyler was answering the ad for the same purpose.

"We'll chip in," said Ross. "Fifteen dollars apiece is thirty dollars. What can we buy them for thirty dollars?" All the way downtown, Ross came up with terrific suggestions, like a new radio, an ivory Mah-Jongg set, a pool table.

The Hotel Saracen was across the street from the Greyhound Bus Terminal. It was red brick, eight stories high, with a rusty fire escape zigzagging up its front and with dark green tasseled shades in its windows. Pretty gloomy. But the lobby was newly painted, with a huge bouquet of artificial flowers on a table in the middle. And the old elevator operator wore a uniform.

The desk clerk was sorting mail as they came up. Ross tried to read the register upside down until Tyler nudged him. Then they both concentrated on the black, grooved, velvet board with inserted white letters spelling out that the Toy and Novelty Association lunch was in Room B. Tyler cleared his throat loudly, but the desk clerk still ignored them.

"We'd like to see Mr. Forbes."

The desk clerk looked as if many others better qualified for the jobs had been there ahead of them. But he pointed to the elevator and said, "Five forty-two."

The old elevator operator waited until they creaked above the second floor before turning to them.

"What's this Mr. Forbes do?"

"Advertising," said Tyler.

"Wait till you see *her*." The elevator operator gave him a big wink.

Outside the door they stopped to fuss over Windsor knots and four-pointed handkerchiefs in their breast pockets. Then, as Tyler knocked, they stood straighter, the way their mother was always nagging them to. The man opening the door in his shirt sleeves must have thought they were a delegation from a Nelson Eddy fan club or something. But he didn't bat an eye. In fact, his eyes were so steady he couldn't bat them if he tried. Everything about him added to this impression of self-confidence—his tan, his thin mustache, the way he combed his hair straight back.

"Mr. Forbes?"

When the man nodded, Tyler introduced himself and Ross. Mr. Forbes held the door half open, studying Ross. Tyler looked over at him, too. The brilliantine had lost its grip, and Ross' hair was spraying up as if he'd just seen the Phantom of

the Opera. Tyler kicked himself for introducing him. He
should have pretended he'd never laid eyes on him before in
his life and that they just happened to arrive at the same
time. Or he should have let Ross go on ahead of him. Now he'd
ruined his own chances.

"How old are you fellas?" asked Mr. Forbes.

"Seventeen and a half," said Tyler.

"Seventeen," said Ross.

"Your mother should be famous," said Mr. Forbes. Then
he opened the door wide and smiled. "Call me Chuck, fellas."
He shook hands firmly with each of them, then led the way
into the room.

"Ruby," said Chuck, "this is Wylie and Russ Bishop."

Before Tyler could correct him, Ross said, "How do you do,
Mrs. Forbes?" So he had to do the same.

"Sit down, fellas." Chuck was lifting some leaflets and cat-
alogs off the one upholstered chair in the room. Ross sat down
in it as soon as it was cleared. The straight wooden chair had
a practically transparent nightgown on it, so the only place
left for Tyler to sit was the edge of the bed.

"How about a little drink?" Chuck moved to the pint bottle
of whiskey on the dresser.

"We never touch it in the morning," said Tyler.

"Good idea." Chuck laughed. "I gotta try that sometime,
huh, Ruby?"

The woman gave a musical snort, and Chuck went into the
bathroom. In the few seconds before he came back, Tyler
took in Ruby.

The elevator operator wasn't exaggerating. This was the
most beautiful woman he'd ever seen. She had blue eyes and
long jet-black hair that shimmered as she tipped her head;
and her lipstick was the brightest of reds and the silk robe
she wore was sun yellow. Yet in spite of all these vivid colors,
Ruby looked sad.

This may have been partly due to the room. Tiny and clut-
tered with advertising material and with a zoned-off map of
the city thumbtacked to the wall, it was the wrong setting for

her. She should have been in a huge satin bridal suite, not bent over an ironing board with the cord plugged into the ceiling fixture. But Ruby seemed impervious to the room. She was even impervious to them sitting there. As she ironed, her robe fell open more, and Tyler could see that her slip had lace edges. Ross had a much better view, but he didn't even look. Instead, he picked up one of the leaflets that Chuck had dumped on the floor.

"Go ahead, read it," said Chuck, coming out of the bathroom, with water added to his glass of whiskey. He gave Tyler one of the leaflets, too. As they read them, he moved around the ironing board and planted a popping kiss on the back of Ruby's neck.

The cover of the leaflet had a cartoon of a huge trailer truck in the middle of a street with a lot of pipe cleaner figures running out of houses toward it. Above this was lettered:

> *'As the suit said to the dress—*
> *When being taken to the cleaners,*
> *make sure the cleaner is*
> *DOORSTEP*

"Lousy copy," said Chuck, "but our advertising manager's a fruit."

The inside of the leaflet told what made Doorstep cleaning different and better. Not only was each garment treated individually, its stains analyzed, its fabric taken into consideration beforehand, but Doorstep Cleaners, as its name implied, did the dry cleaning right on the customer's doorstep. Huge mobile units of the latest equipment were assigned to different neighborhoods on different days. Each garment went right from the customer's hands to the expert hands that would clean it. No being mauled by pickup and deliverymen, no being crushed in dirty bags with other people's clothing, no chance of anything being lost.

"I said, read it, not memorize it." Chuck finished his drink impatiently. And in reaching over to put it on the dresser, he bumped the ironing board.

"Watch it, will ya?" It was the first time she'd spoken, her voice too nasal for the rest of her.

"Okay, okay." Though Chuck said it flatly, she drew back as if he were going to hit her. But he was smiling as he turned to them.

"This lousy bandbox," he said. "We couldn't get near the Statler or any of the good hotels because of all the conventions."

"What conventions?" asked Ross.

"All of them," said Chuck. "This burg's got more conventions than people. But never mind. And don't hold what you've just seen against marriage. It's a great institution—if you want to be in an institution."

Though Tyler had first heard the joke in 1934, he managed a laugh. Ross didn't.

"So what do you think?" asked Chuck, indicating the leaflets they still held.

"Sounds fine," said Tyler.

"How many do we have to give out?" asked Ross.

Chuck turned to him, and he wasn't smiling now. "You ever heard of anybody getting fifteen bucks a week to hand out leaflets?" Ross shook his head. "Doorstep isn't some charity to keep kids off the street," said Chuck. "It's a dry-cleaning company. And it happens to be the best damn dry-cleaning company in the U.S.A." He poked his finger toward Ross on about every fifth word. But his speech didn't carry any more conviction than the leaflet did. Tyler decided this was because of Ruby. Nobody could get very enthusiastic about dry cleaning with someone this gorgeous in the room.

"Our only problem," said Chuck, "is the same one every new company has—to introduce ourselves. And that's my department." He handed them each a crisp white card embossed with the name of the company. And in the corner, CHARLES FORBES, FIELD SALES PROMOTION. "Before the trucks get here,

I've got to see to it that all the housewives in town know about our special offer." He leaned back against the dresser and looked them both over appraisingly. "And that's where you might fit in."

"What special offer?" asked Ross.

"Ah," smiled Chuck. "The *piece de resistance*."

Tyler winced at his pronunciation, then caught Ruby watching him. Luckily, Chuck hadn't noticed. He was facing Ross, getting him to stand up and pretend he was a housewife.

"Mrs. Jones," said Chuck, "how much do you pay for your present dry cleaning?"

"I dunno," said Ross.

"Approximately," said Chuck. "About how much did that suit cost the last time it was cleaned and pressed?"

"Half a dollar," guessed Ross.

"Half a dollar!" gasped Chuck. "You must be a very rich woman, Mrs. Jones, to throw money around like that." Every time Chuck said, "Mrs. Jones," Tyler could hear a little titter from Ruby. But Chuck went right on, and Ross was taking it dead serious. "So unless you *enjoy* throwing money away, Mrs. Jones, you'll be interested in our special offer."

"What special offer?" asked Ross again.

"Mrs. Jones," said Chuck, "Doorstep Cleaners has millions of satisfied customers from Oregon to Florida. But you've never heard of us, right?"

"Right."

"And that's why, in order to introduce our services, we're making you this special offer."

"What special offer?"

"We are going to—" The unbelievability of what Chuck was about to say made him stop and start again. "We are going to dry-clean any ten items of apparel for you for—" Again he stopped to gird himself for the miracle. "For one dollar." He waited for Ross to react, but Ross didn't. "Any item of apparel," repeated Chuck, "except fur coats. That would be asking too much, wouldn't it?" Ross nodded. "And another thing,"

said Chuck. "You don't have to have them all cleaned at once.
These coupons are good for six months."

He shoved a small pad of coupons into Ross' hand. Ross offered no resistance. If he'd had a dollar in his pocket, he probably would have held it out.

"See," said Chuck. "Easier than getting into bed, right?"

"All you think about," muttered Ruby, and he turned to
blow her a kiss.

"Now I'll level with you," said Chuck. "You fellas are the
kind that Doorstep wants representing them. You're clean-cut,
you're well mannered and—" Chuck groped for a third compliment and came up with "young."

"But I don't want you aboard," he said, "unless you really
feel that we're offering the people of this city a damn good
deal. 'Cause unless you really feel it"—he tapped his heart—
"it won't come across at the back door. So what do you say?"
Chuck waited for their decision. But it was all too simple.
Something had been left out.

"When do we get the fifteen dollars?" asked Ross.

The obvious, thought Tyler. I always overlook the obvious.

"It's a straight commission deal," said Chuck.

"The paper said fifteen dollars for five days," Tyler reminded him.

"I know what it said," snapped Chuck. Then he grinned.
"I was trying to impress my boss by keeping the ad to four
lines. What it should have said was *minimum* of fifteen."

"You mean," pressed Tyler, "that we're guaranteed fifteen
dollars, no matter what?"

"Now wait a minute." Chuck held up both hands as if he
was being robbed. "You got a burlesque show right down the
street, ain'cha? Who's there this week?"

"Rose La Rose," said Ross.

"Yeah," said Chuck. "Rose La Rose. So you expect Doorstep
to pay you fifteen smackers while you sit over there watching
Rose La Rose peel four times a day? Take it easy, fellas. I ain't
from Dubuque." Chuck poured himself another drink, but
didn't add any water this time. "Fifty percent commission,"

he said. "Personally, I think the board of directors is screwy, but that's the way they want it. You see, they ain't interested in the buck they get for the introductory offer. The whole thing comes out of the merchandising budget. So you get half, and the other half just goes to defray some miscellaneous expenses like me . . . and Ruby." This made her smile.

"I still don't understand where the fifteen dollars comes in," said Tyler.

"Look." Chuck sounded exasperated. "The way I see it is even if there's a flood and a tornado here this week, nobody could sell less than thirty special offers. So half of thirty is fifteen, right?"

"But what if I sell less than thirty?"

"Less than thirty?" Chuck acted as if he couldn't believe his ears. Then he turned to Ruby. "That guy in Cleveland —what was his name?"

"*Ahhhh.*" Ruby put down the iron and tried to remember.

"A young fella, like yourselves," said Chuck, "only he had an impediment, a harelip, so it was pretty hard to understand him. And you know how many special offers he sold in a week?"

"How many?" asked Ross.

"One hundred and forty-eight," said Chuck, enunciating it slowly. Tyler figured out the commission before he said it. "Seventy-four bucks for one week's work. And I don't mind tellin' you that's a lot more than I made that week."

"And he had a harelip," said Ruby.

It was obvious that Chuck was a bull-shit artist. But she made it all legitimate, even the story about the guy in Cleveland.

When they left, their pockets full of coupon books and leaflets, a man was coming along the corridor looking at the room numbers. He had pocked skin, and his suit was too big, and he wasn't exactly young. Definitely not the Doorstep type. But looking back, Tyler saw Chuck inviting him in.

Tyler had been assigned the South Grand Street section, which had been taken over mostly by Italians. Little Abyssinia, some people called it. Ross' territory was north of the park, the rich-bitch section, and he complained about this going down in the elevator.

"Rich people ain't interested in bargains," he said.

"Not much," butted in the old elevator operator. "How do you think they got rich?"

"A philosopher," mumbled Tyler.

They separated in front of the hotel. Tyler watched Ross plod away to the northbound streetcar stop, then got on a number thirty-one going south. Twenty sales, and he was practically flying a Spitfire. He tried to remember the details of Chuck's sales pitch.

He deliberated over the first house to enter. Then, equating fresh paint with loose purse strings, he went to the brown and white one with the tricycle in the doorway and the broken doll propped in the bay window. The back hall smelled of garlic. He stopped at the downstairs door, faced the baby cries from within, and rapped loudly. Almost immediately the door was opened, and a puny woman, holding her braying brat in the crook of her arm, looked out suspiciously.

He began the history of Doorstep Cleaners, and she started inching the door closed. So he cut out the Oregon to Florida crap and got right to the special offer. Ten garments—one buck, yes or no? The woman peered at the coupons he held out. Then, with her free hand, she unlatched a handbag on the pantry shelf and pulled out a wrinkled dollar.

One attempt, one sale. Chuck Forbes hadn't exaggerated. The special offer sold itself. In a sense it *was* sales promotion more than canvassing. Confident, he went on to the next house.

He made one more sale that morning, just before noon, to a huge woman with four corkscrew whiskers who said he needed fattening up and invited him to stay to lunch. Tyler refused politely, and she bought the coupons anyway. Between her and his first sale, there'd been an endless line of faces, sneering, fuming, flailing him with broken English, slamming doors, silencing him with a no before he could say two words, ordering him out, threatening to summon husbands or dogs or the police.

After each, he told himself he'd try just one more. The whisk-ered woman had definitely been the last. If she'd turned him down, he would have quit. But now he was buoyed up again. His luck had turned. He went to a White Tower and spent fif-teen cents on a hamburger and coffee, eating quickly, anxious to get back to work. There was a dull satisfaction in what he'd done so far. He'd earned a tenth of what he'd come to think of as his RCAF ante. And the abuse he'd taken multiplied by nine was something he knew he could endure. He went to another street and stood at the corner, looking down at the houses of different colors. No picking and choosing this time. Each would be taken in turn. The one thing he'd learned that morning was not to go by exteriors.

At four o'clock he called it a day and went back to the Hotel Saracen. By then he was on the verge of laryngitis and had made six sales.

"Well," said Chuck, "it was your first day." He took out a printed receipt and started filling it in. "But if you don't dou-ble it tomorrow, I'll eat—" He stopped and frowned at the three dollars Tyler held out. "I thought you said six sales."

"That's right," said Tyler. "And I keep half."

"Hey, Ruby," called Chuck. "Come in here." She came out of the bathroom, hairbrush in hand, wearing the same yellow robe.

"Hello." She nodded at Tyler, a bit shyly, he thought.

"Listen to this, Ruby." And Chuck told her about Tyler of-fering him half the money. They both laughed, and Tyler tried to smile.

"I don't get it," he said.

"Listen," Chuck patted his shoulder, still laughing. "Lis-ten, you're thinking shoelaces and matches. What kind of out-fit you think Doorstep is?"

"The best damn dry-cleaning company in the U.S.A.," said Ruby, with a big wink.

"Okay, okay," said Chuck. "Go brush your hair." And after she flounced back into the bathroom, he turned serious. "Look, kid, we got a whole department that does nothing but payroll. You trying to screw them out of their jobs?"

Then he explained how all the coupons were numbered and had to be accounted for. Since Tyler had given out six books of them, six dollars had to be forwarded to the sales office in Chicago, which was separate from the payroll department. Tyler would get a receipt, and Chuck was authorized to issue a check for the total of his receipts at the end of the week. But he could only write out one check to a man. Chuck went to the Gladstone bag in the corner and took a large company checkbook out of it.

"But if you don't trust me," he said, "I'll give you a check for three bucks right now and fare-thee-well."

"How much longer you gonna be?" It was Ruby, sticking her beautiful face out of the bathroom. "I wanta get dressed."

"One sec'," said Chuck. He held his pen halfway between the receipt and the checkbook.

" 'Course I trust you," said Tyler.

He just had time to compare notes with Ross before their mother got home. Ross had quit and given back his leaflets and coupon books. He hadn't made a single sale, and one man had turned a hose on him. His suit hanging in the closet was still damp. Ross couldn't hide his jealousy over the six sales. But he didn't think it odd that Tyler had to turn in all the money. Of course, Tyler had mentioned it offhandedly to show he wasn't worried about it.

Chuck's prediction came close. On Wednesday he made nine sales. The receipts in his pocket that night totaled seven dollars and fifty cents. Five more sales, and he'd have enough.

By two o'clock Thursday he'd made them. But three of them had happened in the last hour, and he didn't want to stop while he was going so strong. By the time he headed for the hotel, he'd made eight more sales. He had four dollars over his quota, and the one-way bus fare to Toronto was only three dollars and seventy-five cents. He wouldn't even have to hitch-hike.

Chuck looked surprised when he asked to be paid. "You've still got tomorrow and Saturday," he said.

"I've got to go to Canada."

"Suit yourself."

Chuck took out the company checkbook and started adding up Tyler's receipts. The fourteen-dollar total suddenly looked small. Tyler projected it to include Friday and Saturday. Fourteen dollars for three days came to almost twenty-four dollars for five days. With twenty-four dollars, he could really go to Toronto in style. He could stay in a hotel instead of the Y, and every hotel had women who made their rent on their backs. All he had to do was slip the bellboy a buck and tell him to send one up.

"They'll cash this downstairs at the desk," said Chuck. He wrote the date on the check.

"Just a minute," said Tyler. "Maybe I don't have to go to Canada until Sunday."

Friday brought the first snow. It settled quickly, and every person who opened a door to him cursed the wet footprints he'd made in the hall. He trudged on, getting steadily more soaked and frozen until it was dark. He'd made one goddam sale, and he was too tired to go all the way back to the hotel just to turn in the dollar. The accounting department could wait until tomorrow.

Ross gobbled down his dinner and clumped off to his dumb scout meeting in spite of the weather. Then Tyler and his mother sat alone. She'd brought home a long, thin package that Ross had started to open until she snatched it away and said it was none of his business. It was propped against the side of the breadbox, and she kept looking over at it as if she wanted to show it to Tyler.

"Dr. Kyriakides is leaving town," she finally said out of nowhere.

"Good riddance," said Tyler.

"Guess who's taking over his practice starting tomorrow."

"I've no idea."

"Dr. Axelrod."

"No kidding." He couldn't keep his eyes on her face. Her hands, clasped on the table, had calluses from sewing button-holes.

"He had to pass the most difficult state examination," she said.

"Is that so?"

"He's a marvelous dentist."

"Probably," he agreed. "Germans are good at pain." That should have made her indignant, or defensive, or something. But she just looked undaunted and tried again.

"I'm helping him fix up the office," she said, pointing in the general direction of the thin package. "Do you want to see what I bought for it?"

"No," he said.

She heaped out a dish of canned peaches and put it in front of him.

"Tyler." She waited until he looked at her. "I've invited Dr. Axelrod to dinner tomorrow night."

"Oh?" He tried to look surprised.

"There's something we want to discuss with you."

"What?" He was giving her every chance.

"We'll tell you tomorrow night."

"Let me guess."

"Wait until tomorrow night."

"Just one guess."

"All right."

He waited, pretending it was a real brain twister.

"Let's see. You want to tell me that you've used my dead fa-ther's insurance to buy yourself another husband."

The faint smile of anticipation with which she'd been wait-ing for his guess lingered for another moment. Then she whacked him across the face.

"Always hitting somebody," he said.

As he went back to his bedroom, she shouted after him.

"Whatever I've done, I've done for my sons. Don't you forget that! Everything I do is for you!"

A few minutes later he heard her go out. Then he got the suitcase down from the closet shelf.

III

HE wrote the cryptic notes he'd been honing in his mind for weeks. The one to Ross was paper-clipped to the cover of *Naked Beauties of the World.*

> *Dear Ross,*
> *This should keep you from making one of the mistakes I made.*

He put the book under the catcher's mitt in Ross' closet.

> *Dear Mother,*
> *I'm off to hell or glory. It depends on your point of view.*

He propped it on her pillow. The lousy thing about farewell letters was that you weren't around to see the expression on people's faces when they read them. He was especially pleased with the wording of the one to his mother. It was a waste to use it only once.

> *Dear Rowena,*
> *I'm off to hell or glory. It depends on your point of view.*

He wrote it more carefully this time, making his penmanship strong and bold. He had decided that signing the other notes was superfluous. But on this one he scrawled a big "Tyler" at the bottom. Then, on a sudden impulse, he added the postscript:

> *Wait for me. I love you.*

He addressed the envelope and put his last three-cent stamp on it.

The suitcase hadn't been used since the Crusades, and one of the latches didn't catch. He packed enough shirts, under-wear, socks, and handkerchiefs to last five days, plus a pair of pajamas, but it was still only half-full. He added both his sweaters. It could be cold in Canada. Then he tied the broken end of the case with string.

He'd left the birth certificate for last. It was fitting that his final moment in this house should be in his parents' bedroom, rummaging in their dresser drawer. It hadn't been touched since he'd looked in it last; the same pictures and mementos, the same lavender smell. His and Ross' birth certificates were folded with the marriage license he knew by heart:

> . . . *between Carrie Beatrice Starkey and Frank Raymond Bishop* . . .

Well, she'd soon have a new one to add to her collection.

He thought of taking the wedding picture to remember them by but decided against it. Then he picked up the wad of tissue paper and felt the dental bridge inside. Where others carried a Bible, he could carry this. A German bullet heading straight for his heart might lodge in it. Saved by a phony bicuspid! He pocketed his birth certificate and the bridge.

The Swerdlovs were still eating, so he had to duck under their kitchen window. Not that any of them ever looked up when they ate. He wished he'd left them a farewell note, too. But his mother would undoubtedly show them hers.

The snow had finally stopped, but what had fallen lay deep and glistening. He wondered how many busybodies peeking out their front windows were making wrong guesses about his destination. It wouldn't occur to any of them that the solitary figure in mackinaw and overshoes, trudging away with a suitcase, was going off to fight their battles.

The slow streetcar ride gave him a last look at familiar places, all peaceful in the snow. A glow of nostalgia began in

him, but was quickly snuffed out as they passed Dr. Kyriakides'
office. He was sure he saw two shadows behind the windows.
She was in there, helping the Fascist sharpen up his instru-
ments of torture, telling herself she was doing it for her sons.

He forced his thoughts away from her and onto the days
ahead, picturing himself climbing into a cockpit with a bulky
parachute strapped on, pulling his leather helmet down, ad-
justing his goggles. The snow outside became tufts of cloud,
the streetcar motor a plane's. Then the reverie hardened.
Machine-gun bullets spit from his wings; black smoke poured
from the swastika-emblemed Messerschmitt ahead; the pilot
threw him a gallant wave before plummeting to earth.

Downtown, he went first to the Greyhound Bus Terminal
to deposit the suitcase in one of the dime lockers. But the goddam string broke just as he came in the door, and his clothes
started falling out. So he had to carry the case across the
terminal like a cello. Then he had to carry it all the way
back again in order to get a dime for two nickels from the old
Negro at the shoeshine stand.

The case was finally in the locker, and the instructions over
the slot said it could stay there for a maximum of eight hours.
The departure board listed the next bus to Toronto at eight
forty-five and another at midnight. Tyler synchronized his
watch with the terminal clock—six minutes to eight. Then he
went into a phone booth.

"Operator, I got the wrong number. I wanted Granite three,
four, seven, seven."

Howie's mother answered and said they hadn't finished dinner yet. But he told her it was an emergency, and Howie
finally came on with a mouthful of food.

"I'm leaving in less than an hour," said Tyler.

"Leaving for where?"

"For the war."

"Oh, Christ," said Howie. "What you pullin' now?"

"I'm not pulling anything. I'm at the Greyhound Bus Station. I just thought you might want to come down and see me
off."

"In this blizzard?"

"Forget it," said Tyler and hung up.

As he came out of the terminal, a post office van at the curb reminded him of his letter to Rowena. He handed it to the mailman emptying the box and saw it dropped into the canvas bag. Then he went across the street to the hotel. The same desk clerk was on duty. Good. There wouldn't be any problem cashing the check. He took the elevator to the fifth floor.

It wasn't until he knocked and got no answer that he realized the Forbes might be out. The other times there'd been an immediate call from Chuck: "Enter at your own risk!" or "Come in and save your knuckles!" But he'd never got here this late. He should have stopped to look in the hotel's small restaurant before coming up. Or they could have gone to a movie. He could see himself running around to every movie house downtown, asking to have Mr. Forbes paged.

Frantic, he knocked again. Still nothing. He turned the knob and pushed, but the door was locked. Another possibility. One of the conventions in town had ended, and they'd moved to a better hotel. The desk clerk would know where. But all the time he invented explanations, he could see Chuck's flashy smile and hear his sugar-smooth voice. Only a backward idiot would be dumb enough to trust someone like that.

Then he heard the sound inside, just a click—but human. He pounded on the door.

"Open up! I know you're in there!"

He moved to the other wall of the corridor and was about to run at the door and ram it with his shoulder when it opened a crack and Ruby peered out.

"It's just me, Mrs. Forbes." He felt like a real jerk.

"What do you want?"

"I'm leaving town." He pulled out his receipts and waved them. "I want to cash these in."

"We're sleeping," she said.

"But it's only eight o'clock."

"Come back tomorrow." She started to close the door.

"I've got to have it *now!*" He shoved and the door flew open.

Sleeping, hell! The only thing on the bed was a woman's aquamarine suit. The room looked different. The shades were pulled all the way down and everything seemed neater . . . and emptier! No leaflets and coupon books scattered around, only some wire hangers in the closet. And Chuck's big Gladstone bag was gone.

"Where is he?" Tyler looked in the bathroom, then turned to her. "I've got fourteen dollars and fifty cents coming."

She looked different, too. Of course, she was wearing a brown dress, and he'd never before seen her in anything except the yellow robe. But it was more than that. She looked *enormous.* Then, as she stepped into the light, he saw the bruise on her face. It was the left side, purple and swollen, her eye half-closed.

"He's gone," she whimpered. "He told me he was through gambling. He swore it. The dirty bastard."

"Did he leave my money?" It was a stupid question, but he had to hear her say it.

Ruby shook her head. "He lost the whole bundle." She raised a finger to the bruise on her face, shuddering wth pain as she touched it. "I told him he'd have to make it good. And look what I got."

It was too much to take in all at once. Fourteen dollars and fifty cents. No. He still had the dollar he hadn't turned in yesterday. One miserable dollar.

"I've got to have that money," he said. But she just went past him and took the aquamarine skirt off the bed. As she stepped into it, he saw the blue hem beneath the brown one. And the rest of the rainbow under that. She sucked in her stomach but could still get the zipper only halfway. No wonder she looked enormous. She was wearing everything!

"The dirty bastard," she said again. She struggled into the aquamarine jacket, then started stuffing rolled-up stockings inside like falsies.

"What about my thirteen dollars and fifty cents?" She stuffed in another pair. "Goddammit!" he yelled.

"I've got my own problems," she said.

"I'm gonna call the cops." He went to the phone, but before he could pick it up, she lunged across the bed and clamped her hand down on his.

"Don't."

"Let go," he said. Her long, painted nails were sharp.

"You weren't the only one," she said. "There'll be twelve other guys up here tomorrow wanting to get paid. One of them's got over fifty bucks coming."

"That makes me feel a lot better." Tyler tried to pry his hand loose.

"Calling the cops won't help."

"They might catch him."

"He's got a two-hour start. He's out'a the state by now."

"I'm still going to report him."

"Why?" she whined. "What good will it do?"

"It can't do any harm."

"They'll just put *me* in jail." She looked up at him pleadingly. "With the hotel bill and everything, I'll get about three months. And I didn't do anything."

He thought of the twenty-eight people who'd given him a dollar, a bushel of faces, all waiting to have their cleaning done.

"The company will have to make it good," he said. He let go of the phone, and she let go of his hand. "I'll write to the head office."

"Yeah." She didn't sound very optimistic. Then she let out her breath like he might as well know the worst. "They folded," she said. "About three weeks ago. He's been handing out rubber checks ever since Indianapolis." She backed away slowly from Tyler's look. "I didn't know. He only told me after he slugged me."

Others had been taken for more; the one who had fifty bucks coming, the harelipped guy in Cleveland. But none could need it as much as he did.

"I wanted the money to join the Canadian Air Force," he said bitterly.

"I'm sorry. Honest." She sounded as sincere as anybody with a nasal voice could sound. But then he caught the nervous look toward the chair in the corner. Her handbag was there, open.

"How much can you give me?"

"Nothing," she said. "He cleaned me out, too."

"Let's see."

It was a race, but he got there first and turned the handbag upside down. Coins spilled out onto the chair and floor—quarters, dimes, nickels.

"Don't!" She had so many clothes on she could hardly get down on her hands and knees to scoop them up. He grabbed some, too, a free-for-all game of jacks. "I need it for bus fare," she moaned. "I gotta get out of this town."

He opened his hands and counted sixty-five cents. The coins she'd snatched up couldn't have amounted to much more. He tossed his down in front of her.

"You know what I think?" he said. She was counting the coins, dropping them back into her handbag. "I think the whole thing's a confidence trick. I think you're meeting him down the street, and you're both going on to Rochester or Syracuse and pull the same stunt there."

"Yeah," she said. "And how about this?" She pointed to her shiner.

"So you had an argument."

"Think what you want." She got up and went back to the dresser. He watched her shove a bottle of perfume in among the stockings. She now had about a fifty-six-inch bosom.

"I'm still going to report it."

That spun her around. "You wouldn't do that to me." She tried to pout it, but she looked desperate—beat up and desperate.

"Wait and see."

"Please," she begged.

"Why shouldn't I do it?"

"Call it a personal favor."

He felt his skin tingling, his mouth going hard.

"And what favor do I get back?"

"Just name it," she said.

He took his time. He wanted to savor every second of this. Surprisingly, he wasn't nervous.

"Take off your clothes," he said.

She stared at him, then looked down at herself helplessly. He wondered how many dresses she had on. Eight? Nine? But eventually there'd be skin. She looked at him again, the realization of what he meant sinking in. Even with a black eye she was still something. Her hand went up to push back her hair, gently slid over her bruised cheek, then stopped at the aquamarine neckline.

"All of them," he said.

"Go fuck yourself, Charlie."

Some people could rat on other people, and some just couldn't. He was one of those who couldn't. It was that simple. No matter how much justification he had, no matter what people did to him, he just couldn't. Not even when a dame who sounded like Rudy Vallee with sinus trouble told him what he could do to himself and kept slugging him with a pillow until he managed to get the door open and practically fell out into the hall. Okay, so he couldn't turn anybody in. But that was no reason to wait in front of the bus station, watching the hotel. The bottom had fallen out of his whole plan, the crap he'd taken at back doors for days had all been for nothing, and he just stood freezing his nuts off and worrying about her. But the flabby man with the red, pitted nose, who he was sure was the house detective, had been in the lobby when he came out. And it didn't seem humanly possible that Ruby could walk past both him and the desk clerk, looking like a covered birdcage, and get away with it. For all he knew, she might have tried it already and been caught. Five minutes more, and he'd give up.

Then what? If it wasn't for those goddam farewell letters, he could go home. Not that Ross would have found his yet. He probably wouldn't touch the catcher's mitt until April. As for the note to his mother, he could talk his way out of that. He'd said he was off to Hell or Glory. So what? "Hell or Glory" could be the name of a war movie, a B picture with William Gargan or somebody. And how about "It depends on your point of view"? He'd claim it was a gag, that she just didn't understand the sense of humor of his generation.

So it was only the letter to Rowena. It was already on its way. And neither snow nor sleet nor the galloping crud would keep it from getting to her. "Hell or Glory" could be the name of a war movie. But you don't write a girl that you love her and ask her to wait for you just because you're going to see a war movie.

"Where the hell you been?"

A hand grabbed his shoulder and spun him around. He was more prepared for the pitted-nosed house detective than the chapped face sunk in the collar of the sheepskin jacket.

"Howie!"

Howie looked amazed when he hugged him. But he wouldn't when he found out why. Talk about arriving in the nick of time when the chips were down. And Howie would have enough money on him. He'd worked all last summer, and he was tight as paregoric when it came to spending any, and he didn't trust his old man, so he wouldn't leave the money at home.

"I come rushing all the way down here," griped Howie, "and I can't even find ya." His ears were too big for his plaid earmuffs, the lobes sticking out and beet-red from the cold. Then, just past the left one, Tyler saw Ruby hurrying out of the hotel. She'd somehow managed to get a coat over all the other stuff—a pincushion on stilts, a robin with elephantiasis, the world's first mother-to-be of octuplets. And nobody was chasing her.

"C'mon!" Tyler hustled Howie into the terminal. Through the steamed window he watched Ruby starting across the street, jumping almost daintily over the mounds of snow. As she got closer, he moved Howie back behind a pillar.

"What's going on?"

As Tyler started to tell him, Howie pulled off his earmuffs to hear better. Tyler stuck to the essential facts—Chuck Forbes, thirteen dollars and fifty cents, and the skipping town. He didn't mention Ruby, but Howie kept looking toward the door whenever he did and saw her come in.

"I almost had that tonight," said Tyler.

"That fatso?"

"She isn't fat."

Howie looked at her again, then frowned at him. "You sure you're over that coma?"

Ruby, shielding her black eye with her handbag, was heading for the ladies' room.

"She's got a terrific face."

"Sure," said Howie. "That's why she hides it."

The wisecracks burned, so he told Howie the rest. Not all of it. Not the "Go fuck yourself, Charlie" and the pillow-walloping parts. Just up to where she had only a few coins in her purse, and he'd let her keep them.

"Sucker," said Howie.

"Who?"

"You. What do you think she's doin' in the john? She probably had a fifty up her snatch all the time."

"You're crazy."

"Yeah? Where do you think broads smuggle diamonds?"

"We'll see," said Tyler. He tried to figure out what to do if Howie was right, if she went up to the ticket counter and plunked down a big bill. Maybe he couldn't rat on people, but he sure could confront them. He'd just grab the money out of her hand and dare her to call a cop.

When she finally came out of the ladies' room, Howie didn't even recognize her at first.

"What the hell happened to the rest of her?"

The rest of her was in the brown paper parcel she carried— the extra dresses, the stockings, the perfume, maybe even a towel or two with Hotel Saracen embroidered on it.

"She ain't so bad," admitted Howie.

"I mean it. I almost had that." Ruby was studying the departure board. Then she went toward the ticket windows. "Wait here," he whispered, and went after her, ducking behind more pillars, then a trolley of luggage, then a cleaning woman wringing out her mop.

Ruby was at window three, opening her handbag. He inched closer, ready to lunge if her hand came out with a bill. Then she began stacking the coins to pay for her ticket, and he circled away toward the luggage lockers. The bus to Toronto was being announced. As he pulled out his suitcase, Howie came up to him.

"I still don't know what you're doin'," he said.

"How much money you got on you?" asked Tyler.

"Why?"

"How much?"

"Couple bucks."

"Come on, how much?"

"How much you want?"

"Loan me thirteen bucks and I can make that bus." He pointed toward the loudspeaker repeating the announcement. Howie listened until it finished.

"It don't cost thirteen bucks to go to Toronto."

"Either that," said Tyler, "or make it nine bucks and I'll hitchhike."

"What you want to go to Canada for?"

" 'Cause the Royal Canadian Air Force happens to be in Canada and I'm joining it."

"Not with my dough, you ain't," said Howie.

"Nine lousy bucks."

"Nothing doing." He'd never heard Howie sound so definite.

"Okay," said Tyler. "Thanks for nuthin'." But it was pretty hard to walk away indignantly when he had to carry the broken suitcase in his arms.

"It ain't the money," said Howie, keeping in step with him. "If it was to get screwed, blewed, and tattooed, I'd loan it to you. But I ain't loaning you nothing to join some dumb Air Corps."

"There happens to be a war on."

"It's a phony war."

"Tell that to the guys who were on the *Royal Oak*," said Tyler.

As they came out of the terminal, the wind blew them to a standstill. They hunched against it, sliding back half a step for each one forward. Then they had to stop, shivering, while a bus came out of the terminal driveway. If it had been the one to Toronto, that would have been the last straw. But it said JAMESTOWN, and as it went by, he was sure he saw Ruby in the frosted crescent of one window. He should have blown her a kiss. A kiss for a "Go fuck yourself, Charlie." That would have given her something to mull over on the trip.

"Tell you what," said Howie. "Wait till next year, and maybe I'll join up with you."

Tyler didn't answer him. It was hard to talk with the cold wind numbing his face. And the suitcase sapped his breath. Howie trudged alongside, never offering to carry it awhile. But when Tyler almost slipped, he grabbed his arm and held him up.

Main Street looked like a picture postcard from Siberia. Only a few cars were out, moving slowly, their tire chains flapping. A man in a lumber jacket plowed past them, a scarf wrapped around his face up to the eyes. Two blocks away, a streetcar was coming. Tyler moved back into the doorway of the United Cigar Store and dumped down his suitcase. If ever he needed to be left alone to think, it was now. But Howie crowded into the doorway, too, flapping his arms and jogging up and down in place.

"I'll bet it's warm in the burlesque show," Howie said. "It has to be if the broads are walkin' around bare-assed."

As if he could think of naked breasts and rhinestone G-strings at a time like this. The streetcar was leaving the next corner.

"I'll ask you once more," said Tyler. "Will you loan me that money?"

"Nope."

He lifted the suitcase and went out toward the tracks.

"I hear Rose La Rose takes off everything," said Howie, sticking with him.

"I'm not old enough to get in," said Tyler. "I'm only old enough to die bravely."

"I'll bet we can get in tonight."

The streetcar braked to a stop, the doors opened, and the conductor looked out at them.

"It's worth a try," said Howie. But when Tyler got on the streetcar, he did, too.

Tyler put the suitcase on the seat next to him, hoping Howie would get the hint. But Howie took the seat right behind him, leaning forward over the back of his and keeping up a steady stream of stale jokes. Tyler stared at his own reflection in the window and tried to weigh his alternatives.

There were only two. He could go home, or he could stay on the streetcar until the city line and try to hitchhike to Toronto tonight. And if he did get a lift instead of dying from exposure, that meant existing for five days in Toronto on one lousy dollar. He'd probably be the only applicant in history to flunk an Air Force medical exam because of malnutrition.

"Did ya hear the one about the fancy diplomatic banquet in Washington?" asked Howie. "There were all these big shots and generals, ya know, and this guy is sitting next to a gorgeous broad who keeps making goo-goo eyes at him all through the meal."

Why kid himself? He was stuck here. He'd have to go back to school and face Rowena and everybody else. He'd have to sit through dinner with Dr. Axelrod tomorrow. There was the sudden, sickening certainty that he'd still be around when they got married and have to watch his mother going off to bed with a Nazi every night.

"Then this broad drops her fork," said Howie. "And when the guy bends over to pick it up, he's looking right at her ankle. So he thinks, 'what the hell,' and he touches it. And she don't even move. So he runs his hand up to her knee, and she still don't pull away. So he keeps right on going."

The days and weeks ahead loomed unendurably. And as if to rub in the torment, they were on Monroe Street, nearing Dr. Kyriakides' office. All that money for a dingy little office, but not one cent for freedom.

"And just when his hand's almost there, she leans over—"

The light in the office was still on!

"And she whispers, 'Don't scream when you come to my balls. I'm a spy.' "

One crappy faint yellow square of hope. Tyler reached up and pulled the cord.

"Where you goin' now?" whined Howie.

"Get lost," he said.

He got off alone at the next corner.

IV

DR. Kyriakides' office was on the "white" side of Monroe
Street, a block past the Liberty. It was a small, shingled struc-
ture with a tar paper roof and could have been a garage once,
the way it was set back from the two brick buildings that
flanked it. It was about the right size for a two-car garage. But
for as long as Tyler could remember, it had the window with
the dirty ruffled curtain and the dentist shingle hanging on
the post outside. He'd never before been inside.

The drill was going, so he closed the door as quietly as he'd
opened it. He was in the waiting room. The cushions on the
bamboo couch and chair had their patterns almost worn off. A
round glass-topped table held a fan of magazines—*Life, Look,
True Story, Reader's Digest, Popular Mechanics*—all new.
And there were two bouquets on the windowsill. He put the
suitcase down and went to the bigger one, pink gladiolas—or
gladioli? He never could remember the plural.

> *Good luck*
> *from Bertha, Morris and Eunice*

He didn't realize it was from the Swerdlovs until he got to
the Eunice. The second bunch of flowers was assorted, mostly
sweet peas.

> *Happy Cavities!*
> *Elena and Paul Kyriakides*

The handwriting looked like a woman's. Elena Kyriakides
sure had a terrific sense of humor. She ought to be on the radio

—in Greece. Then he noticed the thin package, the same one that had been on the pantry at home. It had been opened and loosely rewrapped, but enough to hide what was inside.

The drilling was still going on in the next room. If it didn't stop soon, somebody was going to have a hole right through to the back of his head. He couldn't see what was happening without going right up and looking in the doorway, only a corner of the inside room with a sink and a white jacket on a peg. He'd half expected his mother to come bounding out in a nurse's uniform with an appointment book. Or maybe it was her that Dr. Axelrod was working on. A sadist *would* get his pleasure that way.

Tyler unbuckled his overshoes, took off his mackinaw, and sat down. He could use a few minutes to thaw out before facing his enemy. He hadn't decided on exactly what to say, and he wasn't going to. Premeditation had loused him up enough for one evening. This time he'd be spontaneous. He leaned over to the magazines and picked up *Popular Mechanics*.

Nothing about airplanes. He flipped to the ads at the back. The company in Louisiana was still offering a six by nine printing press with type and ink and everything for only five dollars. That was what he should have sent away for instead of that phony book. Then he could have made enough money printing calling cards and stationery for people, instead of having to ask for it this way. Other ads also taunted him about money.

EARN UP TO $40 A WEEK DOING TAXIDERMY AT HOME!

Stuffing your neighbors.

CHRISTMAS CARDS THAT SELL THEMSELVES!

Then they don't need me.

WRITE SHORT PARAGRAPHS FOR YOUR LOCAL NEWSPAPER!

No thanks. I tried that one.

But dumb as they sounded, they didn't sound any dumber than doing dry cleaning on people's doorsteps. Christ, the drilling was beginning to make *his* teeth ache. It had to stop sometime, if only for the bit to be changed. He tossed the magazine back on the table, hoping the noise would have some effect. When it didn't, he went to the doorway and peeked around.

Dr. Axelrod was bent over the chair in his shirt sleeves, drilling for all he was worth. But whoever he was working on had no legs. No anything! Then he shifted position and Tyler could see the plaster mold he held just above the headrest, right where a patient's mouth would be. Dr. Axelrod leaned back approvingly, then touched the mold once more with the drill, lightly, like a painter adding a last touch to a portrait. Tyler let out a loud cough and stepped into the room.

Dr. Axelrod looked from him to the mold again, but this time as if ashamed of it. Then he put it on the round tray with a scalloped edge that was attached to the drill stand. Aware that the drill was still buzzing in his other hand, he kicked at the foot switch and missed. On the third attempt he managed to turn it off.

"It has been almost three years," he said. "The fingers lose dexterity." He flicked crumbs of plaster off the front of his shirt. There'd been no surprise at seeing Tyler, but now he looked at him with sudden interest and pointed to the gruesome chair.

"Maybe you would like to sit down?"

"No, thanks."

"A dentist's first patient is always a relative."

"We're not related yet," said Tyler. "Besides, my teeth are perfect."

"Let me see." Dr. Axelrod picked up the instrument with a magnified mirror on the end and came toward him, crouching a little to get a better view of his uppers.

Tyler pressed his lips together and backed away. He couldn't believe the guy was serious. But Germans didn't kid around, and the light glinting off Dr. Axelrod's glasses made him look depraved enough for anything. Tyler groped behind for the doorway but felt only some loose, shiny paper on the wall. He turned to face it—a huge, grotesque chart of teeth with red nerves spreading into their jagged roots and magnified illustrations of decay, inflammations, abscesses. He practically ran into the waiting room. But Dr. Axelrod was right after him, still with the goddam mirror. Then he stopped, looking at the suitcase. He turned to Tyler, puzzled.

"We are having dinner tomorrow night, yes?"

"I have to leave tonight," said Tyler.

Dr. Axelrod glanced at the suitcase again, as if to confirm what he'd said.

"Your mother was here before. She would like us to have a little talk."

"I'm in a hurry," said Tyler.

"*Mmmm.*" Dr. Axelrod tapped the mirror against the palm of his hand. "May I inquire where you are going?"

"To enlist," said Tyler. If he hadn't wanted a favor, he would have said, to fight Fascism.

"To enlist?"

"There happens to be a war on," said Tyler for the second time in an hour.

"Yes, yes, the war." Dr. Axelrod motioned to the suitcase. "So you came to say good-bye?"

"Not exactly," said Tyler. "I need some money."

"Of course," said Dr. Axelrod. Of course, what? Of course, that was why he was here. Or of course, he'd lend him some money.

"Thirteen dollars, to be exact," said Tyler. But Dr. Axelrod just went over and sniffed the smaller of the two bouquets.

"From my well-wishers," he said, gesturing to the flowers. Then almost to himself, "My death wishers." He suddenly pointed the mirror instrument at Tyler. "If you go away, with whom will I have contests of intellect?"

"You'll find somebody," said Tyler. "Besides, memorizing a lot of words has nothing to do with intellect."

"I see." Dr. Axelrod sat down and laid the mirror on the cover of *Look.* "Then maybe we should have a different kind of contest."

"Contests don't prove anything," said Tyler.

"Ah, but wars do." Dr. Axelrod sighed loudly.

"Will you loan me thirteen dollars?"

"One thing at a time," said Dr. Axelrod. "You made a statement. Now you must defend it. We will have a contest that does not depend on memorizing. We will ask each other questions of logic. Or maybe you prefer metaphysics?"

"You've got contests on the brain," said Tyler.

"Go ahead," insisted Dr. Axelrod. "Ask me any question, as abstract as you want." He leaned forward eagerly. It was too good an opportunity to turn down.

"Okay," said Tyler. "Why are you marrying my mother?"

Dr. Axelrod blinked twice. "That is not abstract," he said.

"End of contest," said Tyler and stood up. "How about the thirteen dollars?"

"Sit down," ordered Dr. Axelrod.

It was another contest, this time of wills. Tyler went over to the window. Cold seeped in the corners, and his breath formed a patch of steam on the pane. It was his turn to sniff flowers. He chose the gladiolas, but they had no smell.

"Sit down," Dr. Axelrod made it more of a request, and Tyler turned to look at him fully for the first time. The bastard had aged years since that night war was declared. His cheeks were sunken, and the skin under his eyes was loose and dark. The right stem of his glasses had a piece of adhesive tape holding it on.

The hell with it. Staring matches never proved anything either. He had to keep his sights on that midnight bus. If it meant getting the money, he'd humor him. Tyler went back to the couch and sat down, but Dr. Axelrod still glared at him for a while before speaking.

"And why do *you* think I am marrying her?"

"Men marry for one of two reasons," said Tyler. "Physical attraction or money."

"I see," said Dr. Axelrod. "And which reason do you think is mine?"

"Well, she isn't exactly Dorothy Lamour."

"Dorothy Lamour?"

"A movie star," said Tyler. But Dr. Axelrod still looked blank. "The 'Moon of Manakoora.' "

"Manakoora?"

"Dorothy Lamour is very physically attractive," said Tyler.

"Oh." Dr. Axelrod seemed to be retracing their conversation. "Then I must be marrying your mother for her money, yes? For buying me all this?" His hands spread to include the whole room. "Is that what you imply?" Dr. Axelrod didn't wait for him to answer. "Come!" He jumped up and went into the other room, waving Tyler to follow.

Now what? He wasn't getting into that chair, even for thirteen bucks. Tyler went warily to the doorway.

"Look!" Dr. Axelrod was waiting just inside. Tyler jumped back, but he was only switching on the overhead light.

In the bright glare, the torture chamber looked old and falling apart. Several drawers of the wooden cabinet projected screws without knobs, and the marble top was cracked. The leather seat of the chair was almost worn through, and everything else seemed to be peeling—the walls, the pipes, the black and orange cylinders labeled OXYGEN and GAS.

"I had to come across the world for this?" demanded Dr. Axelrod. "I had a hundred times better than this in Germany." He started pacing the room, wringing his hands. "Of course, now we have the pretending. That is the difference. We keep saying it is only temporary, only until we have—" He turned on Tyler. "What is your meaningless term?" He answered himself angrily. "A nest egg. Yes, until we have a nest egg, until you and your brother are older, until . . . until. When is the end of expediency? I have only a small piece of my life left, and I am throwing it away. And you say I am doing it for a few hundred dollars."

"A thousand dollars," corrected Tyler. It was only a guess, but the way it deflated him, it must have been pretty close.

"A thousand dollars," repeated Dr. Axelrod, making a scoffing sound in his throat. Then he went into the waiting room. Three seconds, and he was back with the thin package.

"Your mother brought me a present," he said, waving it. "All the months I have known her, my name is good enough. But last week she tells me it is a bad name for me to have here. In this country, she says, Wolf is a man who pesters woman. That is correct, yes?"

"Sort of," said Tyler.

"She is having this sign made up for the post outside," said Dr. Axelrod. "It is her gift to me on this important occasion. But it cannot say, Wolf Axelrod, DDS, because of the implication of my name. She thinks it is better if it just reads, W. Axelrod, DDS."

"She's probably right," granted Tyler.

"Ah!" Dr. Axelrod raised a stubby finger to silence him. "But she is worried about that, too. She is afraid that just using the initial might make people think my name is Wilhelm, the same as the Kaiser's name. That could hurt my practice too, she says. So look what I agreed to."

Dr. Axelrod pulled the white slab from its wrapping and turned it over so Tyler could see the lettering.

WOODROW AXELROD, DDS.

"She finally made it," said Tyler.

"So now I am a Woodrow." Dr. Axelrod's hands lifted in surrender. "My name I have also given for the thousand dollars. My name, my remaining years, and all I believed."

He shoved a knuckle under his glasses as if there were something in the corner of his eye. Then he went to the tray with the scalloped edge and started straightening up the things on it, the picks and pincers, the little Bunsen burner, the box with the cotton blossoming out of the top.

"For three weeks," he said. "For three weeks, I knew the happiness of living according to what I believed." He was making a visible effort to keep his voice calm. "When Goethe was seventy-five, he claimed he'd only known four weeks of happiness in his whole lifetime. So"— the heavy shoulders rose and sagged—"proportionately, until now I am ahead of Goethe, yes?" He nodded to himself. "Except I will never have any more."

Tyler studied the back of his head. He'd come for a solution to *his* problems, and after all this time they were still talking about Dr. Axelrod's.

"About the money," he said.

Dr. Axelrod turned to him without seeing him. "They couldn't let me be," he said. His voice got louder again. "For my own welfare, they claimed. Yes, like the hounds want the welfare of the fox. First, my cousin and her crying. Then the daughter with the indictments." He enumerated each on his fingertips. " 'How could I sleep on a pile of flour sacks?' they asked. 'How could I survive on the leftovers of the ovens?'" He slapped the fingers down. "These are the false questions of the missionary. How could I live without *their* ambitions? That is the real question." He clenched his fist and shook it. "But I refused to listen. I stood my ground." He glowered at Tyler as if adding him to his tormentors. "Then they sent your mother." The fist unclenched; the hand dropped loosely. "Your beautiful mother."

He said it strangely, mixing bitterness with affection. Tyler felt he should pounce on the bitter part and hold it up as an insult. Or at least correct the adjective. Nice-looking as his mother was, she couldn't be called beautiful. But he'd already made that point with Dorothy Lamour.

"And here I am." Dr. Axelrod shrugged and picked up the plaster mold he'd been drilling. He held it up to the light, turning it slowly. "So I will alleviate a little pain. It is a second-class life, but there are worse." He stopped and considered what he'd said. "See, already I am seeking comfort from comparisons. That is the sure sign of failure."

"You don't have to marry her," said Tyler. His mind leaped ahead to possibilities. Maybe all the money hadn't been turned over to Dr. Kyriakides yet. Maybe Mrs. Swerdlov could get her husband to pay them back.

"But I want to marry her." Dr. Axelrod almost managed a smile. "The writhing, the protesting—these are only to give the illusion of choice. We cannot change what we are or what we want. I thought I could be something more than a dentist, and you see?" He hefted the plaster mold and tossed it onto the top of the cabinet. A piece of it broke off the corner as it landed. "So Spengler is right after all."

"Who's Spengler?" Tyler kicked himself for asking.

"You don't even know Spengler?"

"I don't even know Heinrich Heine." There, he'd done it again. Every time he opened his mouth he got farther away from the thirteen dollars. What the hell did he care about Spengler or Heinrich Heine or anybody else from Düsseldorf?

"Heine was a great man." Dr. Axelrod said it with sad envy.

"Naturally," said Tyler. "He was a German."

He thought he'd managed to make the sarcasm subtle; but Dr. Axelrod's mouth twisted, and a muscle in his jaw pumped his whole face red. "What has that to do?" he demanded.

Midnight bus, Tyler reminded himself. Midnight bus, midnight bus. . . .

"Nothing." But he couldn't back down completely. "I just said that you naturally think he's a great man because you're both German."

"German!" erupted Dr. Axelrod. "You think that is my yardstick?" He didn't give Tyler a chance to say. "In spite of your age, I confide in you. I tell you my honest feelings so that we may begin an honest relationship. And all you can give me back is a label. Ach!" He threw up both hands and fluttered them. "Good-bye! Go to your war! Win medals! Kill Germans!"

"Give me thirteen dollars," said Tyler, "and I will."

Dr. Axelrod stared at him, breathing heavily, his face waning back to pink. He lifted his glasses as if to see Tyler unhindered, then let them drop back on his nose. "You beg money from a German to help you kill Germans?" His voice started

THE PENNY WARS : 244

getting plaintive, but he steeled it. "You are without sensibilities. You have no honor, no shame, no—"

Tyler never found out the last thing he didn't have. A door had opened, the outside door. Someone had come into the reception room. His mother probably, back to hang up her stupid sign or wash out the curtains. She'd already have recognized the suitcase. Okay, then the three of them could have a showdown. But Dr. Axelrod didn't seem to be expecting her. He listened, frowning, then went out to the reception room.

"Is Dr. Kyriakides here?" The woman's drawling voice sounded familiar.

"No. This is now my office. What do you want?"

"See." The woman's speech became distorted as if she had a thumb in her mouth. "Right here . . . candy . . . know I shouldn't eat caramels. . . ."

Tyler only heard them dimly. Dr. Axelrod's last accusations were still caroming in his head, drowning them out. No sensibilities, no honor, no shame. And on top of all that, he'd been accused of begging. He tried to remember if he'd made it clear that the money would be a loan. He was sure he had. Not that it would make any difference. Dr. Axelrod would still call it begging, unless he had collateral to offer. And what did he have? Some old clothes in the suitcase and his wristwatch, which only cost a dollar when it was new. Then he remembered the gold in his pocket.

"If you will have a seat for a moment," said Dr. Axelrod in the waiting room.

Tyler unwrapped the bridge and laid it on the tray just as he bustled back into the room, his face flushed and excited.

"I'll leave you that as collateral," said Tyler.

But Dr. Axelrod didn't even look. The white jacket he snatched from the peg and struggled into was much too small. The cuffs were inches above his wrists, and the seams in the shoulders threatened to split as he bent over the basin to wash his hands.

"Gold's worth thirty-five dollars an ounce," said Tyler.

"Out! Out!" Dr. Axelrod brushed past him, his wet hands

raised as if he was waiting for a nurse to put rubber gloves on them. He opened the bottom drawer of the cabinet with the toe of his shoe, then reached down and pulled out a towel. More drawers were opened and kicked closed until he found the bib that went around a patient's neck.

"I said, 'Out!' " He whispered it, waving the bib at Tyler. "I have a patient waiting."

"How much will you loan me for that?" Tyler whispered, too, pointing at the tray. This time Dr. Axelrod followed the direction of his finger. Then he went over and picked up the bridge carefully, as if it was infected.

"Where did you get this?"

"It's worth at least thirteen dollars," said Tyler.

"Where did you get it?" Dr. Axelrod's voice was still hushed, but there was a storm in it.

"It's my father's." He knew immediately he should have lied. If only he'd substituted an uncle for his father or even a garbage can.

"Why are you doing this to me?" The voice was trembling now.

"I'm not doing anything," said Tyler. "Just give me what it's worth."

"It's worth nothing."

The hand thrusting the bridge at him trembled, too. Tyler looked at the false, stained teeth and tarnished gold. His last chance to get away ended there. He'd failed.

"Keep it," he said. "You've taken everything else of his."

The rest happened quickly—the clink of the bridge as it was dropped back on the tray, the pants pocket tugged at savagely until inside out, the cluster of money thrown at him. One dollar bill fell to the floor as he caught the rest in scooped hands. It felt like more than enough.

"I'll pay it back," he said. He picked up the dollar from the floor and went out to the waiting room.

"Hello, Tyler."

She'd leaped back guiltily from the small bouquet when he came in. She'd been reading the card.

"Hello, Inez."

"You've been out of school a long time," she said, trying to keep her heavy lips drawn over her teeth.

"I've been sick."

Inez Jackson's big eyes were on the money in his hand. He turned sideways to count it.

"Does he hurt?" Inez had lowered her voice and was pointing toward the other room.

"I don't know." While she was trying to figure out how he couldn't know, he thumbed the bills. There was a lot more than thirteen dollars.

"Look what I had to go and do." Her need to tell him was greater than her pride. She grimaced back her upper lip to reveal the jagged half of a front tooth. "And they're givin' me a shower tomorrow."

"Shower?" Twenty-two dollars altogether.

"For my marriage to Richard."

"Richard who?" He'd made it. He was on his way.

"I guess you think of him as Big Richie."

"Oh," said Tyler. "Big Richie."

"If you will come in now." Dr. Axelrod stood in the doorway, bowing slightly, his hands clasped behind his back.

Inez got up nervously. "Can you put a new filling in right away?"

"Yes, yes," said Dr. Axelrod impatiently.

"See you in school." Inez flashed Tyler a brave, broken-toothed smile before going in. But Dr. Axelrod never looked at him.

As he put on his mackinaw, he could hear them mumbling. Then there were a couple of *ahs* out of Inez as if he were examining her tonsils. On this note, he would leave. But, as he picked up his suitcase, the note changed. The *ah* was replaced by the drill. Even more appropriate. This rasping noise would be the last he would hear of any of them. He went toward the door. But before he got to it, Inez screamed.

He would have chalked it up to a nerve being touched and kept on going, except that it wasn't the kind of scream that came out of dentists' offices. It was continuous and getting louder, and the drill hadn't even stopped. Tyler ran to the doorway and looked in.

Inez was struggling to heave herself out of the chair, her arms and legs thrashing wildly. But the bib had her tied to the headrest. Dr. Axelrod stared at her helplessly, pushing his hands toward her screams like a conductor trying to quiet an orchestra. And between them the drill hung like a rattlesnake caught by the tail, hissing and dancing crazily. Then the string of the bib snapped, and Inez leaped out of the chair, spinning around toward Tyler, the side of her face covered with bright blood. She brushed at it, as if it was a cobweb. And for the second that the blood was wiped away, before it pulsed out again, Tyler could see the half a square that had been ripped in her cheek. Her hand went up to it again and stayed there, as if to seal the wound, her screams intermittent now, mingling with long, desperate gasps, as if she would suffocate if she didn't get out of there. Then she pushed past Tyler and ran out.

His first thought was that she'd left her coat. It was draped across the chair in the waiting room, a gray coat that looked new, with a black fur collar. A cry receded outside. Then the buzzing noise stopped. Dr. Axelrod had finally kicked the foot switch, the drill giving one last twitch before hanging limp.

"And did she deserve that?" Tyler shouted the question. "Did she deserve what just happened to her?"

Dr. Axelrod turned to peer at him, then motioned wearily toward the drill. "It slipped from my hand," he said.

As if that were all the explanation needed, he knelt to pick up the blood-streaked bib, then dabbed it at a wet red spot on the floor.

V

SHE'D disappeared.

No distant scream to follow, no drops of blood in the snow. Only the gullies trampled in both directions. He followed the one that led across to the "black" side. Inez would have had to run this way.

The street seemed narrower over here, the snow higher. The few old cars he passed were buried fender-deep. The sagging houses all looked as if they'd foamed from their chimneys and died. Tyler trudged on, his suitcase heavy under his right arm, Inez's coat slung over his left shoulder. The wind, which had been whipping up flurries of snow, suddenly stopped as if turned off. Now the only sounds were his. Ice bubbles popped occasionally under his feet. The open buckles of his overshoes tinkled. Santa Claus was coming to town.

He wasn't sure exactly what he'd say when he did find her. She was bound to be in one of the lighted windows ahead—an anxious mother bending over her, comforting her, bathing the wound. They wouldn't want any sympathy from him. So all he could do was find out how badly she was hurt, return the coat, and be off. Twenty-two dollars were in his pocket, plus the one he'd started with. He could be on his way back to the bus terminal right now. He told himself he was crazy to jeopardize the money. Not just because it was a colored neighborhood. Anybody could get rolled on *any* deserted street so late at night. But he kept going.

Most of the lighted windows were blanked by curtains, one by brown wrapping paper. And the first one that wasn't revealed no one within, just a couch with a couple of springs hanging out the bottom and a potbellied stove. Then an old woman shuffled in, unwinding balled, wet stockings and draping them carefully over the rope he hadn't noticed.

Three houses farther along, a baby was sprawled on a bed like a diapered frog. The woman in this room was young and scrawny and held a green beaded dress against herself as she tangoed in front of a full-length mirror, adoring her every spasm. Then Tyler heard the cry and lumbered across the street toward it. There was some burlap over the lower pane of the window, but by arching up on his toes, he could just manage to see over it.

Two men flanked a checkerboard inside. The cries came from the grisled, emaciated one, more like cackling now that they were linked to his face. He rocked back and forth, his bony hands applauding himself in slow motion, taunting his opponent. But the other man just glared stubbornly at the three kinged reds that had him cornered. Then the cackling stopped. The skinny man was looking straight at the window, his mouth hanging open like a crooked capital *O*. Tyler scrambled away, glancing back toward the house until he was well up the street, but no one came out.

"Oh Lord, what a morning . . ."

The singing came from the house on the next corner. He went toward it. There was nothing to indicate a church, no cross or stained glass. And the picture in the front window looked more like John Carradine than Jesus Christ. Even the hand-lettered sign seemed noncommittal.

ALL ARE WELCOME
SISTER IVY FROM FLA.
BE SAVED!
PRAYER FOR SICK

The last person in hadn't closed the door completely, so he was able to see inside.

"Oh Lord, what a mor . . . ning . . .
Oh Lord, what a mor . . . or . . . ning . . ."

The enormous woman clutching the rostrum was relishing every note, her head thrust back, the doilied bodice of her dress stretching and contracting.

"Oh Lord, what a morr . . . orr . . . ning . . .
Oh Lord, what a morrr . . . orrr . . . ning . . ."

The same line, over and over again, sung straight to heaven. She was born to lead the singing, just as the half-dozen people in the congregation were born to follow. They sat straining toward her from the straight wooden benches, as if their feeble voices could be nourished by her gusty one.

"Oh Lord, what a morrrrrr . . . orrrrrr . . . ning."

Oh, shit, what a night!

What the hell was he doing here, snooping and creeping around with a suitcase and a girl's coat? If a cop came by, he'd have six hours' explaining to do. He moved away from the door. It was only the goddam fur-collared coat that prevented his taking off. He considered opening the door and flinging it toward the singing congregation. One of them might know who it belonged to and where Inez lived. But it wasn't very likely. And for all he knew, Inez's parents were out right now looking for her coat. They could be facing Dr. Axelrod this very minute, adding theft to his other crimes. What a stupid thing to do, taking the coat from the office! He held it out and looked at it. It would be so simple to drop it here in the snow and just walk away. But remembering Inez running out, her face blotched with blood, made this impossible. He slung the coat over his shoulder again and started back.

The lights in the office were still on, the door unlocked. He meant to enter quietly; but he was bushed, and the suitcase thumped against the door. The hell with it. No one was in the waiting room anyway. He walked across and laid the coat on the chair. He was free. Dr. Axelrod could handle the rest with his usual tact. He hadn't even looked out to see who'd come in. Either he was hiding or he'd taken off. That was no longer his concern. Good-bye to little problems! Good-bye to money-grubbing marriages! Good-bye to unimportant people in unimportant rooms on narrow unimportant streets!

Then he heard it, less than a hiss and more than a sigh, like a steady exhalation from a giant, untiring lung. He put down his suitcase and went toward it. And just before he looked inside, he knew what he would see—the bald dome protruding above the twin cushions of the headrest, the black and orange cylinders in their stand wheeled up behind the chair. Tyler moved slowly, keeping his distance, following the curve of the hose until it ended in the triangular cup and the hand embedding it in the face.

What he had to do seemed simple and obvious. He went to the chair to snatch the nose cup away. But the hand clutching it was rigid, and he had to pry at its cold fingers until they suddenly fell open and the arm dropped to the side of the chair. Tyler held the cup to his own nose and sniffed. Then he twisted the valve on top of the orange cylinder until the rancid air stopped coming out. Life was in the other cylinder, the black one. First lesson in science class—without oxygen, the entire planet would be dead in a matter of minutes. He turned the valve on the black cylinder, and when the smell coming out of the nose cup changed, he placed it back on Dr. Axelrod's face.

Artificial respiration. He'd seen it demonstrated many times on imitation drowners. But they'd always been sprawled out facedown on the floor. And the oxygen-giving hose wouldn't reach that far. He had to do what he could from here. He probed the fat stomach. Where did the abdomen begin and end? Where was the diaphragm? Where exactly were the lungs? He pushed the heel of his hand against the ribs, trying to regulate his thrust to the pace of his own breathing. But the lifelessness against his hand, the feel of sacked grain made

him stop. He lifted his fingers to the face, pinched the jowl, the
temple, the bridge of the nose. All felt like India rubber. And
when he took his hand away, the loose gray skin showed no
marks. He followed the eyes, so like those of the stuffed eagle
he'd once been afraid to touch. The last thing they'd seen
was the instrument tray. His father's bridge was still there.
And next to it, the spectacles. The stem which had been taped
on had come off.

Tyler lurched out to the waiting room. The two bouquets
would serve double duty. *Good luck! Happy Cavities!* Behind him, the cylinder was still hissing out its useless oxygen.
He wanted to go back and turn it off. But the strange, sour mixture of gas and death was in his throat, and he was gagging for
clear air. He went outside, pulling the door closed behind him
and leaned back against it, gulping in cold.

There was an optical illusion. You stared at a spot in the
middle of a picture for one full minute. Then you looked at
a blank wall or ceiling, and the picture was reproduced
there. This time he'd stared too long. The image was in his
eyes permanently. Wherever he looked, he saw Dr. Axelrod's
dead face—against the snow, against the black sky, the walls of
the near buildings. There was an accompaniment, too—words
that had been said repeating themselves like snatches of a tune.
He tried to blink the picture away, but it kept re-forming. And
as it did, there was a shrill insistence that he was responsible
for it, not only for this, but for all the anguish everywhere. This
was only one terrible scene out of the thousands he'd caused.
He racked his memory for others, groped for beginnings and
ends. Then, clenching jaw and hands, he hardened himself.

An enemy was dead, that was all. And he'd been just an innocent bystander. Well, maybe more. Maybe a small, unwilling
part of a long chain of circumstances. So what? A lot of more
worthwhile people were going to die before the war was over.
But his jaw wouldn't stay tight. Generalities weren't enough.
There was a lesson snarled somewhere in the night, and
he had to find it. He closed his eyes to narrow the search, but

it didn't help. And when he opened them again, the Negroes were trotting across the street toward him.

There were three of them. Big Richie was in the middle, even bigger than Tyler remembered. The spidery one on the left, with the wool knit hat pulled down over his ears, looked familiar, too. The other man was older. He had a little mustache, gray as his hair, and wore an overcoat. The other two just had sweaters on, as if anything heavier would encumber them. Something dangled from the spidery one's hand, like a stiffened ribbon.

They slowed as they got closer, then stopped completely, breathing heavily, puffing steam.

"Where's that fuckin' dentist?"

It came from under the wool knit hat. Tyler placed him. He'd been with Big Richie that night last summer when they'd stopped him. The stiff ribbon he held was a bicycle chain.

"He's not here." There was more than half a truth in it.

"Then why's the light on?"

All three took a half step forward. One giant step, and they were at the door.

"Get out'a the way." It was the first Big Richie had spoken.

"Is Inez okay?" asked Tyler.

"He coulda blinded her for life," said the older man. Tyler guessed he was Inez's father and aimed the question at him.

"Is she okay?"

"She's a lot better'n that fuckin' dentist's gonna be." The spidery one sounded the maddest. Maybe her brother.

Big Richie shuffled forward a few inches. "Get out'a our way," he growled again.

"It was an accident," said Tyler. "Honest."

He was watching Big Richie's huge arms and fists. So he didn't see the bicycle chain until it glinted. He jerked his head aside, but not far enough, and as the chain clattered against the door, he was sure his ear had been sliced off. He grabbed for it, felt it numb but whole.

"I'm on your side," he said. "But you've gotta leave him alone." As he said it, it became a rule.

"You're askin' for it."

A light went on across the street, and a window was opened. Tyler looked toward the sound, and the three of them sprang. At first he just tried to shield his face. Big Richie's blows were the worst, coming down like pile drivers, one flaring a fire inside his head. When he covered up with his arms, the spidery one danced around behind the others, readying the chain, begging them to move aside and give him a target. Then the old man got hold of Tyler's sleeve and started dragging him away from the door. Tyler grabbed the knob with his other hand, and for a while he was sure his arms would come right out of their sockets.

"Fuckin' whiteshit," someone grunted.

He was bent over now, arms wide and taut. "I'm on your side," he said again. "I've always been on your side."

Though he saw the snow-drenched shoe coming up at his face, he couldn't avoid it. He tasted the wet leather before his mouth filled with blood. Then he toppled forward on his hands and knees. The chain lashed him as he crawled, a lulling rhythm in it. He would have stayed down, taking more; but the door was being opened, and that wasn't allowed. He lunged to his feet, hurtling all his weight against it, and the old man, who'd just got his hand out in time, looked shocked to see him. Tyler shoved against him, saw him skid away, then turned as Big Richie charged.

Somehow he got his head down in time, felt it driven between his shoulders, and heard the air gush out of Big Richie's stomach. He straightened up, still dizzy, and the wool knit hat was within range. It was the best punch he'd ever thrown, a perfect left hook, and for a second he thought the crack came from the dark cheekbone. Then the needles shot up his arm, and he knew his wrist was broken again.

It wasn't fair. At least one of them should have been down, maybe two. But all three were still on their feet. The snow around the door had been trampled flat into a small semicircle arena, and they hovered at the edge of it, wolves waiting for the fire to burn lower. He was aware of snarling back at them,

but he didn't want to. He wanted to tell them again that he
was on their side. Only his mouth was too thick with blood,
and they were coming nearer, closing in.

He threw up his dangling left hand to protect him from the
chain and tried to fight off the others. But for every punch he
landed he took three or four. And there was no reason for it.
All he had to do was fall aside and the pain would end. He
didn't know why they shouldn't go past him if they wanted
to. There wasn't one intelligent reason why they shouldn't go
inside and see the putty corpse with the fixed, dry eyes. He
kept telling himself this. He kept warning himself to fall down
before the rest of his face was shredded and his insides were
hurt too much ever to heal. But when the police car arrived
and the crowd began to form, he was still barring the door.